CHAMBER MUSIC

TOM BENN

JONATHAN CAPE
LONDON

Published by Jonathan Cape 2013

2 4 6 8 10 9 7 5 3 1

First published in Great Britain in 2013 by
Jonathan Cape
Random House, 20 Vauxhall Bridge Road,
London SW1V 2SA

www.vintage-books.co.uk

Addresses for companies within The Random House Group Limited
can be found at:
www.randomhouse.co.uk/offices.htm

The Random House Group Limited Reg. No. 954009

A CIP catalogue record for this book is available from the British Library

ISBN 9780224093514

The Random House Group Limited supports The Forest Stewardship
Council (FSC®), the leading international forest certification organisation.
Our books carrying the FSC label are printed on FSC® certified paper.
FSC is the only forest certification scheme endorsed by the leading
environmental organisations, including Greenpeace.
Our paper procurement policy can be found at
www.randomhouse.co.uk/environment

Typeset in Fairfield LH by Palimpsest Book Production Limited,
Falkirk, Stirlingshire
Printed and bound in Great Britain by
Clays Ltd, St Ives plc

For Mum

I have seen the incipience of intellectual arrogance in you, and sometimes you question the credibility of events. You are entering a new experience. You are writing something unique. You are white. It is difficult for a white person to simulate a black experience. And it is even more difficult to express or interpret something you have never experienced before. Be calm.

Born Fi' Dead, Laurie Gunst

Nothing to Lose, tattooed around his gun wounds. Everything to Gain, embedded in his brain.

Biggie Smalls

1

THE SUPPLIANT

13 February 1998
Friday

'HENRY BANE IS dead.'

I looked up as he said this.

Vic rocked on his heels like a bobby, cleared his throat, lifted his chin, blinked a few times – eyes red and boozy. 'But that dunt mean ee int wiv us. Keepin eye on rest o you lot till we give it up n av the good sense t'croak n all. All o yer knew ee were a good man, our Henry. Ah knew im near nuff twenny years. But ee sodded off fer the las few. Ah were glad when ee come back, though. A sound bloke, ee was. A right jammy bugger. We loved im. Dint we?' Vic cleared his throat again. '*Dint we?*'

His front room said *yeah.*

Vic had been best mates with my old man and I was best mates with Vic's son, Gordon. I was glad to have the do at his place.

So then Vic asked us all to have one on Henry Bane.

'Ee-ah, enry.' Some bloke on the other end of the couch passed me a drop of rum in a short glass. 'Jus one. Do yer good, lad. Elp yer get right in yerself.' I said no, took it off him anyway, held it up to the light. Hard black stuff. The glass didn't glow. I slipped it under the coffee table, untouched, spilling some next to the sausage-roll flakes and dead drinks.

Drip stains swelled and ate the rug.

Everyone was gabbing again.

My old man had been a market trader for most of his years. His last gig was Henry's Records down Arndale Market: 7-inch soul and rhythm and blues classics. Two-for-one every Saturday before twelve.

'Out of Sight' was playing quietly on Vic's dusty stereo in the corner. A James Brown tune – sampled by every rapper since the microphone met the turntable and fell in love.

Out of Sight.

The old man's favourite.

Henry's Records: 1981–1990. RIP.

Henry Bane: 1931–1998. RIP.

It was a mega heart attack outside Ladbrokes – just like that – small winnings still to collect. My mam wasn't too dead to be smug.

Lola Bane: 1949–1990. RIP.

'Out of Sight' faded. We had 'Soul Power (Parts

One and Two)' on next but somebody got up and turned the sound down to zero. 'Coon shite,' they muttered.

I shut my eyes. Soft hands pushed a brew into mine, making sure I had hold of it before letting go. Her fingers stroked my cheek, touched my lips. I could smell her hand cream, her perfume, her B&Hs.

Eyes open: chipped red nail polish.

'Careful, lovey. Hot.'

'Ta,' I said.

'Enry?'

I gulped the brew, put it down on the table between the lager cans and looked up at our Jan.

'Ow we doin?' she said.

'He's not here yet,' I said. 'Gordon.'

Jan rubbed my head, bent over and kissed me. 'No, lovey.'

'Where's Trenton?' I said.

'Ee's in kitchen. Pickin at buffet. Want us ter get yer summat? Yuv not ad owt, av yer?'

'I'm alright, love.'

'Gotta av summat.'

'I will do.'

Jan smiled. Jan worried.

'When yer wanna go ome, we'll go ome,' she said. 'Right?'

'Right.'

She walked out, new heels knifing the bald carpet, dodging the sea of booze.

It was roasting in Vic's with everybody sardined into

the front room, the gas fire going. Above the flames – the brass clock on the mantle said 7 p.m.

On top of the funeral, Gordon was getting out this weekend. I thought he was due back today, but it was a bit late now. Maybe it was tomorrow. His picture by the clock showed him stood with his dad on Blackpool promenade – two scruffy gits, holding up their double 99s. Granite Gordon – six-six, roid gut, squinting at the camera, a jolly grin, the same grin he gave the world when he was kicking some sorry bugger's head in. He'd served ten months of a two-year sentence and I hadn't rung him in four or visited in six. I was bricking it. Maybe he'd be back tonight. Vic would know the ins and outs of it but I hadn't had a proper word since the crematorium this afternoon.

Our Gordon wasn't in my school year – he was a couple of years older. I kept well clear until the summer of '88, when we got friendly through our dads: Victor Payne the bent, sage cabbie and Henry Bane the music man. They were the Cock o' the North, pub quiz dream team. I must've been eighteen, just. Gordon wasn't the brightest bulb but he was hard – a bad lad, a right rum sort, his dad said.

But so was I.

My old man had liked reminding me and all.

I got up with my brew, made it to the hallway, then the kitchen. There was a decent-sized spread on the little breakfast table, some of it still cling-filmed.

Trenton was sat up on the surfaces, still in his scarf, gloves, Adidas jacket, the back of his trainers thumping

Vic's draining cupboard door. He'd turned thirteen last September. Jan's kid. He was mither. But I took care of him and he let me.

'Pack it in.'

Trenton stopped thumping the cupboard and started flicking a Zippo in his hands to remind me he was bored. It sparked but there was no flame.

'These any good?' I said, pointing to a tray of party scran.

'Yeh.'

'Barely been touched. Could be a warnin. Mini sausage rolls? Firm favourite – only two left. You havin one?'

Trenton nodded.

I passed him one and ate the other. He was still pissing about with the lighter.

'Give us that.' I took it off him.

'Oi.'

I put it in my pocket.

'Oi nothin,' I said. 'Y'mam won't want you messin with that.'

'It's ers.'

My dad had never smoked in his life.

We heard the doorbell go. I started on the breadsticks, dunked one in my brew and regretted it.

An old uncle I hadn't seen since I still believed in Father Christmas popped his head into the kitchen.

'Enry, think someone's at door fer yer, lad.'

'I don't live here,' I said.

'Ah said it were yer dad's funeral do n then she said she were after *you*, lad.'

'She?'

'Aye.'

I walked back through to the hall and saw the front door was open. It was dark out and I could feel the draught from there. Somebody was stood on the step but fellers my old man had known were coming in and out of Vic's front room, blocking my line of sight.

'Someone want us?' I said, getting through the traffic.

She'd let her hair grow out.

She'd got thinner.

'Henry.' Her voice still had that soft croak.

The cold bit my shaving nicks. My face cracked when I said her name.

She was bug-eyed in the dark. I shut the front door to and we looked at each other, teeth chattering, brains burning. Time passed. I heard her swallow.

'Henry—'

'It's just Bane now, love.' I folded my lapels up and the frost walked my spine.

'Well, it's still Roisin,' she said.

When I came closer, she stepped back and made up the distance again.

She said: 'Listen. I'll need your help to get him inside.'

She was still gorgeous.

'Who?' I said.

'Follow me.'

Roisin took me out of the front plot and over the road.

There was a battered Fiesta humming on neutral – lights on, exhaust smoking. A bin bag was taped over the back passenger window.

She opened the car door and stuck her head inside, pulled the front seat back and showed me a feller, breathing hard, wincing royal, blood down his jacket.

'Help me then,' Roisin said.

I helped her lift him out the car.

'Who's this?' I said, taking most of the weight.

'This is Dan.' We got him standing. He'd hurt his foot or ankle. He was trying to hop and hold onto us at the same time.

Roisin gripped my arm as well – nails – short but sharp.

Dan said hello.

When he was steady, I had a quick look inside the car. There were tiny crystal squares on the back seat where some of the glass had come in. The door panel fabric opposite had three small holes in it.

'What happened to the window?' I said.

'Kids,' Dan went.

'Bollocks.'

'Henry,' she said.

'Where've you come from?' I said.

'London.'

'Lundon?'

'Freezing,' he said.

'Just help me get him in.'

We got Dan over the road and took him inside – the wave of gas heating making us choke.

Jan came out of the hall loo as we were getting him up the stairs. 'What's goin on?'

'Nothin,' I said. 'Keep everyone downstairs. Be down in a minute.'

She stood there, watching us go up.

'Get him in Gordon's room,' I said to Roisin, Dan's arm over my shoulders.

'Gordon not in?'

'Not yet.'

The three of us reached the landing.

'Oo's that feller?' we heard somebody say from down-stairs.

'N oo's she?' Jan's voice.

Roisin was four summers after Alice, and my first proper bird after leaving school. We were mad for it from word go. She was nothing like Gordon, her big little brother. She was the clever one: bookworm – fancy ideas – studying all sorts at the polytechnic. Gordon didn't seem to mind me shagging his sister and, for a bit, we all got on dandy. Then it got fucked right up. And she left Wythie. Left Manchester. Left the North. This was all a good eight years ago. I hadn't heard from her since that day she checked herself out of the Royal Infirmary.

At least Gordon and I had stayed mates.

I shut the bedroom door and we got Dan onto the bed.

'How long's it been for you two?' he said.

'Eight years.' We both said it together.

Roisin touched my arm again. 'Sorry to hear about your dad.' The crackle in her voice: tyres on gravel, a fucking frog inside the princess. I remembered more and more.

'Cheers,' I said.

Gordon's room hadn't changed since he was a young lad. He was thirty years old and still stopping at his dad's when he wasn't bunking in Her Majesty's cell. There were old boxing gloves hanging from the wardrobe knob. Newspaper cut-outs stuck all over the show – we had Nigel Benn *the Dark Destroyer* and some heavyweights like Herbie Hide. He'd got all creative with it. I tried to imagine our Gordon, sat there with a pair of scissors, Blu-tacking Lennox Lewis and Iron Mike Tyson on his wall – and I fucking well couldn't.

Dan had a go at the zip on his jacket but Roisin had to help him out of it. She kissed the dried blood on his cheek, stopped him flinching. He told her he loved her.

In the light I could see his foot was the real mess and knew that someone had shot him. The top of his trainer was torn but there wasn't any blood pumping out. He was pale as death though, he could've already lost a pint on the way up the M1.

'So what happened?' I said.

Roisin was still sat on the bed, mothering him, his head against her chest, her hands in his hair. She said: 'You're going to have to help us.'

A knock on the bedroom door made her jump.

'Right – clear off, all o yer,' Vic yelled through the door. 'Pub's open.'

We heard his footsteps creak on the landing, voice fading as he went back down the stairs to roll off goodbyes: 'Mind ow yer go. Ta fer comin. All the bloody best.'

'He'll be chuffed when he sees you. Both kids back on the same weekend,' I said.

'Where's Gordon been?' she said.

'Strangeways.'

'Jesus.'

'Again.'

'Again?'

Roisin stood up and came closer. My eyes went to young Tyson on the wall – slugging Alex Stewart, mid-annihilation. Roisin tried to touch my arm but I moved away.

'What did he do?' she said. 'Gordon.'

I looked at Dan – hugging his own ribs. 'What did *you* do?'

There was another knock on the door. Jan opened it, she glared at Roisin then me then Dan then back to me.

'We goin?' she said. 'Vic's pissed. Wants everyone out.'

'I know,' I said.

Jan coughed. 'K, well – me n Trenton'll be in the car.' She shut the door again carefully and we watched the handle turn.

'Who's she?' Roisin said.

2

MENTHOL?

JAN DROVE, HEATER on full to clear the windscreen.

'D'yer eat anyfin?' she said as we pulled out of the avenue.

'We both did, didn't we? Not a bad spread.'

'Plenny lef fer tomorra.' Her eyes went up to the rear-view. Trenton was in the back, holding two trays of cling-filmed scran on his knees. His face was blank misery.

Jan said to me: 'So yer knew um? That feller n is . . .?'

'Yeah. She's Gordon's sister.'

'Dint know that Gordon ad a sister.'

'Lives in Lundon.'

'Ad summat appened?'

'It'll be alright.'

Jan was driving too fast.

'How yer feelin now?' she said.

'I'm gunna go in for a bit tonight.'

'Don't, love.'

'I'll be right. Don't worry.' I twisted round. 'Trenton?'

'Yeh?'

'Open the buffet.'

Jan slowed down for the lights. 'Not in the fuckin car. Av jus oovered it out.'

Green meant go – her fist squeezing the gearstick as she raced for fifth again. I sat back, chewing, covered her hand with mine.

Jan pulled up outside our gaff. Trenton slammed the door and went to the porch to wait. Jan got out too and I slid over to the driver's seat.

'Am waitin up,' she said from the pavement, holding the car door open.

'You're not.'

'Fuckin am.'

I heard her new heels clop on the spot.

'Ah love yer,' she said, leaning in. She kissed me, hard, then slammed the door and clopped up the path, shaking her bag to find her keys.

Hoovered out maybe, but her fag ash was still in the corner lips of the dash.

I tried the stereo, still tasting Jan's Aspalls, and it spat out a cassette. I turned it over, fed it back in – Biggie on the go, RIP. I headed straight for town.

9 p.m. Razdan's Garage, Rusholme. Salvaged motors and twelve tons of gypo scrap in the crammed lot. My

suspension kicked as I rolled up, the potholes in the yard giving it a workout – the tyres probably collecting screws. It was a crooked family business and somehow I was extended family.

Maz flashed his lights twice in the parked van, blinking them over the frozen oil pools, then he kept them on full beam – a sign – telling me that tonight's job was still looking good.

I parked the car next to a nicked Nissan and walked over to the Transit. Maz was behind the wheel, eating home-made butties.

He said as I got in: 'It were a nice service, Bane, wunit?' neck flab shaking as he gulped a butty down.

'Should o gone to the do, mate. Was plenny o grub left over.'

'Bring owt wiv yer?'

I slapped his belly. 'He never stops.'

'This is me tea, this is,' he said. 'Ah swear down. All am allowed.'

'How'd y'mean?'

'The missus won't cook fer us.'

'N why's that?'

Maz shut his eyes, leaned forward and tapped his forehead on the steering wheel. 'Managed to do in four ton at Mint Casino, Wednesday night.'

'Fuck me.'

'Ah know.'

'Remind me o the old man.'

He sat back, opened his eyes. Maz was six-three, seventeen stone and the softest bugger in the game. It took a lot to fuck him off and I'd only managed it the once, donkey's ago. He was like a pregnant Mirror Carp in a navy Henri Lloyd, but our Maz wasn't as daft as he looked.

I said: 'Does he know? Abrafo? Bout me dad?'

'Abs dunt know, no. Wiv told im nowt.'

'Good.'

'Dunno why yer don't wan im knowin. Ee'll be—'

'Everythin alright with tonight?' I said.

Maz finished his last butty and took the handbrake off. 'We're sound.'

I said: 'So how'd you manage to drop four ton? Pissed?'

Maz turned to me, driving. 'Pissed? Never touch a drop, me.'

'Am I hearin this?'

'Gamblin, Bane. Terrible sin, that is.'

'What bout whiskey?'

'Behave.'

Wu-Tang's 'Heaterz' was knocking the shitty van speakers: a grand orchestra beat keeping the blood flowing, Gladys Knight hiding in there somewhere. I maxed the heating unit dial into the red and checked the fans for hot air.

'Packed up again,' Maz said. 'Be fixin it tomorra.'

'How'd your missus find out bout the money?'

'Shiz fuckin voodoo, our Ra. She jus knew.'

'Bet you were talkin in your sleep. Anyway, you should make it back tonight.'

'Aye. Best do. Jus in time fer Valentine's.'

'Rana'll be cookin for you yet.'

I pulled a couple of black bobby hats out of the glovebox and put one on.

'Be needin them,' Maz went, rubbing his hands together. We passed Old Trafford. He swore, one hand back on the wheel, the other pressing a V up to the window. Maz was a diehard Blue.

Trafford Park Euroterminal was up ahead in the dark, lights off over the mile of container yards.

'How's that Jan o yours?' Maz said.

'Roisin's back, you know.'

'Oo?'

'Roisin. Gordon's sister.'

'Dint know that Gordon ad a sister.'

'You did.'

'Older or younger?'

'Older.'

'Fair do's. What she look like?'

'*Roisin*. Christ – you havin a laugh?'

'She wiv *you* at one time? Goin back a bit?'

'She was.'

'Short air?'

'Yeah.'

'Nice arse?'

'Yeah.'

'Ad forgot.'

'Clearly.'

'Bane, what is it wiv you n mates' sisters?'

I said: 'Me n yours only ever held hands.'

'Watch that.'

'She still askin after us?'

'You're askin fer summat in a minute, mate.'

We laughed, and I almost forgot.

An open car park near Westinghouse Road. There was a padlocked barrier over the entrance and I got out with a torch and a spare key. I shook it into the lock, the cold stinging my fingers through the knit-gloves, took off the chains and pulled the barrier back. Maz turned in and parked Van Number One next to Van Number Two, the only motor around. He hopped out – engine still running and I saw the breath in front of his face as he cut across the headlamps. Roll on spring.

I walked to the vans.

Maz was round the second Transit, opening up the back.

'Where were the keys?' I said.

'Behind wrong bloody wheel. Al be avin words.'

He got the doors open.

'She doin alright, then?' he said. 'Roisin?'

'No,' I said.

'No?'

I climbed up and shined the torch over the gear. Maz managed his way in, Caterpillar soles thumping aluminium floor.

'Menthol?' Maz said, poking around, rocking the van.

One of the towers shook and a 200 carton fell but the rest didn't go over.

'Guess so.'

'Owt else?'

He took the torch off me and I pulled out two bottles from the first crate. 'Irish whiskey and Jamaican rum.'

Maz said: 'That's mega, that. "To, me. Love, me." Valentine's sorted.'

'Give us a hand.'

Van Number One. Loaded up.

It was the boss's cherry. Abrafo's score. The deal was worked out before Christmas through a policy of favours for favours. This was juicy, more than just booze-cruise pickings but the more people involved, the steeper the risk rate. We'd had to muscle the price down again – just a quiet word now and then. I missed our Gordon.

'She's brought a feller up with her,' I said, taking the scenic route round town, one eye on the rear-view, nobody following.

'Oo as?' Maz was next to me, already on the whiskey, nodding along to Smif-N-Wessun's 'Bucktown'.

'Roisin.'

'Up from where?'

'Lundon.'

'Oh, aye. *I* see.'

'She's had trouble—'

Maz laughed. 'She's ad *you*, yer mean.'

'No. Trouble. In Lundon. This new feller she's with – somebody's had a go at him with a little shooter.'

'Fuckin ell.'

'He's got a bullet hole in his foot n you should o seen the state o the motor.'

'What happened?'

'A .22.'

Straight over Deansgate, club lights washing the wing mirror. Brave totty in short frocks, freezing their tits off in the queues. I clocked Frank's old place. The Britton was a posh coffee bar these days, where every office suit read their *Evening News* come dinnertime. I'd had a look in on opening week – it was all sofas and sparkle.

I took us onto Peter Street, onto Oxford Road – students and tramps looking alike, only a few puffs making the effort, and then we came off the track and down into Hulme.

Hodder Square was the last of the low-rises. The spot looked different these days. Crescents long gone, Otterburn Close laid to rest – there was no more deck access, no more towers of shit. Cheap new housing was sprouting like weeds between the regular high-rises.

The hippies, gypos and the drug fairies had fucked off. The pubs were ruins. Night-time Hulme was just kids on mountain bikes, black tracksuits and golf gloves – chipped Nokias and Stanley knives and converted air pistols – just kids, falling out with each other over a stare. It made my end of Wythie look like Alderley Edge.

There was a dead tree outside old Hollywood Butchers, roots tearing up the paving. The trunk was chewed, bark splintered, teeth marks and claw marks from Pitbull Training 101.

Hollywood Butchers.

The sign was hand-painted, faded – the shop had only been empty for six months. Glass front boarded up, the boards covered with gig posters and crew tags. But Desmond's fishmonger was still going strong – next door, same building.

Abrafo owned both lots.

There was a tiny walled car park behind the shops and the light was on in Desmond's top window.

I knocked on the back door – no window, peephole, letter box – just *NF* and *black bastard* keyed into the hardwood at eye level, the word *Uprising* etched over them, bigger.

'Bane? Bane?' A voice inside: quick. Wary. Light West Indian accent.

'Thas right,' Maz said. 'It's me, Bane.'

'Fuckery.'

'It's me, Maz,' I said.

'You boys tess me. Make old man vex.'

One bolt, two bolt, three. The back door started to open – got stuck – opened a bit more – swollen in the freeze.

Desmond had a scarf tucked inside the neck of his tatty pullover. It was the first time I'd seen him away from the fish counter without his leather cap. He might as well have been naked.

Maz stepped back and chucked him a 200 pack like it was a rugby ball. Desmond caught it to his chest. 'Menthol?' he said, turning it over in his hands.

Desmond was Abrafo's great-uncle on his Trinidad side. He was black and bald, managed to look skinny with a belly, and let his silver tash and goatee go without a trim. Over here since Windrush – he was more Manc than all of us put together. Abs was always forgiving when he was light on the rent.

We could see past him, up the stairwell, bead dividers swaying at the top. Somehow, Des's gaff upstairs never smelled of fish. More likely Scotch bonnet.

Someone shouted his name down the stairs. A bird.

He took the cigs inside and came back with a folded envelope, passed it me, a handshake first, palm like sandpapered leather.

'We interruptin?' I said, tucking the cash inside my Harrington.

Maz was grinning. 'Well in. Fuckin result. Where y'tekin er out tomorra?'

'Sis a friend. Friend who appreciate a gentleman.' Desmond shut his mouth, had a look back over his shoulder, then joined us outside. I helped him with the door.

'Bane,' he said, pointing to the butchers next door. 'I hearing noises from in there. Like boom boom. Moving through me walls.'

'Since when?'

'Since today. After dark. And they be shouting like fool.'

Squatters.

I said: 'We'll have a look in.'

'You need keys? Me used to have dem.'

'Think we've got a set in the van.'

Maz stuck his thumb in the air as a yes. He was walking to the roller shutters – he bent down, rattled the padlock.

'It's still locked up,' he said. 'You hearin things, Dezzie?'

'Yes. Boom boom! You do not believe me? I tell Abrafo meself.'

'We'll have a look,' I said again. 'Now get back to the new missus.'

He went in.

Maz said: 'Ee does alright, dun ee? Bloody ell. Ee's older than me granddad.'

'Go get them keys.'

3

HAGFISH

WHAT DESMOND DIDN'T know about Hollywood Butchers
was that we'd been stashing all sorts of gear inside its
retired chiller for a good two months. Abrafo's orders.
Desmond was a sharp tool, but if he'd twigged, he
hadn't let on.

We got the back shutter up and had a look inside,
carrying a crate of booze each. I put the bottles down
on the floor and found the circuit switch. The fluorescents ticked – came on one at a time and I closed the
shutter again. It was as cold in here as it was out there.
There were a couple of *Hellraiser* hooks still hanging
above the dusty meat tables, blades dull. A gutter track
ran along the floor, the dregs red ice. Everything was
too still. The place stank of blood and something else.

'You smellin smoke?' Maz said.

I nodded. 'Squatters.'

'Ow'd they get in?'

Des's shop was connected at one time by a set of mutual access doors in the back. The handles were bolted together from this side – I went over and tried them to make sure.

Metal fell on concrete floor. Clanked. Echoed. Then nothing.

We looked about. Maz's eye went wide. He started to say something but I stopped him, held a finger up to my mouth.

Listen, I mouthed.

There was something crackling.

We followed the sound, behind the first exposed wall, towards the chiller.

Maz stopped and picked up a little candle off the floor. 'Fuckin mad, this.' He tipped the puddle of wax and it burned the wick out.

'Look.'

Maybe twenty tealights covered the floor ahead, not all lit – matches sprinkled about like grated cheese – like someone had opened the box upside down.

We found a bin barrel on fire in the prep room – where the candles finished. There were lines on the floor, four red tracks, running under the chiller door and ending by the fire.

'They bin avin a barbecue,' Maz said.

I got closer to the bin, walked round it – the smoke made it hard to see. The flames spat, ashes jumping onto an empty plastic chair on the other side of it – the chair back melting. The four bloodlines on the floor matched up with each chair leg.

'Bastard kids,' Maz said. 'Abs is gunna be lovin this.'

'Ring him,' I said.

Maz dug his mobile out. 'No signal.'

'Try outside.'

He left.

A jacket arm was hanging over the side of the bin, the rest of it burning up. Flames popped and spat bits of hot meat up the sleeve.

There were some tiny bottles on the floor under the chair. I picked one up – glass – boiling next to the heat – dropped it but it didn't smash. I rolled it with my foot, label side up. The label curled. The ink bled.

Berta's Love Tonic.

It was written in marker pen. A cutting of hair was inside the bottle.

I kicked out another bottle and the top was loose and the liquid spilled onto my shoe. The patterns in my brogue started to rise. It stripped the polish then ate the leather. Funeral shoes ruined.

Berta's War Tonic.

'Bwoy.'

I looked up and saw a Rastaman. Some fucking Johnny Too Bad. 'Yah waan some o dat?' he said. 'Yah get some o dat, mon.'

I kept still. He was alone.

'Hagfish hab Obeah tallowah. Dis blud fire. Help a mon t'kill a mon. Make it real nice an nice.'

I said: 'Do I know you, mate?'

'Yah nuh no Hagfish.'

He was a proper Yard Man. Natty spider-leg dreads that grew up before they grew down.

'What the fuck's happened here?' I said.

'Disya bonfire, ra. Thin bite rock-stone. Now he be burnin.'

He came forward. Stopped and stared and smiled. Gold front teeth, two at the top, one at the bottom.

I looked back down at the bottle of acid, rolled it behind me and stepped back, got the fire between us.

He wore a long open army jacket. Buttons torn off. Front pockets torn off. Bare chest underneath – tough, scarred, skinny – a runner's body. I'd say he was older than me. Maybe a rough five years.

'Thin was likkle fryer fish, mon. Thin tess Hagfish an now he a dead mon. An now me a go kill *you*.'

He hadn't blinked yet – he'd been toking the hard stuff.

'Calm down, mate,' I said. 'We're off.'

'Too late to go wey, mon.'

Hagfish took a shooter from the back of his waistband and came towards the flaming barrel. He held the gun at me, arm out, wrist loose, waving it about. Nobody home.

'Bwoy, me show yah Mary. She fed now, mon, but she wanga-gut, she never belly full.' Teeth flashed. His eyes went gold over the fire.

I took my Harrington off and he cocked the hammer. 'Don't be fuckin daft. Y'know whose place this is?'

The smoke blocked him out.

'Me haffi dead you!'

I lobbed Berta's bottle into the bin. It bounced around the drum for a second and then the flames doubled.

He wasted two rounds. Maybe more, it was hard to hear.

I ducked and the barrel went over – either he kicked it or it fell with him – and the gun skated along the floor.

I got close and butted him hard before he could have a swing at me and he took it well, stayed up, his foot nearest the shooter. But I chinned him once and his legs went from under him and I threw a couple more into his face when he hit the floor – until he'd had enough. My knuckles were skinned. His dreads were burning in a patch of fire. His nostrils went wide. The smell of it brought him round.

I picked up the gun and stood over him, my heart still going. It was fancy. Custom-made. A heavy semi-automatic – swirly marks on the slide, gold engravings on the grip, purple cross-hatching, a fake-diamond inlay. All for show.

Hagfish tilted his head away from me – the right eye was shut, bruising. He was swilling blood between his gold teeth.

I took out the clip and had a look in the chamber – saw the next bullet hadn't quite made it and jammed. A botched recoil. The rounds were too small – they'd been wrapped in tape to make them fit a higher calibre shooter. Guns were easy. Ammo was hard to come by.

I put the gun back together and heard something fall behind me.

Maz had dropped his phone.

'We need to get this fire out,' I said.

'Ah were only two sec.' He kept his gob open.

'We need to get this fuckin fire out.'

'Might be some ice in the chiller,' Maz went.

'It's off, dickhead. Remember?'

'Alright, Bane. Fuckin ell. Might be extinguisher in there. Oo's the dread?'

Hagfish was still seeing stars. I kicked out the fire next to him and saved his hair. 'Fuck knows.'

Maz opened the slide door to the chiller and went in.

Hagfish started singing, well out of it: '. . . dragon Mary – she ruff-ruff, Mary . . .' He pushed his tongue out, sang it again. The blood had stopped and he was dribbling white goz instead. He came to life, pulling shapes as he had a fit.

I heard Maz yell from the chiller, howling with pain.

I ran in, shouldering the door wider and slipped on all the blood.

When I was about Trenton's age, there was a lad on our street with a pet iguana. His mam had got it from Tib Street in town. This was before Tib Street became a prozzie corner – when you were shopping for a budgie or terrapin, not a rough shag.

Fuck.

Maz was on his arse too. She had him by the thigh, teeth down – gum deep, jaws shaking his leg, *Jurassic Park* tail whipping like mad. I got up, tried to distract her off Maz.

Daft stubby legs, paddling around, not-so-daft claws.

She let him go, mouth snapping at me, dead eyes –
frightened of us both.

I tipped a shelf unit by the wall, got my weight behind
it and it rocked but was too heavy to go over. A few bits
of junk slid off and bounced and the noise confused her.

I managed to drag Maz out and pull the chiller door
back into the seal.

'Maz, mate. New diet. I'm tellin the missus.'

My shirt stuck to me, blood-heavy.

I propped him up against the door, took his bobby
hat off and the sweat came out of it like a sponge. His
forehead was just water – tears down his face.

'Ever worry bout avin kids, Bane?'

'Kids?'

His cheeks were fat, shaking.

'Aye. Avin kids n all that.'

Blood jetted. The artery warmed our hands.

I said: 'Worry more bout makin sure I'm not havin
um.' Two pound coins in the back pocket for the johnny
machine in the Red Beret.

I sat in his blood. Maz started to sob. 'Could o bin
me fuckin cock in there. Would've bin it. Would've ad
it.' He stopped sobbing. His eyes rolled inside his skull.
I pressed his ruined leg till they rolled back out.

'Don't go yet, lad.'

'Fuckin – ah! Bastard!'

'Need the fuckin van heater fixin.'

I looked over at the fire – barrel on its side – it had
just about burned itself out.

Hagfish was gone.

4

ABRAFO

DRE AND SNOOP'S 'Zoom' demo was ghosting through the speakers – subs throbbing, volume cut back. The rest of the flat was looking bare. Ikea boxes stacked against the walls, hiding the safe, all ready for tomorrow's move. Only the desk, chairs and stereo were left out for the night.

'A dragon?' Abrafo said, slicing the shrink-wrap and taking a menthol cig out of the pack. He settled in his chesterfield, lit the cig first and then put it in his gob.

'A Komodo dragon,' I said.

Three brews, an ashtray and Desmond's rent money were on the antique desk between us.

'Like a fuck-off iguana,' he said.

'Big lizard. Lots o teeth.'

'Ee nab it from the fuckin zoo?'

'Who knows?'

29

Abrafo was living in a converted flat over Lever Street, Northern Quarter – one of those cool loft spaces that were going for a biscuit all of a sudden. It was above a discount-clothing shop which he also owned, but he was moving onto Deansgate to carve himself a piece of the club scene. The new gaff was a plush flat above Billyclub – a nightclub we'd bitten off some puff entrepreneur when he got caught with three ki's of Amsterdam smack and a ball gag in the boot of his SLK. The club had seen a refurb over the last month. 20 February was relaunch night. We'd been x-ing the days off the *Mirror*'s top totty wall calendar.

'Ow'd ee get in?' Abrafo said to me.

'What, the feller?'

'No, the iguana. Yes, Bane. This fish feller.'

'We dunno. Shutters were down. Everythin locked up. Couple o broken windows. Maybe he fancied the climb.'

The missus was stood behind his chair, redoing his cornrows. She tugged his head to one side by his hair, tightening a braid in her skimpies. Short satin dressing gown – thighs a Maldives tan, kitten-heeled slippers, cotton wool between her toes. Ashley. Twenty-two and white. His first wife. Twelve months in.

'Where's Maz?' Abrafo said.

'Royal Infirmary. I took him. He'll tell um one o the lads' pitbulls got too friendly.'

Abs knocked his fag ash into the glass ashtray. 'Ow is ee?'

I said: 'He's in a bad way. What we doin bout this Hagfish?'

'Wiv got the move out o this place tomorra n the twennieth to be thinkin bout. Promotions to get done. Door security still needs sortin. Thin's missin. He's still not got back to us bout lettin his boys do launch weekend.'

'Thin?' I said.

'Yeah. Reckons ee runs the show round Hulme. As a few streets down Moss Side the kids squabble over. Blingy fucker' – *Dickhead* – Ashley mouthed to me, translating – 'yer might know im through us.'

Ashley touched one nostril and then mimed a fat line in the air. She sighed.

'Mate o yours?' I said.

'Nah. Bit young. But ee'll do business. Fucker's not answerin is phone, though. Ah – love!?' Ashley snatched at his hair.

'Soz, babe – gotta be tight an-it?' She bit her bottom lip, concentrating. 'Ee's dead mard, int ee, Bane?' Eyelashes flapping at me again, then back on the job.

I checked my mobile. It was getting on for 3 a.m.

Ashley pulled his head back to start the next cornrow. 'Ow's your Jan, Bane?' she said.

'Good,' I said. 'She's keepin busy.'

Abs's goatee chin went up as she tugged harder – showing me what the beard trimmer can do.

'Well, tell er I asked after er.'

'Will do.'

'Want anuva brew?' she said to me.

I looked at my mug. We both yawned together.

'No, ta,' I said. 'Gunna get some kip.'

'Me too, after this. Oh, Bane, love – think we saw yer dad week or two back. In town.' She nudged Abrafo. 'Where was it, love?'

He stayed quiet.

'Blackjack table?' I said.

Ashley giggled. 'Yeah. Think it were. Ow's ee doin?'

Abrafo said: 'Y'alright fer cash, Bane?' The cig bounced on his lips. He knew. Ashley didn't.

'I'm alright,' I said.

Ashley unpicked a strand of his hair and stitched it down again, nails clicking as she wove. 'Glad someone is. Ee dunt even tip the airdresser.'

Abrafo said: 'Ah tip er fuckin plenny, believe.'

'Best do.' She snapped the last band over the end. 'There, love. All done.' She folded her arms around his neck and pecked his cheek, then came round and pecked mine. She didn't smell cheap.

'Night night, boys.'

'Night.'

We heard a door shut.

'Maz nearly died,' I said.

Abs chain-smoked.

'Still might.'

'Was it robbery?' he said.

'No.'

'Al ask Thin if ee knows owt. If ah ever get old of im.'

'Doctors won't buy Maz gettin savaged by a bullie.'

'Too much fuckin chin-waggin goin on nowadays. Ah like peeps that can shut the fuck up.'

I thought about jammed shooters and missing persons.

'Like you,' he said.

We heard another door shut.

'Got owt sorted for tomorrow?' I said.

'Maz was spose be comin in the van in the mornin.'

Maz might not make it through the night.

'I meant Valentine's,' I said. 'For Ashley.'

'Not ad time, Bane. New ouse. New business.'

'Thought it was your weddin anniversary?'

'Is. But she wants to tek care of it. So I anded over the plastic n let er get on wiv it. Less grief.'

'Our Jan'd have a fit,' I said.

He smoked, smiled.

'Abs.'

'Yeah?'

'Where were you eight years ago? 1990?'

'Ah were still down south. Why?'

'Brixton?'

'Shiftin shooters in a club cellar. Used ter sign fer um when they delivered the kegs. Russian lurry drivers come round sellin twice a munf. Letters on their knuckles, on their ands, up their necks. Big fuckers. N am six-four. We used um ter supply firms all over.'

'Security?'

'Real security. Raves, clubs, anyfin. All them fat white cunts wiv dogs – killin each uva fer the yellow smiley face.'

'I remember it.'

'There were a load of us. Ah were boss's chief.'

'Happy endin?'

'Boss got pinched. Then ee got stabbed. Club burnt down.'

'N you came back home?'

'That summer. Why? Where were you?'

'I was shiftin trainers out o the back o me dad's '75 Consul.'

'You were floggin E as well, ah bet.'

Abrafo was Cheetham Hill born. His old man had died younger than mine. And gun dealing wasn't all he'd done in 1990. When he came up north he moved back in with his mam. His mam went in a daytime hit-and-run on Queen's Road, a fortnight later. I'd heard five versions. The toddler was in most of them. The pigs traced the stolen motor and found a white girl in a Hulme squat – train tracks, crushed windpipe: a three-day smackhead corpse, and a toddler bawling, three days starved. I'd heard Abs called in some local favours and stayed well clear. I'd heard Abs did it himself: choked her dead. There was another one where they found the body in the motor that knocked down his mam – inside the boot, or sat in the front seat . . . There was never any mention of a feller, just the white girl and the little boy. I'd heard Uncle Desmond had been his alibi.

Afterwards, Abrafo clubbed in with Desmond, then bought a shop of his own, then sold it, then bought another. He could prove his earnings, and he kept his cash clean and growing. His rep would never disappear. I joined ranks late.

He put out his cig, halfway through it, moved the ashtray and sat forward. 'Shiz got us cuttin back. Ten a day.' His ruthless eyes quit blinking – went huge. Abs had a face like a lion. I expected him to ask about my old man and the funeral. But then he smiled it away, and said: 'Right, fuck off. See yer tomorra.'

5

BISTO

WYTHIE. TRYING TO get the key in the door – hand shaking like some fucking Arctic explorer. I was almost in with the milkman again and somehow, maybe that kept me feeling young.

1990: twenty years old and living with the old man. Mam came and went, came and went, for years, before she went for good, that winter. I remembered getting in at this time of night, that summer, after seeing Roisin. Stinking of her. Walking on air. Too sore to sleep.

I emptied my pockets on the table in the hall, dead quietly, so as not to wake Jan.

I hadn't told Abrafo about Thin. What I'd seen. What that Hagfish had said. It was Thin's bloody jacket cooking in the barrel – along with the rest of him – after he'd had his arse torn off by Mary the pet Komodo dragon. I filled the kettle, knocked over a jar of Jan's Nescafé and found the PG Tips.

The old man gone. Maz nearly with him.

I sat at the kitchen table with an empty mug and a fancy shooter. Waiting.

'It'll keep yer up,' Jan whispered.

She was by the door. Half asleep. Eyes more shut than open. I tucked the gun away.

'Enry?' Then she saw that I was crying and said 'Come ere,' and she came over and touched my face, hugged me too tight.

'Yer miss im,' Jan said.

Henry Bane.

'Course,' I said.

'God – what's appened to yer and?'

Ashley had given me a bandage for my knuckles.

'Nothin,' I said. 'Knocked it at work.'

'Knocked some twat out yer mean.' Jan rubbed my tears with her fingers, then she leaned on me. She was standing up but with her head on my shoulder, bed-warm, almost asleep. She smelled grand.

I said: 'Take you out tomorrow night if you fancy it.'

'. . . Ay?'

'Nice little bistro just opened in town.'

'We're alright fer gravy, love.' She said it through a yawn.

I laughed and her head flicked off my shoulder, eyes open again – heavy, dopey.

'Bed, love,' I said.

The kettle boiled.

She nodded and took my good hand.

6
THE YELLOW COAT

July 1990

THE WORLD CUP was already over. I was running most
evenings. Bit of exercise. Did me good. I lapped the
estate and my lungs started to feel it. The Mr Whippy
van was outside the shops, ahead. Kiddies queuing
for a choc ice, the older lads by the new BT
box: techno trackies and bovver boots in this heat.
They were minding a nicked stereo – last month's
ram-raid spoils – a New Order 'Fine Time' remix on
the go.

I clocked a looker coming out of Forbuoys, holding
a broadsheet, struggling with the pull-door. She stepped
outside and stopped to fold the paper up. I slowed
down – our eyes met as I jogged past. Charcoal round

hers. Christy Turlington nose. Bed hair. No tan. Well put together.

I carried on to Gordon's.

'Bobbies bin after yer again, lad?' Vic let me into the hall, fresh fag in his gob. His trilby was on the coat hook.

'Is he in?' I said, still panting.

'Aye. Front room. Doin bugger all.'

'Me dad said to pop round in a bit. He's got them Sammy Davis records you've been after.'

Vic on Sammy: *only coloured wurf knowin.*

'Nice one. Jus tell im to bring um round pub. Can't be arsed trekkin to yours. Cab's in the garage.'

'You want some o these, Vic?' I said, wagging a white Reebok. Straight out the box. I still had fifty pairs of knock-offs to shift. Just a punt buy from working the market stalls with my old man. I hadn't a clue what I was doing.

Vic scratched his bum chin. 'Thema alright lad, int they?'

'Sort you a pair if you want.'

'Do ah buggery.' Vic was laughing. He took the trilby off the hook and put it on, rim tipped down, then he opened the front door again. 'If yer dad rings the ouse, tell im to get down to the Cock o' the North. N tell Work-Shy in there to get off is bloody arse.'

Gordon was sprawled on the sofa in the front room – sport news on the telly, a Carlsberg in his hand. Two empties on the table.

'Iya, Bane.' He'd shaved his temples, greased the short mushroom-cut down. Oliver Hardy meets the Guv'nor.

I said: 'Could o got the door for your old man, mate.'

Gordon took a swig. 'Ad yer tea?'

'Yeah. You?'

'Chippy.'

He switched channels. Spencer Tracy on the box.

'Ever seen this one, Bane? Ee's only got one bloody arm n ee's kung-fuin shit out of um n allsorts.'

'That's right,' I said. 'He fucks up Lee Marvin in a bit.'

'Me dad, right – fuckin loves this shite.'

So did I.

'So does ours,' I said.

Judo throws inside the saloon. The tables collapsed. The baddies glassed themselves.

Gordon switched the telly off and stood up and I followed him into the kitchen.

Our Gordon was a bruiser. Twenty-two and bouncer big. Meathead through and through. He didn't get out of bed if it wasn't to misbehave.

He tipped the dregs of his can into the sink and we sat down at the table. There was a little yellow coat over the back of his chair.

'What we doin tomorra?' Gordon said.

'I'm workin with me dad in the mornin. After that: Bullring. Try n sort out some gear for next weekend. Get back what's ours.'

He was nodding at me like he couldn't wait. 'Al come find yers in Arndale.' Then he crossed his arms on the table, scratching a new glass scar on his bum chin.

'Johnny got stabbed,' I said.

Gordon stopped scratching. 'Fuck off.'

'Should read the locals.'

'When was this?'

'Last weekend.'

'Where?'

'Civic. Not even town.'

Gordon raised his Conan shoulders – shrugged – carried on scratching. 'Av t'find im what did it. Fuck im up. But knowin Johnny – cunt probly ad it comin.' He left his chin alone. He cracked his knuckles. 'Mad bastard, im.'

'Whose is the coat?' I said.

Gordon twisted round, Conan shoulders knocking the yellow coat onto the floor. He picked it up, creasing it more, and dropped it on the table. 'Sister's. Shiz ome from uni.'

'Didn't even know you had a sister.'

'Hassle,' he spat.

Next morning. Arndale Indoor Market. Minding the stall. We had 60s Jackie Wilson on the vinyl player, painting the high notes like a don – smoother than the needle would allow – no sweat, no effort. The tosser who had the rave-gear stall opposite hated us for blaring out the oldies all day. But I'd had the Ruthless Rap Assassins on the go, Saturday before last, and he was still giving us the V.

Jackie sang.

A few shoppers browsed the cassette box and walked off.

Jackie sounded gorgeous, on top of his game, giving it large for the closer, a last stand – sounded like his death rattle.

The old-timers shuffled over – flat caps and wheelie trolleys – trying to whistle.

One of them dug out a Percy Mayfield LP and wiped the dust jacket. 'Oo's this feller, then?' he went. He looked like Joe 90 at ninety.

I started to speak but my dad's voice came out instead: 'Don't ask this one. Knows nowt, our lad. Let us tell yer bit bout ol Percy Mayfield.'

Henry Bane came over to the counter side, just back from the caff by Shudehill, carrying two Styrofoam brews and two bacon butties, a betting slip in his top pocket. He passed me my brew, took the Percy Mayfield from Joe 90 and started gabbing.

'Wrote the its fer Ray Charles, ee did . . .' My dad was a scruff in his tea-brown shirt, stained summer pants, battered Harrington. His wardrobe hadn't seen an iron since Mam left. '. . . no relation to Curtis. This is a real blues singer, this is. Now we don't stock a lot o this but . . .'

Then the volume went down on my old man.

Another customer. She was five-four. Maybe a couple of years older than me. Bed hair. Charcoal round her eyes. Christy Turlington nose. An open yellow coat, slipping off one white shoulder.

'Do you have the Banshees?' she said to me.

What a fucking kitten.

'Siouxsie Sioux?' I said.

'Yeah.'

'Try Afflecks, love. We're more Soul Power down here.'

'Any Prince?'

I flicked through the Ps, showed her the goods. '*Parade . . . 1999 . . . Dirty Mind.*'

'Got them,' she said. 'Do you like rap music, Henry Bane?'

'Sorry?'

Browsing: 'EPMD, De La Soul, Big Daddy Kane?' She pulled out LL Cool J–*Radio.* Her short fingernails were rainbow varnished – each one a different tester shade.

I said: 'How'd you know me name?' The sign just said *Henry's Records.*

'*I* like rap music,' she said. ' "Ladies First".'

'*All Hail the Queen,*' I said, and showed her we had it.

She laughed. Soft. Strange. Croaky. 'I'm Roisin.'

'Gordon's sister,' I said.

'Well done.'

'Where's the big brute?'

Roisin smiled, cocked her head. 'Over there, flexing his pecks. He'd like a little fan club.' Her eyes led me across the market to a sunglasses rack. Gordon was in his fuck-off Lonsdale vest, taking his time. There were poor sods waiting to try on new shades in the mirror squares. They waited patiently.

'You coming then?' Roisin said.

My old man put the Percy Mayfield in a bag and gave Joe 90 his change. Joe 90 looked at Roisin.

Roisin gave him a wave.

Dad looked at me.

'Go on,' he said. 'Bugger off.'

We moseyed down Birchall Way, the three of us, heading to Hulme Crescents.

I said: 'So how come you're taggin along?'

She turned and shot me a sunshine grin. I saw myself in her heart-shaped glasses. 'I'm seeing a friend,' she said. 'Old flatmate.'

She was in tall cherry Docs and denim short-shorts – showing some decent leg. The yellow coat flapped in the breeze, belt loop broken, sleeves pushed up. Tangled bracelets. Green biro scrawl on her inside arm.

'Want one?' she said, scoffing an Opal Fruit, offering the pack.

'No ta.'

'Where's mine?' Gordon said. It was the first thing he'd said since we'd left the Arndale.

'You eat enough,' she said, then to me: 'He's too big to be my little brother. Our mam used to say he was the wrong size.'

'She use to say you was a fuckin accident.'

Roisin snatched his hand, still smiling when he snatched it back. 'Bet we both were,' she said.

Gordon huffed. Gordon gozzed on the pavement.

Clopton Walk Chemist had been bricked in – main

window a spider web. They needed bouncers to keep the junkies away.

The Bullring smelled of bonfire. It was dead busy, all the squatters out in the sun – white lads and a few birds with their baggies off, blonde dreads tied up, toking joints. Tunes sounding stale in the tape decks – the cassettes wearing out. It was still all that D-Mob bollocks and 808 State, booming through the Crescents. Not my speed but I could live with it. There was a West Indian posse chilling in the courtyard. You could tell the Brit-borns from the Tivoli Garden lot – the ones puffing sensimilla through their missing front teeth from the ones still rocking the Terence Trent D'Arby look. Original Yard Men were just muggers – robbing each other, robbing other dealers. Dishonour amongst thieves. Dripping gold, a ratchet blade down their pants or even a Glock 17 next to their bag of gear. It was crack they were shifting. Not what we were after. Gordon was going to try his luck one time and mug the muggers, but I warned him off.

Some Haçienda heads were toasting on the dead grass bank, a sleeping dog with them – its belly to the sky. A few hippies were bobbing about the place and Roisin waved at this flock near a camper van missing wheels. Her bracelets jangled. They waved back.

Gordon said: 'Looks dead rough but they're all fuckin fairies round ere, Bane. Even coloureds.'

Roisin poked him. 'Say that louder, chick.' She fixed her bracelets with perfect hands, checked her nails.

We walked up along the trash heaps, bluebottles

whizzing everywhere, clouds of them making shade, and headed to the second concrete stairwell: graffiti paradise.

'Right, boys. I'm up this way.'

'To see a friend?' I said.

Roisin nodded, biting her lip, making fun of me. 'To see a friend.'

'Who's this friend?' I said.

'A Mr Nosey.'

'A Mister?'

I had her smiling, even if it didn't take much.

'Well, what are you boys here for? *Really.*'

'Like you. Seein a mate.'

I was doing my best but she was the one playing with me.

'How long you up for?' I said.

'You mean back home?'

'Yeah.'

She lifted her shades and shot Gordon daggers. 'Couple of days. Long as I can stick it.'

'Might see you again, love.'

'You might. Think you could keep my little brother out of trouble? Apes don't like cages. But he'll end up in one.' Her voice crackled louder: 'Behind bars.'

'Fuck off, cow,' Gordon said.

She grabbed him by surprise, stood on her tiptoes and pulled his face down to kiss it. 'Love you too.' Then she bounced up the stairwell to the upper deck and tossed us a wave.

'That one's a smiler,' I said.

'Hassle.' Gordon rubbed his face. 'Love ow she reckons yer the good un. Dunt know yer as bad as us.'

'Worse.' I pushed my T-shirt sleeve up and made a fist. Gordon mellowed.

Gordon let him have it – the bastard's head up against the concrete wall in the underpass – the three of us hiding from the sun. He scraped the poor sod along by his hair, tracing a line of graffiti that read *PRAY FOR WAR* – yellow to red. We could still smell the paint.

'That'll do,' I said. 'Christ.'

The bloke had slapped me about a month back, when I paid him a visit after realising I'd handed over three ton for a bag of fifty worming tablets. He'd held a Turkish razor to my throat and sang me the verse to 'Blue Monday', then given me a backhander. And I took it. I didn't bruise easily.

We were dealing in the clubs, me and our Gordon. Casual. Not part of a firm. Risky business. We had a couple of friendlies working the doors getting ten per cent of what we made on the night – but we were only young lads making pocket money. Gordon needed to get the abacus out to count to ten. But I could do the basic arithmetic. Flog them for twelve quid a go. Double or nothing gross profit. Sorted.

The bloke slid to the floor in the underpass. He was a white lad in a Public Enemy T-shirt. 'Got nowt,' he said. His left eye had popped – his whole face gone fried tomato. He coughed a tooth out. 'Got. Fuckin. Nowt. S'fuck off, fuckin twats.'

Gordon jumped on his head. 'Cuntcuntcun—'

I shouldered Gordon off him, just enough to save him from one last boot. I couldn't shift Gordon far.

The bloke tried to move, gave up. His back pockets were full. I emptied them.

A silhouette appeared at the end of the underpass – saw us, changed its mind, and did one.

'Tellin us porkies,' I said.

He had four ton on him. No pills. Just the notes rolled up in his bird's elastic hairbands.

I shaved some twenties onto the floor next to his mouth, and just took a refund, not a penny more.

Gordon kicked the wall to clean his sole, leaving his own tag.

'Ta-ra, Blue Monday,' I said.

7

PARACHUTE JUMP

14 February 1998
Saturday

ALMOST NOON – she was half an hour late. I was waiting in a little caff in town for Roisin, so we could go and see Maz together. I was the only customer in, finishing off a brew and butty, thumbing through a local, solving crimes:

Pg.1: A Halifax robbery in Sale. *Masked thugs make off with thirty-five grand.* The pigs had nothing. Stan Barker had been planning that job for months. I'd heard the driver was a brickie from Sharston.

Pg.4: A drive-by shooting in Longsight left three wounded. *Both suspects in the silver Honda were described as young black males.* It was anyone's guess, it wasn't my turf.

Pg.8: *Three fawns have been found alive and well in a skip in Trafford. RSPCA baffled.* Hagfish?

I skimmed the rest: no lizards on the loose.

The forecast said snow.

The old caff had sticky blue tables, windows washed with grease, a handwritten specials board – spelling mistakes even our Jan could spot. I'd only been once. I didn't know why I'd picked here.

The feller behind the counter was tapping fag ash onto a plate of cold scrambled. He coughed and put the radio on.

'Ever get busy?' I said, folding my paper up.

'Not at weekend,' he went. 'Got lads comin in durin week, what wiv um doin up Withie Grove. God knows what they're buildin there now.'

New cafés.

'Cinema,' I said.

'Thell clear us all out in the end. Am jackin it in, me. Can't mek it pay.'

At least it was warm inside. The posh caffs had fucking air con on all year round.

The door jangled and Roisin came in, the cold with her. She took her scarf off and sat down.

'This what I think it is?' she said, twisting to find the radio.

I told her it was. LL Cool J–'I Need Love' on the go – naff hearing it now.

'Must be Valentine's Day,' she said. Her smile was the same, but her eyes had grown.

'Must be.'

Big black jumper, slashed wide at the neck. Grey skirt, tights and boots. She took her mitts off and put them on top of the scarf. Her skin was like milk.

'Want owt?' I said.

She shook her head. 'Late breakfast.' Then: 'Do you know how he's doing?'

'Maz? I rang um this mornin. Said he was better.'

'That's good.'

'How's the lovebird?'

Her face went hard.

'Don't ruin it,' she said.

'Well? How is he? Lovebird.'

'He doesn't go by "lovebird".'

'"Knobhead"?'

She didn't even blink. 'No. He's called Dan. Doesn't go by his surname either.'

One-nil.

'So who shot him?' I said. ''N why?'

The feller on the counter looked up.

Roisin hunched forward, collarbones out, eyes screaming.

'I said who shot him?'

She picked my hand off the table and stood up to go, taking me with her.

'Fucking child,' she said.

Hospital. Maz was looking rough but he was still with us. He was even awake.

'Were plannin to get a bit o golf in over weekend,' he said. 'Cocked it right up.'

'Flowers?' I said, turning the vase to the sunlight –
window open a crack. 'The missus?'

'The boss.'

'Where's Rana?'

'Jus missed er. Shiz back tonight to watch telly wiv
us.'

'You remember Roisin?' I said.

'Do now. Bloody ell, love. Yuv kept well.'

Maz tried to sit up as she kissed his cheek but he
couldn't find the strength. He winced. We sorted his
pillow.

There was a telly unplugged in the corner, and a
little card on the windowsill opposite the flowers.

Maz -

Hope you get well soon.
All our love & best wishes.

Abs & Ash.

Ashley's handwriting – office-girl formal.

'So what they sayin?' I put the card down and pulled
up the visitor's chair. Roisin sat on the bed.

'It's infected,' Maz said. 'Bacteria or summat. But it's
not comin off. Av told um.'

Roisin said: 'How big was this dog?'

I said: 'What they got you on?'

'All sorts. It's bloody mega.'

'You'll be tap dancin soon. They feedin you?'

'If that's what yer wanna call it.' Maz winced again. He turned to Roisin. 'Love, can you do us a favour – shut that window?'

She smiled. 'Course I can.'

I leaned in close to Maz when her back was turned. *I'm gunna do him*, I mouthed.

That dread?

Yeah.

Roisin fixed the window and came back.

Maz sat up – managed it – itched his face, in need of a shave. 'Ay, Bane – ad this male nurse come in this mornin, givin it proper chat, ee were. Sayin ee were doin this n that – tryna raise five undred fer some charity to do wiv rescuin cats. Got a parachute jump nex week. Parachute? Ah said ad give im a fuckin grand to jump wivout one.'

We all laughed.

He looked at Roisin and said: 'Pardon the swearin.'

She felt the drip stand. 'Blame this.'

Maz said: 'So where've yer bin idin then, love? Lundon?'

'What's he said?'

'Nowt,' Maz said.

'I'll believe that.'

'Yer workin down there, was yer?'

'For a charity.'

'Rescuin cats?' I said.

'And dogs.' She said it to Maz's leg.

Ward corridor. Chemical-cleaner stink. Foreign porters squeaking linen trolleys down the mucky vinyl floor.

Roisin walked ahead of me. She still had a perfect arse. I stopped to push a quid in a vending machine.

'B2 or D9?' I said.

She stared. 'I'm always after the bad lads, aren't I?'

'What, you on a diet now?'

'No.'

'That's twice you've turned down scran. There was nothin of you back then, now there's less.'

'Well, there's more of *you*.'

'There's no fat on me, love.'

'There's more of everything else.'

'Wait till you see our Gordon. He back yet?'

'Dad said afternoon. D9.'

I handed her a Twirl and we walked out together.

'Nippy,' Roisin said, hugging herself up Oxford Road.

The pavement was packed. We were dodging the ice puddles, the students, the shoppers, all the mopey buggers – wrapped up to the nines.

'So let's hear it,' I said, glove hands in pockets. 'What's Knobhead got you involved in?'

'Nothing. Nothing.'

'What happened?'

'Dan found himself witness to a bit of trouble on Thursday, that's all. He's taking some time off work. We both are.'

'Bit o trouble? Twat's almost had his foot blown off.'

She could walk and glare. I couldn't. I missed a lamp post, shouldered oncomers into traffic.

'What does he do?' I said. 'This *Dan*?'

She turned her head to a book sale outside the SU and then looked at me again. A mouth peeked from behind her scarf. 'Customs officer at Heathrow.'

'Nice.'

'Give,' she said.

I took my hand out of my pocket and she hooked our arms together to keep warm. 'Henry, I want your help. We both do.'

'So tell us what needs doin?'

Her eyes were massive, dead pale, barely a colour. 'We need a place. A flat or something. In town – anywhere – just temporary. Just somewhere so we can sort out what's what – get from under Dad's feet.'

'I'm not bloody Travel Inn.'

'Thought you were some big hard man up here now?'

'I'm not bloody Al Capone.'

'And you're not Al Green, either.'

July, 1990. Summer of love. Singing 'Love and Happiness' in the bathtub with her. Just the two of us alone in my dad's gaff. Lovey-fucking-dovey. She had me remembering it all. She let me cut her hair that night. Sad bastard – I'd asked her if I could keep a piece.

I asked her again: 'Say it, love. Tell us what happened.'

Roisin squeezed my fingers.

I said: 'You didn't see it, did you? He just hopped his way home. You got him in the Fiesta n fucked off straight up the M1.'

Squeezing, squeezing, I felt her bones click through mine. 'I'm scared, Henry! Alright?! RIGHT NOW. RIGHT NOW.'

Heads turned, passed us, kept watching.

Roisin hid in her scarf.

'Your nose's gone all Rudolph,' I said.

She let my hand go – stuck it out for a bus.

I said: 'You busin it to Didsbury? I'll just give you a lift.'

The bus stopped for her.

'Roisin.'

No answer.

'Oi.'

No answer.

'Sure your Dan'll be tap dancin soon n all.'

She got on, went straight to the back.

'Ta-ra, Rudolph,' I said.

8
APOSTLES' WARNING

2 P.M. BACK of Billyclub. I was waving the removal van in – the poor feller reversing blind. Orange light twirling, reverse alarm going. I could still hear the chants over it, coming up from the main road. Protestors. Some bird with a megaphone, yelling up Deansgate in a patois.

The van stopped and we unloaded the next lot – Abrafo watching it all from the back step, fag in his gob, arms crossed in his Adidas warm-ups and cashmere scarf. I took one end of a couch and got things moving – then after a bit I let somebody else take over.

'Stressin?' I said to Abrafo.

'Bin alright.'

'No Ashley?'

'Shiz shoppin. Thank fuck.'

'Need owt doin?'

The bird was still yelling. Something about gun crime. Noble causes.

Abs dropped his cig on the back step and crushed it. 'Sort out that racket.' He went in, clocking how the movers handled his Bang and Olufsen surround system.

The pigs had already done the job and told them to move on.

Two bobbies versus nine of them, all women, yelling as one. They were blocking the pavement and had a banner, megaphone, the works – a little angry mob.

Kendals shoppers carrying box-bags weaved through everybody, complaining.

A fold-out table was set up near the shop window – a tenth girl sat behind it – black, young, gorgeous – collecting names.

I said: 'Hello.'

'We're jus after women's signatures today,' she said. 'But cav a leaflet if yer want.'

They were flogging charms and trinkets as well but she was packing them away. Bones and gemstones and rainbow feathers and wooden beads.

I took a glass bottle off the table.

Berta's Love Tonic.

Handwritten.

'Who's Berta?' I held the little bottle between thumb and finger.

The woman holding the megaphone came over.

'Roots tonic,' she said to me. 'Make yah irie.'

'Tenner a bottle?' I said. 'Best do.'

She was a big girl, short and wide, a Mother Goose in a bloke's parka – hood up, almost over her eyes. 'Yah waan fi donate?'

I said: 'Not today, love. Can you tell us bout this Berta?'

'Berta? She local woman. She help wit a community.'

'Whereabouts?'

'Gwey. Yah no go deh.'

A pig called her back over.

They were giving the others a hard time, asking them to roll up the banner:

Stop the Shooting.

Mother Goose left and the girl finished packing up.

'Them real?' I said.

She looked down at her chest.

'The skulls,' I said, pointing to the table. They were tiny songbird skulls in a cardboard box, mixed in with the beads and shiny tat.

'Bring yer good luck,' she said.

She was nineteen, twenty at a push. Gloomy black eyes – camel lashes, clear skin, too much make-up, hair sleeked inside her Bench hoodie.

'Yer need any luck?' she said.

'Try n make me own.'

'They proper work, these. Sometimes.'

'If I get all the good luck,' I said, 'who gets the bad? Some other sod?'

'Can do it that way.' She passed me one. 'If yer want.' There was a red mark on her hand, shaped like letters: *A* and *W*. Raised – like a new scar.

'Who gets the bad luck?' I said.

'Anyone. Yav to pick.'

The skull was soft like paper, weighed nothing. I dropped it back in the box. 'Not convinced. Don't sound like you really go for this yourself.'

'Ow'd you know what ah go fer?' She was stewing about something. And it wasn't me.

'What's your name, love?'

Still stewing.

'I'm Bane.'

'Sorrel,' she said.

'Sorrel?'

'Yeh.'

'That's gorgeous.'

'Oo a'yer?'

'I wanna know bout Berta.'

'Fuck off.'

'I'd like to know, love.'

'Why?'

I put the bottle down. 'Cos I've seen what the War Tonic does.'

Sorrel looked at the other girls – keeping warm, tussling with the pigs. One of them tripped and fell to her knee. She stayed on it, screaming *ASSAULT*.

'Truth seeker,' Sorrel said.

'What?'

'Truth seeker. That's what Berta would call yer.'

'You feelin alright?'

She smiled, gob closed. Her eyes went wet. 'No,' she said.

'Got a feller for Valentine's?'

'Ee's missin. S'why am ere.'

'Look – I'm sorry.'

'Not your fault, is it?'

Sorrel was blinking, trying to keep tears from eyeliner.

The pigs threatened to nick everyone. Things calmed down.

I said: 'What's this about – today?'

'Tryna stop the murders down our way. The gunnin n drugs n that. They called it *AW Women Unite* . . . Cos there's too many dead lads round ours.'

Noble causes.

I said: '*AW*? This a charity?'

Sorrel looked at the scar, touching it with her other hand. 'Me congregation. Apostles' Warnin.'

'Berta?'

Nod.

'Where can I find her?'

Sorrel traced the *W* slowly with her finger.

'Come on, love,' I said.

'Church Place. Flat 39.'

'Hulme?'

Nod.

'Cheers.'

A couple of the other women were watching us chat.

I was ready to go.

'Bane?'

'Sorrel?'

'Bes not see yer there.'

The ladies folded the banner up:
Stop the Shooting.
Stop Shooting.
Shoot
ping.
.

The pigs were smug as fuck.
'Good luck with all this,' I said.
Sorrel smiled, gave up – let her make-up run.

9

GORDON

GORDON CHUCKED HIS knock-off Lacoste jacket on the back seat and put his seat belt on while I pissed off Saturday traffic. He was a monster in a grey stretch T-shirt. His arm was a map. White spots and Hulk veins: roads, places, glass scars, bullet wounds.

He looked pleased, ugly as ever. I drove us round town.

'Told Abrafo,' I said. 'He knew you were comin out.'

Our Gordon laughed, chest out here. 'Can't fuckin believe it, me. Only inside ten munf n now yer workin fer coloureds? Magine what Frank'd say? Fuckin ell, Bane.'

'Frank's not around,' I said.

'Ab-rah-foe? Jungle bungle or what?'

Gordon opened the coin tray, roughed compartment lids, pulled out cash wads, cassettes. 'This a new motor?'

'Ish. Listen, there's a job goin if you wanit. Specially now with Maz . . .'

'What's appened to im?'

'Out of action.'

'Ay?'

'Komodo dragon.'

'Yer what?'

'Big lizard. Lots o teeth.'

'Fuck off.'

'Serious.'

'Ee get a bit close to the bars at Chester Zoo?'

'Some Yardie last night. Tryna go one up on a Staffie.'

'Fuck me.'

'I know.'

Gordon snapped a cassette case with his thumb, trying to open it. 'Oo was ee?' He took the tape and tried to feed the player.

I switched it on for him. 'Let's find out.'

I stopped at the next lights and had a proper look again. A monster. I wondered if he was mad I hadn't visited much. 'You're lookin good, mate,' I said.

Gordon patted my shoulder. Grinned. 'N you, mate. Nice to be fuckin back. We jus need to do summat bout weather.'

'Gunna snow soon.'

'Bloody ell. Bes get me winter wardrobe sorted.'

'Since when did you mither bout clothes?'

'Since ah did the bird, mate. Not a fuckin fashion show in there, ah tell yer.'

'Seen that sister o yours yet?'

'Nah. Me dad said she were back though. Our Roisin up north? Hassle. Mus be after summat.'

'You met that Dan?'

'Ah met some twat. Stoppin in our room, ee were. Cunt.'

'What's his story?'

'Dunno. You tell *us*.'

'She won't.'

'Fuck er. Fuck um bowf. We'll sort it out.'

'So you fancy workin or what?'

'Met couple o Salford lads inside. Got pally wiv this one – our Keith. Looked after im, n that, yer know? Were tellin us to go see is boys outside. Plenny o work goin in security. Ed doorman job if ah wanit, like. Sayin ah could run me own crew n that.'

I said: 'Do what you want, mate. Just let us know.'

Bonsall Street. It was late afternoon, the sky like mud. Church Place loomed ahead, a pub boarded up opposite – car park just weeds and rubble. The newbuilds behind it didn't belong.

'S'what we doin ere, Sherlock?'

'Gordon.'

'Fuckin rescue mission?'

'Gordon.'

'Afro Man know yer pissin about the show?'

'Doesn't know I'm here yet, no.'

'Knew it. Fuckin Frank all over again.'

'Told you. Maz nearly got done by some Johnny Too Bad. I'm gunna find him. Settle it.'

I parked up.

'Lives ere, does ee?'

'Let's go see.'

It was a bog-standard 60s high-rise. Nothing too grim, nothing too mad, but I was pretty sure the kids ran the show come night-time.

Find Berta: find Hagfish. It was worth a shout.

Gordon put his jacket back on and I opened the boot.

'Oi,' I said.

'Ee-ah, what a'them?'

'Little welcome back present.'

Four bottles of Jamaican rum.

'Cheap get. Yuv nicked um, ant yer?'

I had my hand up on his shoulder. 'Keep you warmer than a fake Lacoste.'

'Sez the lad on the Kalibers. N ay, fuckin real deal, this is. Wan't cheap.'

I brushed his shoulder off.

We headed over to the entrance – Tango cans, broken glass. The buzzer doors were locked, but we caught someone on their way out, a young bird in khaki combats and a lad's bomber, chewing chuddy with her gob open. She gave us a dirty look. She wanted to let the door shut but Gordon put his hand in the way. She skulked off into the courtyard, looking back.

They were coming and going from flat 39. It was a fucking drop-in centre. It was Heartbreak Hotel. Druggies, prozzies, all sorts – local faces, mostly young. Rubbing the walls as they came up, zigzagging when they saw us, antsy stares before we'd said hello.

All women. Only women.

We couldn't get past the door.

I knocked on again.

SLAM.

I nearly lost my fingers.

The fluorescents in the hall were dodgy, flashing above the door and giving me a headache, making the sign sparkle: *AW* was keyed into the wood.

Flies were butting the light tube, buzzing round our heads. A great big spider off work in the ceiling join, not doing his job.

AW.

Apostles' Warning.

I wondered what the gaff was like inside.

I knocked once more.

The door opened an inch, still on the chain. 'Get fucked. Not tellin yer again.' Her eyes were acid-pink.

I said: 'Can you help?'

'Yer fuckin need elp, you do.' They were shiny without sleep.

'So help me,' I said.

'Elp police. Beat yerself up.' There was crack smoke in her lungs, tuffs of it still falling out of her bugle, toffee-sweet.

I said: 'I'd like to see Berta, love.'

'Not wivout a woman yer not. Piss off.'

'Rules o the house?'

'Dead right. Our rules.'

I kept it cool. Kept it polite.

'If I get us a bird down here, love, you'll let us in?'

She opened the door another inch and maxed the chain out, then left. A new face appeared in the gap. A white girl. Sixteenish. 'We might,' she said. She stared me out: green eyeshadow on top, blue bags underneath. She was bouncing a baby on her hip. We saw glimpses of him: the chubby feet, the tiny face.

'Ta,' I said.

She looked up at Gordon. 'Ee's not, though.'

'He's harmless,' I said.

'Ee can fuck right off.'

Gordon blew her a kiss.

SLAM.

The tot wailed from behind the door.

Gordon laughed. 'Am fuckin third wheel again already. Like I ant bin away.'

The flies buzzed. My mobile joined in. 'Ashley.'

'New missus?' Gordon said.

'Boss's missus.'

'She forget, does she?'

I ignored him and answered it. 'Ashley.'

'Iya Bane, love. Ow was Maz?'

'Alright, yeah. For now. He likes the flowers.'

'Aw, good. Can yer tell im Abs n me'll visit Monday?'

'Will do. Listen, you still shoppin?'

'Till ah drop.'

'Can I borrow you? Once you've finished.'

'Av shopped. Near nuff dropped. Where am ah needed?'

*   *   *

I rang Abrafo next, and walked back to the stairwell to talk.

'Mek sure there's no trouble,' he said.

'Shouldn't be. It's just women, far as I know. You heard from Thin?'

'No. Keep eye on Ash. N keep us in the know.'

I came back and saw our Gordon, watching another bird leave the flat, scaring her high away. He was picturing his First Shag Since Freedom. She swayed past me into the stairwell. He was still undressing her after she'd gone.

I said: 'Is it love?'

'Ad pay tav that, me.'

'Ask her what her goin rate is.'

He scratched his bum chin, found the scar. 'She wan't on the game, that one.'

'You can always tell, you.'

'Always,' he said.

I could smell her perfume climbing the stairwell before I saw her. She stuck her hand over her brow like she was staring at the sun. 'Anyone needin t'borrow me?' Echo.

'A taker right here,' I shouted down.

She laughed. 'Iya, Bane.'

'Iya, love. Happy Valentine's Day.'

She came up to the fourth floor. 'Appy Valentine's to you. What yer get fer your Jan?'

'Meal tonight is the plan.'

Ashley smiled. Nice teeth. 'Good boy. Bring flowers.'

She was wearing flats for a change. She was in a tight

grey split skirt and a black turtleneck – no shopping bags with her. Her engagement ring was out – twenty carats cramping her finger. It was anniversary day.

I'd sorted Gordon a twenty before Ashley came so he could taxi it home.

I took us to 39, knocked on the door and found Apostles' Warning as good as their word. Ashley hadn't a clue why we were there, she was just making friends.

10

DEM NAH GWAN SHOOT AT WE TODAY

A VIRGIN MARY roped up on a nail, showered in bling – outlined in sequins, feathers, cuttings. She'd been customised like a Golf MK3 decked out by one of Maz's cousins.

It was a kitchen/living space. There were two half-caste girls, about twelvish, sat on a manky rug, giving each other henna tattoos. Ashley bent down and said: 'Oo! Thema gorgeous.'

'We're witches,' one said.

'Can I be a witch?'

We clocked the old madams burning foil at the break-fast table – monged-out, twitching, rushing the next toke – the rest of them on the couch: sad dopey cows, just in a right pickle.

Not quite the face of the campaign I'd seen outside Kendals.

Ashley gave me a look like she'd make a good mam, then she sat on the rug and crossed her legs, brushing away the crack crumbs, while the kiddies drew up her arm with sticks.

The bird who'd let us in was fixing up some tot formula by the sink, baby dribbling down her shoulder, fast asleep.

I was the only tackle in the place. They whispered, smoked. They didn't stare. Ashley made the most noise.

Apostles' Warning: crackheads and gullible maidens. And fish: a laughing skull at the bottom of a tank opposite the window – Paradise fish doing laps through the eye sockets.

There was a sheet of paper tacked on a closed door next to the kitchen space. The Venus symbol biroed thick inside a pentagram. The door opened – no handle on this side, just a black hole. Mother Goose came out – minus parka and megaphone, rattling with cheap jewellery. She saw me and froze, then put her hands on her spare tyre.

'Berta,' I said.

'Aright. Aright.' Cleavage jelly-danced. Berta waddled back in, so I followed.

I cleared my throat – smelling dust, weed, incense, spicy grub, winter damp. There was a small table and two chairs in the corner, a sweaty mattress on the floor next to a canvas wardrobe. A bed frame against the wall – springs mangled like barbed wire. Berta shut the door and told me where to sit.

I just walked the room, eyeing her, eyeing the tat.

She plonked her arse on a chair. 'Sidung.' Her hair was a thinning afro. Brown skin, browner freckles. She wore lipstick, a cartoon shade.

'What is it you lot do here?' I said.

Nutcase digs. More pentagrams, stacks of leaflets, lit candles about to slip off wonky shelving, dream-catchers, a briefcase full of novelty coins – naff shite. Charms everywhere, trash in every corner. I thumbed through plenty just to give her grief. I spied the tops of a row of bottles behind some books.

Once the gob opened, plenty fell out. She started shuffling a pack of cards on the table. Tarots. She moved the cards throughout the speech. I listened, tried to follow, but it was all over the place. She played up the patois. I had to break it down into something simpler.

Apostles' Warning is a *Sistren*.

'Ooman need help fi belief in demself . . .'

Women are sufferers.

Women need a way out.

Women need faith.

Women need to understand that they can say no when they're asked to stash a shooter or mind the gear in a safe house or be expected to shag a feller bareback.

Women are sufferers.

When the violence ends . . .

'. . . Dead mon dem. We be lef. Ooman an dey pickney.'

Kiddies.

'So we say we priors.'

Prayers.

'Dat dem nah gwan shoot at we today.'

Then I stopped her mid-flow and said: 'You know a dread – goes by "Hagfish"?'

She'd stacked three cards up, the rest fanned in front of her.

'Me nuh no Hagfish,' she said, fibbing like a champ. 'Ya chatty wi Sorrel. She tell tings an now yah follow we. But we follow da Science, troot seeker.'

'She kept it zipped, that one. Said nowt. Got um well trained.'

'Sorrel we say prior fa. Er mon be missin. Thin mess wi bad mon bidness.'

'Thin?' I said. 'That her feller? She Thin's bird?'

'Sorrel nuh say?'

I gave up. 'A beauty like that – swallowin this bollocks – tears me heart out.'

Berta lifted up a tarot card – showed it me.

'That one mean owt?' I said.

'Jusdiss.'

Justice.

The baby cried from the front room. Berta looked to the door.

I came up and nudged the table – knocked the tarot stack over, took the top off a War Tonic and poured it over the cards in a snail swirl. She got her hands away in time.

The cards smoked.

'What does that mean?' I said.

Maybe she was just a fruitcake trying to help. Maybe she did a bit of good – gave them all a place to hide, to kip, to be safe. The fuckups. The unlucky birds, still hanging on – those who'd made their choices, or had them made for them. Berta wasn't judging anyone, unless they had a cock. But the tonics said she was up to more.

Ashley gave the kiddies a quick squeeze and one of the mams waved her off, the rest of them just sat around, watching the fish tank, staring at candles – too far gone.

I was still the Invisible Man.

'Poor babies,' Ashley said, outside the door. 'No justice in the world.'

'Dead right.'

We walked back to the stairwell.

Ashley said: 'So oo yer lookin fer?'

Hagfish.

I said: 'There's a bloke they're hidin.'

'A *bloke*? They *were* full o shit then.'

'You hadn't twigged?'

She was smiling again. 'Was chattin to the mother o one o them little ones. She were a right prozzie – nice enough – but God elp them girls. Anyway, she said that Berta's a proper Good Samaritan. Tellin us ow shid fed er daughter, sorted um both out.'

'Call that in there sorted?'

I held the fire-escape door open for her.

'She were tryna rope us in. They all go same congregation.'

'Cast a few spells?'

'Summat proper weird like that, yeah. But it's all ush-ush. Could see the uvas dint like er gabbin. Guess where they av it?'

'Hulme Hippodrome,' I said. 'Tonight. True believers break in after nine, have a service once—'

'—a fortnight. Ow'd yer know?' Ashley reached into her skirt pocket, showed me a crinkled note.

I dug one out of the Harrington, showed her mine. 'Dint know you had pockets.'

Ashley slapped my arm. 'She jus give yer one o them? That Berta?'

The date had been crossed out twice and changed on both.

'Did she bollocks. I lifted it. They must pass um round.'

'Jammy sod.'

'Ay?'

'Yer don't even need us, Sherlock.'

'What's the plan tonight?' We were outside, both of us stood by the buzzer doors. 'Heard you were surprisin the boss. All very modern.'

'What's ee said?!' Ashley laughed, fixing her hair. It was shoulder-length, rinsed dark.

'Nothin.'

'Am tekin *im* out, yeah. Got a swanky otel booked. Jus in town. But room service, Cristal, Valentine's hamper . . .'

'Nice.'

'Ee's fuckin paid fer it.' She had her shoulders up with the cold – fixed her turtleneck – henna squiggles down her fingers.

'Need a lift?' I said.

Ashley turned to me, gave me a wicked eyebrow, glossy lips split open.

Did she fuck.

One of Abs's other boys beeped the horn, his Lexus reversing round in the courtyard. It was Lenny behind the wheel – a keen lad, not too sharp – kept on a short leash. But he'd been Abrafo's designated driver since before my time with Frank. Ashley reached up – kissed my cheek, wished me luck for dinner with our Jan, then jumped in the back of the Lexus. Lenny gave us a nod and drove off.

It was nearly dark. Half-four. The caged light above the entrance stuttered on. I took the note out and read it again.

The Hippodrome. Tonight. True believers only.

So Sorrel was Thin's better half. Only half. Poor cow. But I was pretty sure she'd be better off.

I got back in the motor and blasted the heater on full. Gordon's booze was still in the boot and I thought about dropping it round his.

Roisin.

I put it off.

11

JUKE BOX JURY

JAN WAS IN her towel bathrobe – slicked hair, roots showing. A black sequin frock hanging off the bathroom door handle, a size too small. A fake-tan bottle on the top stair. She had different earrings in each ear. She asked me which one I liked best. I told her. She asked me why. I told her. When she came downstairs she was wearing another pair.

All Saints–'I Know Where It's At' was blasting out of my front room on repeat. She was doing my head in. Bass down, treble up – she'd even fucked about with the settings again. There was a blip over the bubblegum, and I thought for a second that the tune was wearing out, but it was the doorbell instead.

'Can we have it down, love?' I said.

She'd unplugged the toaster to dry her hair in the kitchen while she got Trenton's tea ready – make-up bag next to Birdseye. She couldn't hear me, or the door, or her fucking tune.

'OI!'

I pressed eject. The tape spat out. I flung it on Jan's pile.

They started knocking on the glass when I got to the hall. Jan popped her head out of the kitchen, clueless, shouting *what?* as I opened the door.

Officer Dibble didn't look old enough to shave. He was lanky, no chin, the reflective jacket too wide on his shoulders, his belt overloaded with police issue.

He said: 'Evenin, sir.'

I said: 'Well?'

He cleared his throat and went through the motions: 'This lad belong to you?'

Trenton was next to him, stood just off the step. He folded his arms, rushed past me to get in, kept his head down.

'What's he done?'

'He's bin caught nickin lead off the rec centre roof.'

She'd kill him.

'Again?' Jan's voice. 'Get ere yer little bastard! Al fuckin leather im!'

Banging up the stairs. The officer looked past me – his eyes chasing Jan, chasing Trenton.

'Is he gettin a warnin?' I said.

'Told me he was thirteen. That right?'

'That's right.'

'He's had a formal reprimand before? For thievin?'

'That's right.'

'This could be his final warnin.' His chest radio sneezed.

'Look, his mam'll deal with it,' I said.

'He frightened of her?'

A scream came from upstairs. Jan's not Trenton's. We both looked.

'Wouldn't you be?' I gave him some details, said ta-ra, then watched Dibble struggle with the front gate. I shut the door.

Jan started down the stairs, holding a round hairbrush – the weapon of choice. Her lips were smudged, hair half dried, mascara on one eye: picture of fury.

'How is he?' I said.

'Ow is ee?' she said, stopping on the middle stair.

'He sorry, or what?'

'Sorry? Av give im sorry.'

'Calm it down, love.'

'Ah try n try n try. Everythin ah say ee says no. Ee says fuck off. Ee says fuck off t'me! Us! Is fuckin mam! Ah do me best wiv that lad.'

'No,' I said. 'You don't.'

She changed colour. 'Yer what?'

The doorbell went again.

'Don't.' Her gob opened, shut, opened.

It went again.

'Fucksake.' Jan threw the hairbrush down the rest of the stairs and it bounced over my foot and hit the letter box. I picked it up and answered the door.

Roisin saw the hairbrush and we both smiled.

'What does Henry Bane sing in the mirror?'

I watched her breath smoke. I forgot how to speak.

'Am I coming in?' she croaked. That voice.

I stepped aside.

She came in and scrubbed her boots on the mat. Jan stayed on the stairs, wrapped the bathrobe round her tighter – tits out, head up, stiff, about to crack. 'Iya.'

Roisin took her hands out of her pockets and said hello back. Silence.

I broke it: 'This is Roisin. Our Gordon's sister. Roisin, this is our Jan.'

A second round of hellos.

'Anyone havin a brew?' I said.

Roisin: 'Thanks.'

Jan: 'No, ta.'

Me: '. . .'

Jan came down and snatched the hairbrush from me – using her hand as a blinker when she passed Roisin. She went in the kitchen to finish her face.

Roisin read me as she took her kagool off extra slowly, then I showed her into the front room.

'What did you do?'

'Sorry,' I said.

She looked shy. Awkward. Immaculate. 'I can go.'

'No. Sorry – about before.'

'Oh. Me too.' The bubble roosted in her throat.

'You doin alright, then?' I said.

'It felt weird being in town today.'

We were both whispering. Jan's hairdryer seemed dead noisy.

I said: 'Weird cos it's been bout eight years since your arse graced Manny?'

Roisin smiled at the two Valentine's cards on the chipped mantle and kept whispering: 'Maybe. Maybe more like weird as in it felt like my arse was being watched. Just a horrible feeling. Like there were eyes on me. Like I was being followed about.'

'Swear down?'

'Yes.' She said *yes* again when I said nothing back.

'Even when I was there?'

'Even then.'

'You never said.'

Roisin sat forward, over her knees. She was about to laugh or cry.

'You tried to.'

She nodded.

'Can we have a real chat?' she said. 'Look, I'm not trying to cause trouble—'

'Where?'

'Anywhere,' she said. 'Not at mine, though.'

'Pub?'

She nodded.

We heard Jan's hairdryer stop.

We both shut up but kept eye to eye. Roisin turned away first, and leaned over the end of the couch to see my stereo. The back of her jumper rode up and I saw the milk skin, the top of her knickers.

'All Saints?' she said, reaching back to thump me. 'This is heartbreaking.'

'Hers.'

'"The missus"?' she said – Manc accent back on the go – voice tuned to blokey.

'Don't be a snooty cow.'

Roisin chewed her lip, dying to laugh.

Jan opened the door with her foot. She was holding two mugs and I took one off her.

'D'yav sugar?' Jan went.

Roisin said: 'Not for me, thanks.'

'Same as im.' She perched on the other sofa – feet together, toenails scraping the carpet.

I got off the couch and said: 'Actually, love – think we're gunna pop out for a bit. You'll be gettin ready for a little while, yeah?'

Jan looked up at me, blinking. 'Well . . . yeah, but—'

'Won't be long,' I said. 'Honest.'

The Red Beret. Blow-up hearts and stick-on arrows on the specials board. Pink tinsel round the jukebox. Roisin came back from the loos and sat on my bench of the corner booth instead of opposite. 'Rod Stewart–"Stay With Me",' she said, crossing her legs. 'So how long have you been with her?'

We were naming the tunes. A ten-second time limit for the intros, but this one was nearly over.

'Faces–"Stay With Me",' I corrected. 'Jan?'

'Yeah. Jan.'

I sipped a Kaliber. Roisin on house red. 'Eighteen month.'

'God.'

'Off n on,' I said.

'Right.'

'How bout you n Danny boy?'

She shrugged, looked away, all casual. 'Dan? Same. About eighteen months. Off and on.'

'Right. So what you think of her?'

'Jan?'

'Yeah.'

'Very *you*,' she said.

'Sorry?'

'Blonde. Big boobs. Open for business.'

Our Jan had been a blonde since New Year.

'Piss off,' I said.

'Henry. You were always a *breast* man.'

'Well, what bout you n us?' I said, inspecting her mosquito bites till she gave me a frown.

'Bowie–"Modern Love". You and I were a special case.'

I said: 'You're cheatin, you are. You cued these on the way in while I was at the bar.'

Roisin gasped. 'I never.'

We kept it up like this.

'She's got a kid,' I told her. 'Jan.'

'Yours?'

'No.'

'You sound pleased.'

A punter came up and asked if he could nab our ashtray. He sneezed before he could take it. Roisin said 'Bless you' and passed it him.

'I dunno,' I said. 'It's alright – me n Jan. Steady. Nice n steady.'

Roisin finished her wine glass, giggled. 'Bloody hell.'

'What?' I said. 'What?'

'Nothing.'

'What was Gordon like when you saw him?'

'He was lovely.'

'"Lovely"?'

'Yeah. "Our kid! Our kid!" He gave me a big hug. Swung me round. Tears in his eyes. Said he'd missed me like mad.'

'Like the bloody deserts miss the rain.'

'That was it!' She was laughing again.

'Soft bugger,' I said. 'Knew it.'

Roisin started tugging my arm. 'Aw, leave him.' She turned to the jukebox. 'What's this?'

Five seconds in.

'Everyone knows it.' Her hair flicked as she looked back at me. It was still dark, but I preferred it shorter. 'God, what is it? Is it a cover?'

Fifteen seconds in . . .

'Easy. Isaac Hayes,' I said. '"Walk on By". Better than original, the old man used to say.'

Roisin clapped. 'He's not lost it after all.'

'Never.'

Silence.

'What?' she said.

'You happy down there? Settled? Made a few mates?'

'A few.'

'Yet you still come knockin on our door.'

'I knocked on my door. You answered.'

'You asked for Bane.'

'I asked for Henry. My round?' She stood her empty glass with mine.

'I'll get you one more, love – n then you're gunna tell us what really happened in Lundon. N who might've followed you up here.'

Her face changed. She pinched my wrist under the table and said: 'You believe me?'

Course I did.

'Convince us,' I said.

I took the mobile out while I queued at the bar to give the Royal Infirmary a ring, to try and find out how Maz was keeping. They wouldn't say – just told me his missus was there. I told them to get her to ring me back.

Three minutes later and I was getting two quids' worth of drinks change back in coppers when she rang. The barmaid was ginger, apologetic.

'Iya, love,' I said to Rana, still filling my pockets. 'How's he doin?'

'Bane?' She was in tears.

I told her to take her time.

She said they'd moved him to another ward, hooked him up to the big machines and kicked her out of the way.

'What happened?' I said.

He was in a coma and had been since the lottery results.

12

SHOWTIME

ROISIN REALLY DIDN'T know a lot, but it was enough to get me spooked since it came from her.

She said somebody had waited for Danny boy to get off work on Thursday. She'd been waiting too – in the car park to pick him up. A black feller had knocked on her window, mimed a lighter. She'd shook her head, told him she didn't smoke. He'd left her alone.

Dan-Dan-Heathrow-Customs-Man. The knobhead clocked out half an hour late, some mither with a drug mule – an interview took longer than expected. She was fucked off. She asked him why he hadn't rung her and let her know he'd be late. Dan said sorry and they drove away. They were followed home. They were shot at soon after.

Roisin still wanted a safe flat up here.

I said I'd talk to Abrafo.

＊　　＊　　＊

Black clouds, dead low, no moon out.

I parked up closer to the main drag and walked onto Royce Road with a bobby hat on, a crowbar from the boot down my pants, gun-weight in my Harrington – a fancy shooter, the chamber cleaned out, four rounds left.

I called Gordon's gaff and got answerphone. I let him know I was here.

Hulme Hippodrome.

It was like the Ardwick Apollo but more flash in its day and half the size again. It was something forgotten about – hiding something grand.

It'd been shut twelve years and was begging for the wrecking ball. Music hall, 1901 – bingo hall, 1962. They'd tried to open a corner of it as a community theatre but it'd lasted five minutes – the place was too big, too much needed doing. Outside, it was iced over with white cladding, chunks flaking off, red brick under-neath, weeds poking out of the snapped drainpipes.

I lapped round it, looking for a way in.

An empty road. There was no through traffic this end. It was quiet round here, especially on the far side – even the tramps stayed clear.

Windows were boards instead of panes. Everything sealed up tight, at least on the ground floor. Maybe they were below me – Apostles' Warning, following the old tunnels, canal not far off.

I sucked the cold into my lungs and zipped the Harrington over my throat to keep the heat in.

Three lots of stage doors were barred shut down

the rear face which was set back, arches above each door so nobody got pissed on when they went out for air.

I kept well clear of the street lights and crowbarred a window by the gutter pipe. The wet fibreboard gave. Pure rot. A nail tinked on the pavement. Worming out another one I saw the corner of a grill plate underneath. Berta wasn't climbing through a fucking window any time soon. There had to be another way.

I looked up.

Snow.

Just a sprinkle. No wind. No sound.

I found the steps up to the old box office and sat in the dark at the top, watching it fall.

Silence. A car alarm in the distance but then that stopped. Silence. I had a think, felt Trenton's Zippo digging in my pocket – took it out and played with it. Not even a spark.

The door hit the wall hard behind me and bounced back shut. Something ran out in a Playboy bathrobe, blood over the bunny.

She slipped on the last step. Her legs split at the bottom and she went out, barefoot in the snow, flapping to stay up.

I ran after her – grabbed her.

Sorrel.

She almost butted me trying to twist free – pure fucking hysterical. I covered her mouth with my hand and she bit through my glove. I shook her – clamped her gob shut and threw us both into a backstage doorway. She pressed herself against the boards and I held us together – I couldn't see her face, two inches away in the dark.

I whispered – calm: 'It's Bane. Good luck. Remember? I won't harm you, Sorrel – I swear.'

Heartbeat like a songbird.

Robe thrashed loose.

No knickers on.

Feet kicking me – wet with snow.

She relaxed her jaw and my hand left her gob.

'Don't rape us yer bastard.'

'What's gone on?' I said.

She came forward, wiped the snot running over her lip. 'Nowt. Jus – jus fuck off.'

'You'll freeze to death, love.'

I pulled the robe round her.

'Get off us.'

The sweat on her forehead was shining. Her eyes were still missing, just sparks when she blinked.

'There's blood—'

'S'not ours,' she said. 'S'not fuckin ours. It's . . .'

'Whose?'

'In there.'

'Sorrel!' It was Berta's voice. We both pricked up even more – Sorrel's gloomy eyes appeared, wider than ever.

We saw nothing but snow – heavy now. Sorrel sunk back into the doorway again. Her piss steamed.

I looked out and saw our footprints were melting, almost covered over.

Berta yelled: 'Go fine she!'

'Please . . .' Sorrel said.

I held a finger up for her to be quiet.

I pulled out the shooter.

She stopped pissing and shaking and her face glazed over. She said: 'That's our Thin's gun, that is. Yer fuckin bastard. *You* killed im. Dint yer!'

'No,' I said. 'I didn't. They did. They did.'

'Yer lyin,' she sobbed – losing it again.

'Just stay here,' I said.

I ducked out the doorway, saw nobody. Not a footprint in sight.

I heard panting. Fabric moved behind me.

Sorrel had bolted.

Fuck.

A barefoot sprint. She was already hard to make out in the snow. She fell at the top of the road – up again – out of sight.

I hugged the wall, stepped through the guttering to keep my treads from showing. The box-office steps were in shadow, the entrance door shut but unlatched.

An echo reached me. They must've been outside, round the other end, calling after Sorrel. God help her.

I went inside.

13

UP IN THE GODS

I DROPPED DOWN, found more stairs and came up behind the stage: tealights burned the way. Furry walls, leaks glowing. It was thick with dust – air like ice.

The old dressing rooms were doorless or unlocked and I snuck in the darkest one, the gaps in the walls letting me see along the row. A wall behind me was half missing – ceiling swollen, burst, dropped in on one side. Water dripped constant, fell in a single candle, splashing the wax, knocking the flame about without killing it.

I snuffed it myself and then clocked Hagfish through a hole to the next dressing room. He was topless. His ribs showed. His skin was oiled up, practically silver by candles. He didn't seem that mithered with the cold.

I watched him work. He pulled up a stool by some surviving shelving and used it as a table. He was slotting rounds into a box magazine, one after another. Then he stopped and held a bullet up to the light, sniffed the gunpowder, itched his dreads, and then carried on loading till he'd brimmed the fucker. He reached down, grating something on the floor, trying to pick it up. When he did, he held it high and slapped the handle, posing for nobody.

Hagfish licked his gold teeth. Thin's shooter was still in my hand – this customised semi with four decent rounds – one in the chamber.

Vs.

A fucking MAC-10: full clip, suppressor threaded onto the barrel.

At least they both had a history of breakdowns.

Abrafo still kept a few, but I got nothing out of guns. That didn't mean I was a novice.

Berta came in the dressing room – no door to knock on first.

Hagfish didn't turn around.

Berta didn't seem so arsed about gun crime now.

She got behind him and started giving him a massage – humming as she lifted his dreads to work on his neck. She throttled him till he purred. She must've been three times wider than him, easy.

'Sorrel—' she said.

'Nuh no matter. Me ready get Thin. Is done, sight? Tanks fi dat ooman. She a go tell yuh is bludclot secrets. She a go tell yuh when an wheer.'

Berta took a candle next and poured the wax over his back as he talked. He was too high to flinch.

She bent over him and landed a kiss upside down. 'I-rey, sis,' he said, licking her mouth.

Then he batted her away and stood up. I could see she was still keen. They copped off again and he started pawing her, pointing the shooter down her tits. She went mad for it. She tore her kit off. There was plenty to see. Enough to make you go blind.

I left them to it.

A bleat echoed through the place. Another bleat. Another bleat. A wheezing, fizzy noise, like a talking doll crying backwards – but it sounded alive.

I followed it to the front, kept back and saw it, saw them all. A baby deer, bleeding centre stage.

The battery lamp gave her a spotlight. She was punch-drunk, razor-slashed. She stalked the stage, wetting it.

There were more candles dotted around, tonic bottles: Love and War, bloody hoof-smears in the light.

The congregation was a half-circle around Bambi – cold air, sweaty faces – all of them were sat down with their arms folded, legs crossed. Nobody was decked out in magic-ceremony hoods – we were talking: pyjamas, vests, trackies, one or two bathrobes. Coats and that piled up at the side.

There were eight women and spaces for a couple more – all monged out from passing the pipe around – the fumes even filling this place.

I looked up and – fuck me – felt small. Hulme Hippodrome was swanky, enormous. The stage lamp was just enough to glimpse the old glory.

I u-turned and went out into the stalls, worrying

more about being heard than seen. I climbed to get a decent view of the show, stuck to the dark, made the stairs alongside the stalls, made the back balcony at the top. It was all cobweb chandeliers, fancy gold crests, faded palace colours – a hundred rows of red seats. Some of the seats were missing – sucked down into the collapsed flooring.

The balcony whinged as I moved across it and found a spot. I kept still, waited, came forward and spied over the edge. I didn't do heights but it wasn't too bad in this dark.

I'd been hoping for a song and dance but it seemed like it was going to be a sit-down performance. Still, a good job our Ashley hadn't made it down.

I watched poor Bambi get up, skate about without going anywhere – fall again and call it quits.

This wasn't Ashley's scene.

Hagfish and Berta came on stage. She was holding a candle. He had his jacket on – both hands empty.

He said a few words – arms out, high and mighty – softened his slang. He made us all feel welcome.

I took the gun out again and pulled the trigger. The deer went barmy – kicking itself back from the dead. Hagfish nearly took one in the nadgers. Candles went over. Berta got a hoof in her spare tyre and fell too. The tonics smashed, sparked quickly – washed Berta in flames: cue screaming.

Hagfish had his tool stuffed at the back of his waistband. He got it out and opened fire on the empty crowd. He was shooting blind – down at the stalls – up at the

gods – spraying the wings, but no near misses. The
noise was unreal. He left the trigger alone. A million
echoes.

He looked out into the black – fat chance of finding
me. He bellowed: 'Raatid! We put serious Obeah pon
yah, likkle mon! Yah hear me now, yah ras-clat? Eaz
haad! Yah messin wit real bad mon bidness, yah nuh
see?'

The birds were sobbing in disbelief. Some had scrambled for their clothes during the madness and wrapped
Berta up to stamp the fire out. Others were just stood
around – brains smoked, still spacing with the noise
and light.

I aimed again.

Not breathing.

I squeezed the trigger and fluked it royal – put one
between Bambi's eyes instead of his – just to shame him.

She keeled over and her matchstick legs went stiff
and twitchy. Hagfish saw the flash and took rough aim.

I scarpered.

The air was full of noise, dust, woodchip – then it
peaked and I couldn't hear a thing. Bullets ripped through
the balcony, tore up the broken seats and then things
started to sway. I saw my foot go through the flooring
but only part way. I tried to pull it out but I was wedged
in a treat – bastard splinters through my shoe.

Hagfish was up in the gods in no time. I heard him
panting, saw him between the seats a few rows up. The
bits of him poking out of his army jacket were still
shiny with oil.

I managed to prise my foot out of the front row without using the crowbar. There were cuts on my ankle I felt, but couldn't see. I plucked daddy splinters and then kept low, kept moving.

Hagfish. I knew I could have the fucker if I got close enough – took the shooters out the equation.

Hagfish picked a row, shimmied closer to me without knowing it – I had one eye on him, one eye on the exit. He was buzzing. Scraps of light bounced off his teeth: 'Yah be nuh dupi ghost, mon. De bwoy be flesh n bone.'

I popped up in his face when he reached the front row, and he shot back with a fright, squeezing the trigger, firing at the floor.

His leg went through a new hole.

The MAC-10 went over the balcony.

Both of us reached for it in midair – miles off.

I got hold of him, dragged him out onto the seats, fired Thin's gun next to his face, through the nest of dreads, nearly taking his ear off. The fight left him and he relaxed and stared me down.

A black eye on black skin. I'd already given him a good hiding and up close he still looked rough from yesterday's punch-up.

'Me know yah, bloodclat. Bane dat fatty bwoy call yah, nuh? Hahahahaha . . . me de Don-Dadda now, mon. Troot.'

I said: 'You're nowt, son. Just a bit doolally. N now you're dead n gone.'

'Yah can box Hagfish but yah cyan kill Hagfish. Obeah protek.'

I thumped him again and got an elbow in the mouth. His jacket collar slipped out of my fist.

He came up and I landed another left on his jaw – he staggered over the seats and fell onto the next row. I pointed the shooter, aimed for his heart and fired. The last round jammed – a waste of time.

Hagfish was up and running. I chased him, followed my row to the exit – gun still in my hand – the old balcony rocking like it was about to go any minute.

I could hear Hagfish's jacket flapping as he raced up the stairs, shouldered the entrance door and disappeared outside.

The snow had stopped. It was untouched, a clean sheet. I took off after him, racing him towards Alexandra Road, crunching the snow, stepping in his footprints, watching him kick up the sheet.

We sprinted for five minutes – ten minutes – felt like hours. I was bored. He was panting regularly, and I could hear the goz building in his throat like it was mine, making his breath ratty until he spat it out. His skinny legs were going strong. My ankle gave me trouble but I kept up the pace.

We headed into Moss Side.

He ran out into the road as a van drove past – horn beeping – brake lights colouring in the snow. Hagfish turned a corner and scrambled over a wire fence onto a lit path that cut across the back of a new cardboard terrace row. I heard another car horn behind me. I ran over and cleared the fence – Hagfish still in sight.

A few white lads were dealing at the side of the path,

caps on under their hoods, spliffs glaring in the dark. Their eyes went up as I bolted past – Hagfish already on the main road again.

We ran forever.

Dreads bouncing, he never looked back.

I was the fitter man but he wouldn't give up the game. My chest was tight – crushing the air out of my lungs, the ankle killing me now, plus a cross-country stitch. But I was gaining.

The estates were dead – white-roofed maisonettes – a winter bloody wonderland, just our gasping ruining the peace.

Alexandra Park was 200 metres away, but he ran past the locked gates and headed towards the next lot of housing.

There was a gang of them outside a shut chippy, stood under the street lamp. Just blobs at first, my eyes streaming in the wind. Hagfish shouted something, the blobs parted. Hagfish collapsed but they helped him up, got him inside a gaff next door to the chippy – the front door opening from inside.

I got closer and I saw a couple of Staffies minding the BMXs.

They were just young blokes, no birds in sight. They came forwards and made a wall. I skidded to a stop and dropped to my knees in front of them – clawing for air.

'What youz fuckin doin round ere?' one of them said.

I tried to speak but was too knackered for words.

'Hag – fish,' I managed.

Another lad stepped closer – his jaw going like mad. He chewed his tongue: 'Agfish be – fuckin don . . . fuckin top dog . . . fuckin big man, inney? Thin's gotta be dead. Ee's fuckin new man now.'

The Staffies barked.

He pulled out a six-shooter, fired once into the snow. The dogs whined. 'Shud up,' he said.

One of the lads put his hand down towards me. I took it and he cut my palm with a blade.

I pulled him to the floor and belted him so hard I felt his cheek break. I got the gun out and held it to his head.

His hat had fallen off. He looked about twelve.

He started to laugh and the laughter became tears, then he was crying his eyes out – begging.

The lad with the six-shooter laughed, too.

'That's Thin's piece init?' he said. 'See. Thin's fuckin dead. Told youz, dint ah?'

'Jus fuckin do im,' another one went.

I heard a car engine scream but couldn't see a car.

The lads looked over me. Headlights dazzled them, lighting their faces before they scattered.

I saw what happens when a Staffie tries to maul a moving Fiesta wheel.

It was *the* Fiesta – the back passenger window broken, covered with a bin liner.

It made a handbrake turn, bounced up the pavement and came to a halt. The lights were blinding – stuck on full beam, the engine still running.

The chassis rocked. Snow settled. The driver door opened.

'Ee-ah, dick ed – get in!' It was our Gordon behind the wheel.

I jumped in the front seat and took my bobby hat off. 'Why dint . . . didn't you . . .'

'Ah did, mate. Fuckin beeped the orn n that but yer jus went after im.'

We lurched off the pavement. Gordon missed the gears. I put my seat belt on.

'Gunna snuff me a few monkeys while am down ere, Bane. Look at um do one. Smart cunts.' He tried to run them down, turning the wheel at the last second, doing donuts in the snow. 'HAHAHAHA. Let's av yer.'

We clipped one lad and lost a wing mirror.

Gordon was pissing himself.

I held the dash, seeing his joy at seeing the world spin.

'Get us fuckin out of here,' I said.

'Ome?'

'Town. Billyclub.'

'Right then. Looks like am tekin that job.'

'Ah were followin yer down the road. Watched yer chase some cunt arf way round town . . . oo yer ringin now? Afro Man?'

I had the mobile stuck to my ear as Gordon drag-raced Sikh cabbies down Oxford Road.

'Yuv lost it, mate,' he said.

'I lost *him*. He was the one that got Maz.'

'Feller what as a dragon?'

'Aye.'

So Hagfish had taken over Thin's crew. He'd killed and spooked his way to the top. Only, I couldn't picture him staying there – too nutty – no head for business. But he'd planned this. He'd come from somewhere.

Gordon snorted. 'Mate, what yer fuckin doin?'

'Watch what *you're* doin,' I said as he went through a red light.

I heard my name. Abrafo's voice on the phone.

'Abs,' I said. 'Thin's dead. Hagfish snuffed him.'

But he talked over me and said: 'Come to the Renaissance otel. Room 190. Top floor.' Then he hung up.

14

BAD FOR BUSINESS

I PUNCHED THE button and the console lit. The hotel lift was too smooth – I couldn't tell if we were moving. Trapped between four mirrors, Gordon was checking his form. My shoes were mucking the carpet.

A bird in a frilly cocktail dress got in on the second floor and lit the button below ours. She was a right looker – all legs – five-inch heels – calves getting a workout. Gordon parked his back against a mirror wall and gave her the middle. She took some lippy out and gave herself a touch-up.

Mint arse on that, Gordon mouthed to me, eyeballing her.

I nodded.

Prozzie, he mouthed.

No chance.

Bet yer.

Bollocks.

Tenner?

He raised a never-ending eyebrow in the mirrors.

Tenner.

'Ow much, love?' Gordon said out loud.

'What's that, chicken?' she said, without turning her head.

'You erd.'

'More than yuv got on yer, fuckin scrubber.'

The lift pinged. She snapped her new lips and heel-strutted out onto her floor. Doors closed, we could still smell her shampoo.

Gordon laughed. He put his breath on the mirror she'd used and wiped it with his forearm. He checked his form again: Mr Universe. 'Told yer.'

I opened my wallet and coughed up.

The top floor was a short corridor with pale carpets and hot radiators. This black porter was counting bank-notes outside room 190.

'You im?' he said to me, stuffing the money in his back pocket.

His tie was off, top button undone – scruffy – bad for business.

'Dunno – who am I?' I said.

'Abrafo's white lad.'

'That's right.'

'N im?'

'New employee.'

He looked us over. 'Tek yer shoes off fore yer go in. Both o yer.'

We did.

He said: 'Av seen nowt but tell im am callin police in two minutes.'

'Don't get cocky,' I said.

He dropped the keycard in the slot, elbowed the handle down and pushed 190 open.

We went past the ensuite as we walked in – the door was open wide. There was a crack in the mirror. A tooth in the sink.

I kept off the rug which had soaked up the spilled Cristal – a silver ice bucket, upside down like a sand-castle.

Abrafo was stood by the window in his new tux, lighting up. 'Don't touch owt,' he said, breathing out smoke. He took a huge drag, tapped the ash into his hand.

You could smell the blood as well as the fags. It was a right horror show.

She was still cuffed to the king-size bed, gripping the bars of the headrest, the ends of her fingers missing – cutting today's henna patterns off. Tape over her eyes, tape over her gob. They'd slashed her out of her new slip and made her ugly. They'd made a Valentine-pink bedspread dark and wet. They'd painted the walls with her.

'When?' I said.

Abrafo looked at his wife, looked at me. His eyes

were red, his voice tiny but solid: 'Got ere late, bout ten. Thed left er fer us. Like this.'

'We can cover her. We should.'

'Don't touch er.'

'I'm sorry.'

'Ah dint spew. When ah come in. Ah dint spew. Strong stomach we all av, ay? Look at er, yer cunts. Look at er.'

'We'll find um.'

'Ah know.'

Gordon's face was stone – he wouldn't let me catch him staring.

'They leave anythin?' I said.

Abrafo: 'Nowt.'

I was speaking low, but still too loud. It felt disrespectful to her, like I was vandalising the room. I made myself look again.

'What do we do?' I said.

Abs smoked. He ignored me.

'We stickin around?'

He said: 'Fer the pigs?'

'Yeah.'

'*I* will. Yer best fuck off wiv im. This the big lad?'

Gordon nodded.

I felt kitten-weak.

'Oi, Bane,' Abrafo said.

'Yeah?'

'Erd bout yer dad.'

'Did you?'

'Am sorry.'

'I'm sorry.'

He took a last drag and reached the filter. His anger came. 'This down to you? Is it? Is it fuckin cos o you?'

'What?'

'Bin nosin about fer sake o Maz.'

'I didn't get her involved. I was careful.'

His anger went. 'Tomorra. Yer tell us everyfin again.'

I said: 'Abs, listen – Ashley was—'

He put the cig out. '—She *was*.'

3 a.m. – back home in Wythie – Gordon had dropped me off. Jan's note was on the back of a takeaway menu on the kitchen table.

> you made me feel so embarased you made me feel like shit ~~you could of rung~~ gone town with sharon dont want you in are bed when I come in

I cleaned my knuckles in the sink, then sat down and rested my ankle on the next chair, gulping a brew. I took the spring and follower out of Thin's gun – stuffed a pipe cleaner up the barrel to clear it, pushed the empty magazine back in and binned the last round along with Jan's note. I wrote her a new one on the back of an envelope and trapped it under a can of gravy granules from the cupboard. I left it on the table and went to bed.

15

THE COACHMAN

July 1990

SHAGGED HER? I hadn't so much as copped off with her but the old man must've been wary – he'd started dishing out the good advice. He reckoned she was a bit of a bright spark – an intellectual bird – *all them big words, big ideas*. He'd only seen her twice – both times yesterday – once at the stall, then that night, in the Cock o' the North. He and Vic shared the booth and had a quick pint with us all – but that was it. The old man had listened to her talk while I'd listened to her laugh. He watched me eyeing her up, and said to me in the morning:

'If she's after a toy boy – some fancy man – then let er bloody get on wiv it.'

Roisin was three years older than me. Not exactly Maggie May.

'She's oneathese. Knows it all. Knows ow to mek a pig's ear o things, more like. Er dad's ad it up to ere, lad. She's a right one.'

'What's our Gordon then? The good son?'

'They're both a bloody pair.'

Dad kept all this shut around Vic – he wasn't going to start mouthing off about his daughter.

Roisin.

My dad was miffed I hadn't kept with our Alice. But it had fuck all to do with him.

Sunday afternoon – quarter past twelve. Gordon's. I knocked on the front door and Vic opened it on his way out again.

'Is he in?' I said.

'If ee is, son, ee's not doin much about it.'

'Ta.' I went inside.

I could hear the radio on in the kitchen – a straight line down the hall. The DJ was gabbing over 'Doctorin' the House'.

'Alright, lad,' I shouted through. 'Get anythin last night?'

The radio went quiet. 'Lad?' A voice. Soft. Strange. Croaky.

Roisin appeared in the kitchen doorway without make-up. She was in a baggy T-shirt that finished high on her thighs. She cupped her tits through the material. 'Lad?' she said, pulling her best ugly face.

I laughed but it didn't come out right. 'Sorry, love. Thought you were our Gordon.'

'Still in bed.'

'How are you?'

'Still offended.'

I came in the kitchen and she turned the radio up – eyes following me, having fun. I saw the charcoal was still round them, washed out but there.

There was a blood-streak smiley logo on the back of her T-shirt. She had it on back to front. 'Would you like breakfast?' She rubbed her permanent bed hair and then finished cutting a loaf.

'It's bloody middle o the day.'

'Dinner then,' – pouring apple juice into a fat polka-dot mug.

'I'm alright, love. Been up hours.'

She giggled. 'Doing what?'

'Nowt,' I said.

'Then why get up?'

I fetched a tub of low-fat margarine out of the fridge for her.

Snap! – 'The Power' came on. She bounced like a fitness instructor – hopping about as she made her breakfast – too full of beans for hangover day. Dancing badly, unembarrassed, she shook her arse – all go. I crossed my arms and made like I was disappointed. 'This your sort o thing?'

She kept moving. 'Nope. Not really. But it's good to dance every day.'

Her legs were bruised, her feet tiny.

'Thought you were into Siouxsie Sioux, n that?'

'I am into Siouxsie Sioux, and that.'

'Can't dance to that shite, either.'

'You can,' she said. 'Same as this.'

I leaned against the cooker – feeling worn out just watching her. 'Was it a late one? You go town after we left?'

'Yes. We did in the end. You?'

'Oh aye.'

She was wiggling with her back to me now as the toast got buttered. 'Take it you found a young lady to drag home.'

I said: 'Please. I'm like a monk, me.'

She turned round and stopped bouncing, started grinning – a little out of breath. 'Are you now?'

'Yeah.'

'Bollocks,' she said.

'Aren't you a snooty cow.'

'Am I?'

'Tryna hide it but there's a bee in your bonnet. Who was he? Not left his number?'

Roisin dropped the bread knife on the plate and made it clatter. She turned the radio off. Her face went calm and hard to read.

She was fucking gorgeous.

'I think you're worse than him,' she said. 'I think you're what he'd like to be.'

'Who's this now?'

She glanced up at the ceiling, another smile growing. 'Our Gordon.'

'N what does he wanna be?'

'A ladies' man,' she said.

'He's more Lee Marvin than Errol Flynn, is our Gordon.'

'Errol Flynn? Hmm . . .' She folded her arms, copying me. 'Dad thinks you and Gordon are *bloody villains*.'

'Heard you're an angel.'

'Are you trouble, Henry?'

'What do you think?' I said.

She had great big laughing eyes someone had forgotten to colour in. She had it all going on upstairs.

'I think you'd like a brew,' she said.

'Love one.'

She had the back bedroom, facing out over the plots that were crying out for a weeding – but the curtains were still drawn.

A massive poster of Siouxsie over her wardrobe, chopped through the middle so she could open the doors. Posters of films I hadn't seen, and one or two I had. She liked Pixies, the Fall, Nick Cave and bloody Morrissey.

'Can't stand that soppy bugger,' I said, pointing with my brew.

'The last bloke I was with was mad on him.'

'Puff?'

'Funny, that.' Roisin crawled onto her duvet and sat with her legs crossed open like a Buddha.

'Funny why?' I said.

'He decided he was mostly gay.' She gulped her apple juice. 'I always thought his hair was too nice for a bloke.' Cradling the mug with both hands, she kept it inside her legs – pressing her shirt to cover her modesty.

I went through her tunes. A copy of Janet Jackson's *Control* . . . Prince–*Sign O the Times*, the case empty. It was a start. I switched her portable stereo on at the wall and pushed Janet in the deck.

There was a broken shop dummy tipped against the corner by the window. He was missing a leg, wearing a frilly lampshade as a hat, and she'd painted his nails – written WILL NEVER MARRY across his abs.

'Where's that from?' I said. I took a gulp.

An outstanding brew.

'I nicked him from this factory loft I squatted in with my ex.'

'The puff?' I said.

'Another ex.'

'You get around.'

'Hardly.' She was nodding along to Janet.

'Bollocks.'

A clever grin. 'That what you think?' She put her juice on the bed table and the mattress squeaked. She shut her legs, shut her eyes. 'Listen, I'm chaste!'

'Chased? Chasin who?' I went.

Roisin fell back – shrieked with laugher.

I sat on the edge of the bed and went to touch her hand – almost – but then I bottled it. 'What you got on this afternoon, love?'

She opened her eyes.

My blood jumped.

'Nothing planned. But, shit – I've just remembered I left my coat at this party in Hulme.'

'Unlucky. Might rain later.' I stood up and peeled the curtain back. Blistering sunshine.

'Might do,' she said, covering her face.

'We'll have to go fetch it,' I said. 'Y'coat.'

'Will we?'

'Aye.'

'You are different,' she said.

Janet sang about nasty boys.

I said: 'What?'

'Gordon.'

'Shall we get him?'

'He's still asleep,' she said.

'Dunno how.'

'He sleeps through anything. It's all he does.'

I downed my brew. 'Best go now then. What am I doin? Waitin around?'

She stood up on the duvet – stretching like a cat. I wanted to break off a bit of her and eat it. 'No,' she said, yawning. 'You're staying here and watching me get dressed.'

What have you done for me lately?

'Sounds good,' I said.

'Downstairs. I'll be ten minutes.'

We got the bus into town. I gave her the window seat.

She'd had a quick bath but didn't mither with drying her hair. A perfect springy mess – dyed black, plug-socket frizz, chopped above her jawline.

We talked about the music she didn't like. The food

she did. She took her heart-shaped sunglasses off and pushed them over my eyes. 'Do you like trying new things, Henry?'

No.

'Depends,' I said – the lenses were tinted red, grubby with fingerprints.

The Bullring. Sunny Sunday afternoon. Roisin went up the stairwell first.

Cherry Docs. Tartan miniskirt. The rest of her lost inside one of Gordon's gym polos.

There were marker-pen scribbles up the wall:

♀ **we live in fear of rape why is there no light on these stairs??**

~~SEE U TONIGHT SWEETHART~~ ♥   ← Fuck off
                                     twat what
                                     wrote this

I took the shades off and pocketed them. 'You wanna be careful round here.'

'I am.'

Roisin knocked on a door. She laughed and hugged the bird who opened it. She introduced me to Sally – white, late twenties, purple hair, tall and gangly, ironed-on grin. Sally took us into the flat and we said hello to the room.

The flat was a bombsite.

A tubby black feller in circle shades and a Kangol

cap stuck his thumb up at us from a sofa chair – a mini suitcase next to his knees.

'I-ney.' A spliff bounced on his lips.

I said: 'Alright, mate.'

Roisin giggled.

There was a white couple necking on the couch, blowing smoke into each other's gobs. Students. Party streamers in his blond dreadlocks – his bird twirling his rosary necklace round her fingers.

Another white bloke was dossing on the floor, underneath Roisin's yellow coat. His tongue was hanging out – dipping in some fag ash. His arms were round a bottle of Strongbow like some kiddie sleeping with a cuddly toy.

Sally yawned through a grin. 'Still avn't ad a tidy up fer las night.'

'Still haven't chucked out the dregs,' I said.

'Ay, we live ere,' said the lad on the couch.

'Just testin,' I said.

Sally offered me a hash pipe and a brew and I told her I'd just take the brew. She gave the pipe to Roisin and then went into the kitchenette, after a clean mug.

Disney's *Pinocchio* was on the box – a big black and white set in the corner.

'I love this,' Roisin said, sitting on the rug. Her arse found the only clear spot.

'Best cartoon,' I said.

'You reckon?'

'Yeah.'

'Why?'

Kangol reached down to pass her a silver lighter – his face split open – bright white teeth, 'Dehya go, sis,' and he sat back in his chair.

I squatted down next to her as she lit the pipe – eyes on *Pinocchio*. I said: 'You've Honest John n the tabby cat as the bad buggers at first, right? Tellin Pinocchio to wag school, n that. But then they get clued in on the Coachman. We thought they were the baddies, *they* thought they were the baddies – then they meet some shady bloke down the pub one night n straight away they know he's the fuckin don. They're terrified of him. We're terrified of him. All of a sudden, Foxy n tabby go straight down the food chain. We all just shared a pint of ale with pure bloody evil. Lesson for the kiddies isn't don't tell porkies – it's there's always a badder man. He'll try n do you harm. N he'll get away with it in real life – just like he does in this.'

Roisin gave back the lighter. 'I prefer *Jungle Book* now.' She inhaled – coughed it straight up. 'Fucking hell,' had another go and offered it round.

'Not for me, love.' I nodded to Kangol. 'You live here n all, mate?'

'Nuh. Me be here fi bit o bidness. But wi satta dem. Yah waan try ryal ganja, mon? Nuh lie.'

'Henry. Not right now, ta.'

'Call me Dudley, mon,' he said, spliff burning up. He was holding his beanbag gut like he was due twins any minute.

I said: 'What's in the case?'

'Save us a bit on that,' someone said. It was the feller

who'd been roughing it on the carpet of cigs. He was up – Roisin's coat on his shoulders. He held his hand out for Dudley's spliff. He looked like death.

Dudley gave him a toke. He choked on it, swore – gave it straight back, said he was going for a slash.

Roisin nudged my hand and we saw the back of her coat – stained to shit – disappearing into the bathroom.

I said: 'I'll get him to cough up for the dry-cleanin.'

Roisin shook her head, right up close, smiling.

Sally put a brew in my hands. The mug was scalding – last night's lipstick on the rim. I shifted some rubbish, made room for it on the rug, while there was another knock on the door. Sally let a West Indian feller in – short dreads, black Adidas suit, gold chains round his neck, gold rings on every finger.

Everybody came out of their haze to give him the eye and give him a shifty hello.

'I-tes,' this one said, winking at us – teeth either missing or gold.

Nobody introduced him. He kissed Sally's cheek and she wiped away some empty lager cans and sat down on the other side of Roisin.

'Know him?' I said quietly.

Roisin shrugged, watching Disney.

Dudley got a tap on the shoulder by Goldie. 'Hot steppa,' he said laughing so much the twins were kicking. He was the only one happy to see him. Dudley stood up and dropped two fat pre-rolls – one into Roisin's lap, one into Sally's.

'Fi me ready gyal dem.'

The two Yardies went into the kitchenette together – Dudley hauling his little suitcase along with him. He shut the door to.

'Dint know ee were back,' the lad on the couch said, miming the words out in a big whisper.

'Wonder if ee's still goin wiv that girl?' Sally went.

'Thought ee got deported.'

'Dudley?' I said.

The lad's tongue was dozy with weed but he knew the story: 'Nah, the uva feller. Dealer. Big time. Is flat got raided round Christmus. Dibble spose to av sent im back to Kingston. But ere ee is.'

Roisin – blinking happiness.

Figaro – fishing with his tail.

'Ee ad a row wiv Stan Barker's security firm las year,' the lad said. 'All got a bit rough in the end. Couple of um went missin. Wound up dead.'

'That's him?'

'That's im. Horace.' He groped his missus. 'She'll tell yer.' He patted her fishnet thigh. 'She works açienda bar. Knows all the goss, this one.'

She yawned and didn't take her cue.

He carried on: 'Know Stan Barker? Salford Stan? Nasty fucker.'

This Stan became chief doorman for two clubs last summer. He left gruesome warnings for the old bouncers. He stabbed the ones that still came to work. He replaced them with his own crew the same fucking night. He muscled the management. He dealt his own gear. I knew one of his lads who let us make some small change in one of his clubs, but I'd never seen Stan, though I'd heard he could give our Gordon nightmares. I'd heard some Yard Men had tried their luck and it'd ended in stalemate.

The pigs had something on Stan, and he was inside now, pending trial. But business still boomed.

'They're puttin im away – Stan.' The feller tipped his head to the kitchen door. His hand a gun – trigger to temple. 'Be why ee's back. Horace. T'tek over.'

Sally said: 'Forget yer nittin needles, you lot? Give it a rest.' Grinning again: 'Av never seem im shoot anybody. Av never seen anybody shoot anybody.'

'Sally's right,' said his bird on the couch. 'Leave um. Leave um all to it.'

Roisin was glued to the box – watching Geppetto smoke his way out of the whale.

Sally lit her joint and felt Roisin's skirt. 'Likin this,' she said. 'Where'd yer get it? Afflecks?'

'Sue Ryder.'

'Gorgeous.'

I said to Sally: 'That dickhead in the loo has ruined her nice coat.'

Sally tutted. 'Ah think ee's fallen in. Ay, cav one o ours if yer like, love. Got loads o shit people leave ere. Wanna try summat on?' She pushed her spliff into Roisin's gob and broke the spell – Roisin's eyes left the telly. Sally grabbed her hand. Roisin grabbed mine and we stood up and waded into the poky bedroom – clothes hiding floor.

*   *   *

'Bit warm for leather,' I said, letting them put my arms inside it. 'No chance,' I said, getting a quick look in the mirror. It was a Canal Street Special. The girls loved it – rolling about on the bed, having a fit.

'What's she like, out there?' Roisin said afterwards, popping the collar on a tatty Levi's jacket and stroking the sleeves.

Sally looked up, rooting through another pile of outfits. 'Dave's new one? She's quiet.'

'Feller neckin on the couch with his missus?' I said.

Roisin: 'That's not his missus.'

Sally: 'Glad ee's got rid o that slapper.'

'Was she a looker?' I said.

Roisin sniffed. 'Blonde and bulimic.'

'Now we're talkin.'

'Don't be rank.' Roisin found a lighter on the dressing table and relit the joint.

I put her sunglasses back on.

Sally couldn't stand up – fucking high as a kite. Roisin wasn't doing much better. We buried Sally under some rain macs and went back in the front room.

The place stank now – enough to knock me sick. The West Indians were still in the kitchenette and my brew was still on the rug, not touched. Dave and his new missus were conked out flat. Roisin was past hysterical. They were all rat-arsed on skunk – it seemed our Dudley was flogging some serious herb.

I took the brew in to get rid of it – pushed the kitchen door open and they both looked my way at the same time. Dudley was trying to shut the suitcase but the zip was stuck – it was full of feathers – a dock-off bird inside. A proper one. I thought it was a chicken till I saw its head. It was a hawk, maybe an eagle.

I stumbled up to the sink like I was munted, making out I was away like the rest of them. 'Fuckin hell, mate. That thing dead?'

Dudley pulled his Kangol cap over his brow, winked over his shades. 'Nuh worry. She jus sleep.'

Drugged.

Horace gave me another once-over. 'Cut y'eye,' he said.

Dudley grinned. 'Nuh, disya mon be cool. He hol ih dang.'

There was a tiny budgie cage looped on a hook in the kitchen ceiling. The budgie started going mad – flapping its wings, chirping war – as if it was having a go at Dudley.

Dudley laughed and slapped the cage – it swung about – a tornado of feathers.

'Scuze us.' I washed the mug out in the sink and nudged between them both – clumsy and merry – putting the mug up on a shelf. Dudley gave me a pat on the back and I left them to it.

The feller who'd gone AWOL with Roisin's coat was back on the sitting-room floor in his spot. Roisin was in front of the telly again – last one standing.

I went in the bathroom, put the plug in the sink – ran the cold tap, then took Dudley's wallet out of my pocket. Two dodgy passports sandwiched between the market leather. One slid out and nearly fell in the sink.

Jamaican citizens. I had a flick through – neither picture was him, though one might've been Horace.

Roisin came into the bathroom and shut the door.

'Thought I locked it.'

'Didn't.'

I stopped the taps.

She tugged her knickers down to her Docs, lifted the toilet lid and took a seat. I watched her, watching me as I pocketed a wad of real notes. Some went in my empty wallet, the rest in my sock.

Dudley had two driver's licences on him, a fake student visa and a handwritten campus ID with no expiry date. He had three names and two dates of birth.

Roisin's forehead was shiny. Eyes soft, pupils missing.

I listened to her piss.

'Feel sick?' I said.

'. . . Not yet . . .' Her head bobbed like she was about to drop off. Elbows slid off knees.

After she'd finished, I helped her stand up. Then I helped her stay standing up. She was cooking. Hair stuck to her face, sweat down her cheeks. She breathed on my lips and when I spoke she rushed for a kiss.

I turned away.

A bang out in the front room made me notice the telly was off. 'What?' Roisin said. 'Don't you want to?'

I said: 'Bout time it kicked off.'

I sat her back down and opened the door an inch.

There was another posse lad in the flat. An outline

of Africa on a huge pendant chain and a *Learn Swahili* slogan vest – a phrase dictionary printed down his belly. Horace had the black and white set in his arms and he passed it to Swahili who went out the door with it.

Dudley was collecting wallets from sleeping victims, jewellery off fingers. He sifted through the tat around the gaff for anything worth pinching. A few bottles of spirits, a stereo without speakers, the VCR, Roisin's coat. It all got shifted.

I came out of the bathroom and tried to shut the door on Roisin but she followed me out. Dudley pulled out his ratchet – blade sharp, a decent size.

He held it to my throat.

I took my wallet out, emptied it – gave him half his money back. Laughing, he put it in his top pocket and slapped my face gently like a pissed uncle at a wedding.

Roisin started to cry.

16

GODSEND

15 February 1998
Sunday

ROISIN WAS IN the back with Dan. I drove. 8 p.m. Dashboard lights turning my hands blue.

The radio was off and nobody had any conversation, making it an awkward do.

We listened to the hailstone gunning the bonnet, slush under the wheel – I could barely keep it on the road. Their suitcase in the boot wasn't helping – it made the back sluggish. I eased off to thirty and took us down Cornishway. Roisin – face to the window, squinting at the Red Beret pub as we drove past.

I kept eyeing Danny boy in the rear-view and he kept eyeing me back, trying to size me up. I couldn't tell what he was made of.

He had a thin Irish face, naff boy-band haircut, cheeks thick with designer stubble covering bad acne scars. His eyes were dead pale, like Roisin's, but there was nothing going on in there.

Then he said: 'I'm trouble. She knows that.'

Roisin didn't look.

'This isn't the first time,' he said.

'What isn't?' I said.

'That she's rescued me.'

Roisin didn't look.

'It's how we met.'

'You were gettin shot at?'

'I was being mugged. Night like this. Hailstone. Middle of winter. This junkie outside Oddbins asks me for a light. I gave him it and then he pulls out a boxcutter and asks for my Nokia. Someone over the road shouts "Oi," and he runs off, and these three gorgeous women come rushing to my rescue. And guess who's the prettiest? She looks at me and says, "I know you. You used to get on my bus." I remembered her. Told her I haven't seen her get on for a while. She says she bought a car. The girls have brollies and Roisin wants to walk me home, so they do. We both live in Chiswick. She says bye at the door and goes off with her friends. That's it. No phone number, no second date. I'm too stupid to ask her out there and then. So I dream about her every night for a fortnight. Then one Saturday morning: there she is.'

'Where?' I said.

'I took the bus,' Roisin said.

The gritters were out at the ring road. I put my foot down and sped off for town.

The safe house was in a converted industrial block behind Store Street Aqueduct. Most of these flats were still empty. I pulled into the roofed car park, tyres slipping on the ramp and found a quiet spot, a dozen to choose from.

Dan needed a hand to get out of the motor. I got their case from the boot and we walked him to the lift – Roisin acting as crutch.

The lift churned.

Dan spoke. 'First proper date. We went to a friend of mine's, who had this studio. He was having a private view.'

I said: 'Of what?'

Dan laughed.

Roisin cringed for me. She fucking bled. Dan didn't notice.

'It was like a party,' he said. 'This friend – used to paint. People actually paid him money. Real money. For his paintings, I mean. They were mad enough to. For example . . .'

Roisin smiled. 'Heavy discount.'

Dan smiled. 'Heavy frame. Remember putting that up?'

Fourth floor. I went first and let them struggle, tossing her the flat keys when they made the corridor.

'It's nothin swank. One bed, a few mod cons.'

'Thanks for this.' She tugged her scarf off. 'I mean

it, Henry.' Her hair was tied back. She looked tense and drawn but was still managing Shagable in lace-ups, woolly tights, a black kagool for a dress.

'This one,' I said.

Dan limped. 'You're a godsend, Henry.'

'Bane,' I said.

Roisin rattled the key into the lock and we helped him inside first.

Dark—

We shuffled in and I shut the door.

'Shit. Where's the light?'

'On the wall, love.'

'Which wall?'

'Keep goin.'

'Which wall?'

'Left.'

'Whereabouts?'

'Bane?'

'Other left.'

—Light.

There was a meathead in a leather coat and balaclava sat on the bed. The mattress was dipping – pity the springs. He lifted his hand and checked his balaclava. The coat squeaked – I could smell the fresh leather.

There were two more blokes by the window with balaclavas on as well.

Roisin twigged it in a heartbeat.

I heard her take the breath.

'N—'

I pulled her back to me, covering her gob to cut off

the *NO* before her lungs supplied it. Jerking like I was electrified, she clawed my face from behind – nails short but sharp.

One of the lads by the window came forwards to give Dan a good hiding. Dan took one slap and fell against the wardrobe and a picture came off the wall.

I let Roisin go – pushed her onto the bed, into Gordon.

She snatched his balaclava off and tore at his neck. Gordon picked her up without a word and carted her out of the flat over one shoulder, kicking and shrieking.

Lenny and I dragged Dan onto the bed – the nylon rope, ready.

Roisin's voice scraped through me: 'Complete bastards! Bastards! Both of you! Henry! Don't. Hen— fucking wait! BANE!' She was popping that bubble in her throat. Tearing the frog apart. Gordon shut her up.

We heard the front door slam.

Dan stared me out from the bed, panting through his bloody teeth. His wrists tied together, his nose a mess.

Abrafo kept his balaclava on.

Lenny lit a cig for him.

Abrafo gave us the nod – the whites of his eyes too white.

17

WHITE WIFE

'LET'S CALL THIS an interview,' I said, holding his stare.

We'd shit Dan up a treat but he kept it together, strapped to the bed the same way Ashley had been. I thought Dan would be in pieces the second we looked at his foot. His bullet wound was dressed up to his ankle, toes pushed into a new Fila shoe, the laces taken out.

Ashley had died because somebody had mistaken her for Roisin. I didn't know it for sure, but I knew it just the same. It meant somebody wanted Roisin dead, enough to come up to Manchester, to rape her, open her up, leave her there as a message. This was somebody dangerous enough to do the deed – to tail me yesterday, clock Roisin leaving hospital, Ashley leaving Church Place – but daft enough to get the wrong missus – which made them more dangerous.

It couldn't have been a personal job – must've been work for hire. Hairdo aside, up close there was no taking Ash for our Roisin. Not a fucking chance.

'Who wants yer both snuffed?' Abrafo said quietly, tapping his fag ash onto Dan's shirt.

Dan told the same story Roisin had told me, but filled in a few blanks. There was a drug mule on an Air Jamaica who tried to skip Customs with White Wife inside her fucking coconuts. Dan had stopped her. The posse she was bringing in for were twiddling thumbs in arrivals. A phone call would confirm she boarded in Kingston and the lounge screens would tell them the plane had landed. So when she didn't show it kicked off.

But why take the trouble to get the airport workers marked?

I said: 'Shit hit rate for mules at the best o time. Why was this one special? They bring in a bit o gear – little n often, right? We're not talkin enough to cry about, are we?'

'Half a kilo,' Dan said, then: 'Where's Roisin?' The words were right but there was nothing desperate in his voice.

'Roisin? She's sound. Doin better than you, son. Now what happened to the mule? Where'd she end up?'

'Don't know.'

'Don't know?'

'I'm up here, aren't I?'

'We keep um or do they get booted straight back home so they can sort um out?'

'Depends. It – it varies. Don't know.'

I sighed. I walked to the bottom of the bed and took Dan's Fila off. The bandage on his foot wanted re-dressing.

Lenny put a big toe between a pair of Halfords bolt cutters.

Abrafo held Dan's legs and I went back and covered his mouth.

'You're chattin shit,' I said, my face half an inch from his. 'Why they really after you, Danny boy? How'd you get um fucked off enough to wanna kill your missus like that? Slash her to bits. All sounds pretty personal, to me. Does it to you, mate? Nod if it does.'

Dan nodded. Dan squeezed out a tear.

Lenny snipped the nylon rope instead of a toe and we let him free.

I said: 'Well then?'

'Don't know! I don't! I swear!' He sat up, clutching his foot. 'Don't fucking hurt Roisin. Please!'

I started to speak but Abrafo held my arm – signed me out. He sat on the bed and offered Dan a cig.

'Who are you?' Dan said.

'Oo am ah? Am ere to tell yer a bit bout our Ashley.'

'Who?'

'Me wife.'

'I don't know your wife.'

'No yer don't. N yer won't. Ever. Cos it's too late to say: "Don't fuckin urt our Ashley."' Abs held out a hand and Lenny passed him the bolt cutters.

*　　*　　*

The rooftop was a flat concrete floor, sparkly air vents – packed up with ice. Gordon was sitting on a sand bin, wearing his balaclava as a hat when I came out from the fire escape.

The sky was black but the hailstone had stopped. Town was wide awake – lit up, giving the night some colour.

I plodded through the wet and sat next to him, got my arse soaked through.

We said nothing. We watched town lights blip.

'Bitter out ere, init?' Gordon said after a bit.

'Where is she?' My lungs needed defrosting.

'Over there.' He pointed.

Roisin was sat with her legs over the edge, her back to us, kagool hood up, shivering in the dark.

'Y'didn't belt her?' I said.

'Did ah fuck.'

'She gunna jump?'

'She fuck. Ant got the bottle. Icy, though. Could slip off ledge wiv bit o luck.'

'Don't say that, mate.'

Gordon folded his arms, turned his head and gozzed in the slush. 'Don't give a fuck, me.'

I pinched the balaclava off his head and walked over. By the time I'd reached her, my shoes were white, twice their size.

I peered over the edge, down the old brick face of the building, feeling like a yoyo. I couldn't even blink, couldn't take my eyes off the view. The wind was biting my legs – blowing me forward, my rubber treads inching over the ice until I was off the ledge.

Eyes closed – my legs firmed up. I was standing still. I knew that I was standing still.

'You still don't like heights,' Roisin said.

I opened my eyes and sat down, my legs dangling over. I nearly took her hand but didn't. I was sweating and it was minus three. She turned away.

'Ee-ah,' I put Gordon's balaclava in her lap. 'If y'stayin out here.'

Then she turned to me. 'Fuck. Off.' Teeth rattling. Cheeks wet. Even in the dark I could tell her nose was Rudolph red.

'Ro—'

'Ask me if I'm alright. Just ask me. Go on. Dare you.' She flung the balaclava over the edge. It took off with the wind and did a loop-the-loop, but it was too far down to see it land. 'If you've touched him. If you've so much as touched a fucking hair on his head. I'll murder you. I'll murder you. I swear on your dad's grave. Do you hear me? Did you just hear what I said, Henry?'

'Bane.'

'HENRY! Your fucking name. Is HENRY.'

Then she covered her gob with her hand and her eyes wrinkled.

I turned away – embarrassed for her. Gordon wasn't on the sand bin anymore. The fire escape was shut.

Roisin gripped my arm to make me look at her. 'How could you set us up? Set me up? I can't believe you could do that. After everything . . .'

'Had to. Had to find out what he knows.'

'Because he has a normal job and a normal family and he's a Southern fairy from the Big Smoke?'

'Cos he's a liar.'

'Because he's not some bloody drug dealer.'

'Cos *you* didn't love *them*.' I'd twisted the knife.

'Because he's not *you*.' She dropped my arm, wounded. She tried to stand up but I wouldn't let her.

I said: 'He got my boss's missus killed. They snuffed her last night.'

Sobbing hard: 'Who did?'

'Ask Dan.'

'Why did they kill her? Why?' Roisin shook her head at me in a daze, made the last *why* stretch.

I told her. 'They thought she was you.'

Back in the safe flat. Happy couple on the bed. Roisin shoving Kleenex up Dan's bugle. Everybody's toes still attached.

Abs pulled out a fat roll of notes, leafed out a few and slapped them on top of a chest of drawers. 'Get um sorted out. Food n that. They don't leave ere fer time bein, less ah say.' He said it to me like neither of them were in the room. Abs pointed to Gordon with his silver lighter in his hand – a gift from Christmas gone, engraved: *Give up – love, Ash.* 'N big man, let's see what yer can do tomorra.'

Do what tomorrow? Something I wasn't clued up on.

And whatever Dan had told Abrafo, it had squared it, he was satisfied. Abs gave Lenny a nod, and Lenny got the door and left with him, bolt cutters under his coat.

Dan started breathing again.

'Have a quiet one,' I said to them both. 'We'll drop off some grub in the mornin.'

Gordon lifted the cash and headed off.

Roisin – too disgusted to watch us go.

I turned around on the way out and saw Dan, sat with her, pushing her face into his chest, watching me holding the door. Blank, no fear now – Knobhead wouldn't look away.

18

YOU SNATCH A TUNE

July 1990

OUR HOUSE.

'Your dad not in?'

'Pub,' I said.

'Probably with mine.'

'Aye.'

We went into the kitchen. Pinched pint glasses upside down on the drying board. A daddy-long-legs underneath the Guinness glass. I turned a John Smith over and filled it with tap water.

Roisin said thanks – took a sip, shivered – tipped the rest away.

'Still rough?'

'Bit better.'

'Sorry bout your coat,' I said.

'I got off alright. Sally. God. The bastards took every-thing.' She still looked thirsty. 'What if they'd taken more?'

'They didn't, love.' The broken record on the wall was a clock the old man had lifted from a car-boot sale. 'Half-eight? Boys in blue be round there soon.'

'Four hours late.'

'Rapid for them.'

I lifted my leg back and stood like a flamingo – reached into my sock and pulled out Dudley's cash. 'Ee-ah,' I said. 'For the coat.'

'I can't.'

'Not ours is it? It's his. Let's just say he bought it off you.'

She flicked through the wad, then waved it back at me. 'A hundred and eighty quid?! It only cost me three pound.'

'Sue Ryder?'

'Arndale Market.'

'You're laughin,' I said. 'Brew?'

'No.' The notes jumped back into my hand.

'Cheer up,' I said.

I pulled the neck of Gordon's gym polo, and dropped the cash inside.

'That's been in your sock.' She danced it down her, grinning again. Thank Christ.

I boiled the kettle. She put her arse on the worktop – swung her cherry Docs, skirt riding.

I took the milk out of the fridge and had a whiff. It was good for another day. 'What?' I said.

She eyed me like a kitten.

'What?'

'Thank you.'

'Can get yourself a decent haircut now.'

Her Docs went still. 'Beg your pardon?'

'Think you heard, love.'

'Right.'

'Right, what?'

Roisin pounced on my back.

'You're a cheeky shit,' she said.

Legs round my waist.

'Thought you felt rough!' I said.

Hands over my face.

I spun us round – she didn't weigh a thing – shaking the laughs out of her until I lost my balance and knocked something noisy. The glasses went over and smashed on the lino, but we didn't stop.

She snaked round me – Docs still off the floor, fingers in my eyes and mouth. Then we both fell and ended up horizontal on the lino. I could just hear the laughter – croaky, soft – our Roisin. I pulled her fingers away to see her. She laughed until she was out of breath, until she was safe.

The kitchen was out of focus. A scribble brushed past my nose: daddy-long-legs making a break for it.

I sat up and a shard of pint glass sailed from my foot. I kicked the rest away. There was a cut on Roisin's shin – just a nick, a couple of new bruises arriving next to the old ones. She sat up, inspected them, patted the dust off. Sly smile.

'We alright?' I said.

'Still here.'
'That's good.'
'Henry?'
'What?'
'Today. You were scared?'
'Yeah.'
'Good.'
'Why?'
'I'll have that brew now.'

10 p.m. Bathroom. Two johnnies floating in the bowl. A sink full of hair. Bathtub clean for a change.

'You not cold?' I said.

Snip. Snip.

'No,' she said. 'You?'

'No.'

'When's your dad back?'

'Ages yet. Sunday lock-in. Might not even come home tonight. He's been a right stop-out since . . .'

Snip.

Her eyes flicked up and found me in the mirror. They did the asking first.

'Forget it.'

'Your mam?' she said.

Lola Bane.

Mrs Henry Bane.

I said: 'Yeah.'

'You've got nice skin,' she said.

'I'm darker than you.'

'Everyone's darker than me.'

'Milky Bar kid.'

'Least I'm not fucking blonde like him.'

Snip. Another strand fell in the sink. 'Bleachin's gunna be the next job.'

'Will never marry. Will never bleach.' Grinding me hard, she said: 'Even if we've got all night – you better show me the goods soon.'

'Think you've just seen um,' I said.

'Funny.'

'I feel used now.'

'Yet that's how you conned me round in the first place! To see the collection.'

'Got you round to see summat else.'

She folded her arms – crushed her little tits. 'You're a pig,' she said.

'You're a snooty cow.'

'You love this snooty cow.'

'I don't.' I threw the scissors on the worktop. I licked her neck – tiny hairs, tiny freckles – said things I really meant, even without my cock nudging her. She beamed through the mirror.

I put it in and took it out.

She melted.

She bent for more.

She had small animal bones. They moved her skin – surface swimming.

'How am I doin?' I said.

'Terribly.' She cleared her throat – coughing sanity back: 'Haircut. Focus.' Then she said: 'This what your ex looked like, then?'

I stroked out another lock of her hair – scissors ready again. I must have chopped four inches off. More.

'Give over,' I said.

'Can't believe I'm letting you do this.'

'I missed me callin.'

'I look like a lad.'

'Fuck off. You look gorgeous.'

'Are we nearly done?'

'Sorted.'

I put the scissors behind the taps and stepped back – enjoying the whole view.

Roisin stood naked, on her tiptoes, and roughed up the front in the mirror, checked out the sides. 'Dead short,' she said. 'But even.'

'What's the verdict?'

'Love it.'

'Told you.'

'It's ace. Better than a salon job. He's got skills, has our Henry. Not just a decent shag.' She scooped the offcuts from the sink, binned them and went back to preening. 'It's like Mia Farrow's in *Rosemary's Baby.*'

'But not fuckin blonde,' I said.

Her head shot round – gobsmacked. 'Keep this up.'

'Can do that.'

She turned round. I started low and tried to make it to the top, but it was all a bit of a struggle.

She saw the trouble I was in and came over with a kiss, grabbed my cock, tugged me forward, walking backwards to the sink, giggling away. Her ears were on show now – five holes in each – two silver studs, the rest empty.

I picked up the scissors and cut one last piece of hair.

'Can I have . . .?' I somehow made it sound casual, like I was pinching an Opal Fruit.

She nodded.

I stuffed the lock in an old contact-lens box and hid it on a cabinet shelf.

'Get in the tub,' I said.

'We should fill it first.'

I dropped the plug in and squeaked the taps round. The fixtures were loose and the pipework had a hissy fit. Hot water came out after a wait.

'Have a soak, love. Plennyosuds,' I said. 'Be back in a sec.' I patted that perfect arse, left the bathroom and went downstairs.

'Where you going?' I heard her shout down.

'I'll put us a taster on.'

Al Green singing downstairs. We listened from the tub. I'd cranked him high enough to hear the dust trip the needle.

Roisin lay back on me – her knees bobbing above water like mini icebergs. I touched every part of her narrow body.

I said: 'He croaks like you do.'

'Aw, cheers, love. That's what the ladies want to hear. That they sound like an old reverend.'

'*The* reverend.' I kissed her hair.

'Anyway, thought you were mad on him?'

'Too right. Can't go wrong with a bit o Al Green.'

I cupped her tits. She purred. 'True.'

'". . . You be good to us . . . I'll be good to you . . . We'll be together . . . We'll see each other."'

Roisin cracked up. She said: 'You should do that more often.'

'What?'

'Sing for me.'

She flipped over, made a wave – suds gliding off her shoulder blades.

'Can't sing for toffee apple, me.'

'I still love it,' she said.

Her chin was on my stomach, lapping at water level, her eyes up at me – mucky thoughts colouring them in.

I said: 'Me dad keeps them in back room.'

Roisin got out of the tub, slowly, without a splash.

We watched each other as she towelled herself. She made a show of it.

'Not puttin knickers on?' I said.

She wiped her forehead like she'd forgotten there was no hair in her eyes. 'Do you *want* me to put knickers on?'

I got out and she threw the towel over my head and started scrubbing me dry.

'Well?'

'Won't say another word.'

I gave her a kiss when she was done and took her downstairs – both of us still in the buff.

Back room. Side A had finished – needle up, record

spinning. The stereo was behind the door because there was no space for it – album towers on top of the speakers. I put The Reverend back in his sleeve and switched it for a Stax volume. 'Green Onions' on the go.

Boxes of vinyl were piled to the ceiling. The old man had been grabbing anything he could get his hands on lately. He kept his ears open, listened for anyone round our way that was having a clear-out. He'd blanket buy, then chuck anything afterwards that wasn't soul. He got it all for cheap. He always had some cash to bet come Saturdays.

'Let's find you some Siouxsie,' I said.

I gave Roisin a box to go through and she knelt down, ran her finger over the spines.

'You into Stone Roses?' she said.

'Shite. The Mondays I can stomach. One or two tunes.'

'Sounds better on E.'

'Never touch it, me.'

'You sell gear, though.'

'Gordon been blabbin?'

She looked at me sideways, still rooting.

I said: 'Didn't have you as a raver.'

She looked down again. Dust showed on her arms, she was that white, that clean. 'Deep breaths,' she said.

I'd been staring too long.

I opened another box and clocked a Juice Crew LP between the novelty ballads. I'd be pinching it before it made the stall. 'Any gems?'

She squeezed out a record. 'Costello? Do you like him?'

'"Watchin the Detectives" I'm alright with.'

'Me too.'

She passed it me to put on, and sat back – legs open. 'Gordon said you don't drink.' Her toes played the bassline.

I was dying to touch her.

She said: 'Fair enough.'

She split her cunt.

She said: 'You're quite straight for a bad lad, aren't you?'

'Deep breaths,' I said.

She giggled again and stood up. 'Let's have a dance, Henry.'

'You've already had one o them today.'

'Not with you.'

19

OUR KID, STANLEY . . .

16 February 1998
Monday

THEY WERE THE last of the Salford Mob. A scrap of the old Firm, plenty of mileage on the clock. Perrys without decent music taste. Gordon and I dropped off food shopping at the safe flat first. Roisin had thrown it in the cupboards without saying a word. Dan was on the bed, watching telly.

I asked Roisin if she was sorted and she wouldn't look at me.

I left her a pack of toffees, a newspaper. Gordon tore the sport out in front of us.

When we headed off she said: 'Bane, you forgot the milk.' Bane. Not Henry.

* * *

I pulled into an estate near Langworthy – blank sky, no traffic, Gordon giving me directions.

'One o these, down back, ee said it were.'

A squash of red terraces – rooftops wearing white, front doors next to the road.

I said: 'I'll leave it here, mate.'

I parked by the main street, deep in slush, and got out and put my Harrington on.

A football smacked my front wheel on the pavement side.

'Oi, mistuh. Ow much t'mind yer cah?' Three young lads were stood against a wall, skiving off school – hoods up, scarves over their gobs. The football rolled to the middle lad, but I wasn't sure which one had spoken.

I said: 'Do that again – you won't find out.'

Gordon opened the passenger side. They did a double take and sat on the wall.

'Oo yer seein?' a lad said.

'Yer fuckin mams,' Gordon went.

The lads kept it buttoned.

Gordon dug out some change and handed it out. 'Get some Dolly Mixtures n fuck off.'

It was nice to see a slice of Gordon-brand peace-keeping. But there was something new, only I couldn't work out what it was. He'd have handled it just the same before he went inside.

I started to walk along the stretch of housing, getting my bearings. A scruffy local was on the other side of the road. There were clean shapes in the car park under the weekend snow – ditched motors like Greggs ice buns.

Gordon jogged to catch me. He squeezed fists into new leather pockets. 'Ay, Bane – me dad said yer still seein that Jen?'

'Jan.'

'Stickin wiv that one, a'yer?'

'She's livin at mine.'

'Since when?'

'Time ago.'

He laughed, shaking his head. 'Daft cunt. Bes not be out the fuckin game. Shameful, mate.'

'You don't even know what the game is, son.'

He stopped laughing, kept shaking his head. 'Yer gunna av t'sort us out.'

'What with?'

'A missus. Get us on fuckin *Blind Date* or summat.'

'You need a shag, not a missus.'

'Bane, av lost the plot, me. Wiv birds. Am tellin yer.'

'Bad do last night?'

'Am not goin there.'

'You were stewin from what happened with Roisin n Knobhead. Y'mind wasn't on the job. We get you back in the saddle n you'll be right.'

Our Gordon lifted his chin, stuck his roid chest out and switched it on again. 'Aye.'

'We'll be runnin Clubland in a week. You'll be gettin plenny.'

'Best ad.'

The red row finished and we came off the main road and onto a cut-through. Paving slabs seesawed:

pensioners beware. There was a matching red terrace row at the bottom end.

'It's down ere,' he said, too sure to be right.

Some of these gaffs were empty, decorated.

Boarded windows read good riddance.

PAKI tagged on front doors.

WOGS OUT – nice and sloppy, paint weeping.

Gordon rang a doorbell three down from *FUK OFF BAK HOME*, and a dog barked from inside.

There was a young bird having a cig on the front step, next door. She took a long drag – blue eyes fixed on us, then turned the other way to exhale. She had pink socks and pink combats on and a packet of Lamberts sticking out of her waistband. Her hair was napalmed blonde, a tight ponytail. She looked back at us on the next drag.

'Oi,' she said.

The dog kept barking but nobody answered. I rang the bell again.

'Fuckin deaf?' she said.

Gordon: 'What?'

'Cav yer number?' she said.

'Ours?' He pointed at himself.

'Nah. Is.' Her face was hard and pretty.

'I'm spoken for, love,' I said.

She smoked without blinking, eyes never off me, then dropped the fag on the step and went in.

Gordon leathered the brickwork in between the two front doors. 'FUCK ME! This is what av bin sayin!' He left his fist against the wall and shut his eyes. He was grinning.

I knocked on again and the door opened a few inches, a tan bulldog sniffing through the gap.

'Yeh?' A short feller with silver sideburns and an angry face kept the chain on.

'You Smithy, mate?' Gordon said. 'Keith Town's cousin?'

'Yeh. So?'

'Gordon.'

'Simon.'

'Keith spose to av said summat ter yer.'

Simon took the chain off. Red polo, turn-up Levi's, gold necklace. He grabbed the bitch by the collar as she went up on her back legs – tongue out, choking. 'Ee did. Yer was doin time wiv im wan't yer? Keith's a fuckin cunt but ee knows oo is mates are. Get in big lad. N oo's this?'

'Bane,' I said.

We shook hands. There were swallows up his forearm. He was five-four with his trainers on. He let go of the dog collar and she dropped, barking again until she sneezed on my shoe. I stepped over her and she whacked herself on the door, chasing her docked tail.

'Dippy bitch.' Simon yelled through: 'Judy! Got guests. Get fuckin kettle on.'

The missus in the kitchen: 'Yer what, love?'

'Fuckin brew up.'

'Right, love.'

Gordon made the bridge. I crossed it, made the chat.

'We've taken over Billyclub in town. Know it?'

Simon put his brew on the arm of the couch. He sniffed before he spoke like he had a heavy habit. 'Tenner a drink. Stuck-up slags. Fullofaggots.'

'That's the one.'

'Fat chance o findin a shag in there.'

I said: 'Best not let the missus hear you talkin like that.'

She was still in the kitchen, rattling the pots and pans. Simon slapped the front-room door to without getting up. 'She dunt listen, that cow. So yer needin a few lads then, yeah?'

The bulldog started panting on the seat next to him, inching forward to put her head on his lap.

'Door security,' I said. 'Experience ideal. Our Gordon'll be runnin the show, though.'

Simon mimed a gun at Gordon, his thumb taking a quick bow. 'Top man.' Sniffsniffsniff.

Gordon winked.

'Jus fer first night or summat regular?' Simon said to me.

'Get launch weekend out the way smooth n we'll take it from there. Wanna talk percentages?'

'Sweetshop? Nah. Not yet. Let us mek a phone call. See what ah can sort out. Shift.' The bitch took her head off his lap and he got up and left the room. She sat in his spot, smiling with her tongue out.

The front room was standard – it reminded me of my nana's. Fish tank, flower wallpaper, net curtains, heaped ashtray, the carpet covered in dog hairs. I put my brew on the stained doilies, looked at Gordon and leaned back, tipping my seat. There was a sawn-off twelve bore gaffer-taped to the back of his brown leather sofa chair. It was taped barrel down, within reach. I stretched round and felt the handle. It was warm against the radiator.

I showed Gordon the shooter and he grinned. He sat back in his chair, dipped half a Rich Tea in his brew and held the biscuit to the floor. 'Come on, then,' he said.

But the bitch just whined.

Gone noon.

The young lads were still on the wall when I unlocked the motor. They jumped down in height order and Gordon started slap-boxing with the shortest, his giant hands like pads. He was bulldozing forward on the little man, who kept throwing them wild. Simon came up and clipped the lad's ear a little too hard.

'Daaaad!' The lad rubbed his hood off.

Gordon gave him a pat. 'Ee's a right champ, this one.'

'Get t'fuckin school,' Simon said. 'Now. Rest o yers n all.'

They spat, dawdled.

We followed Simon's 306 to another pub down the road. There were alkies hovering by the entrance. One poor bastard was trying to roll a cig but the jitters wouldn't let him. He was my old man's age, maybe younger.

'Gone noon!' another sod went, giving the frosted glass a thump.

A shadow inside pulled the bolts out of the floor. 'Ang on.'

We shuffled through with the alkies and Simon introduced us to the landlord: Stan Barker – ex-club-bouncer, ex-Securicor-van-hijacker, mid-forties, carrying his weight well. He was Gordon-big, with skin like boiled ham. He wasn't pulling pints, and he wasn't pulling jobs himself anymore. He had a couple of these pubs, a security firm, and plenty on the side. Last week's Halifax robbery had been his doing. And the Barker boys visited post offices more often than pensioners.

I'd heard he was sitting on half a million. Cash. His watch said it might even be true. I'd heard his missus was queen though, and he was the bee. But if looks counted, he hadn't lost his sting.

'Straight through, fellers,' he said, pointing behind the bar. He didn't follow us up.

Gordon swooned, too at home with these devils. 'Fuckin champion,' he said, thumbing twenties – a wad thicker than a Thomson local.

'Thas jus ter say ta fer lookin out fer our kid Keith inside,' said Kara Barker, Queen Bitch.

Gordon looked over at Simon by the open safe. He was stood nodding, his arms folded, his eyes small.

'Where's y'husband gone?' I said to her, sat in a hard chair next to our Gordon's.

Kara leaned over the desk. 'Stanley? Nipped out. Business.'

'When's he back?'

Kara yawned. 'Inabit.'

'We gunna play dominoes meantime?' I said.

Kara leaned back in her throne. Kara said: 'You're a soft cunt, aren't yer, babe?'

I said: 'Sorry, love? Didn't catch that?'

'Said you're a soft cunt, babe, aren't yer? What yer reckon, Gordon? Soft cunt?'

He said nothing.

'Look at im.' Kara pointed at me with a salon nail. 'Ee dunt like that does ee?' She had a machine-gun laugh. She had too many teeth. 'We'll do fuckin security fer yer fuckin disco! Don't worry, babe. It'll be alright on the night!'

I cracked my neck, sat there and stewed.

This Kara was a hateful witch. She'd taken a shine to me the second we made eyes. She was tan-bed gold, forty-odd, almost gorgeous once. Crow's feet. Crayon eyebrows. Roll-on blouse. Pamela chest. Bra frill showing.

She shot us another laugh and her eyes went back on Gordon – nail still pointing at me. 'Ever push is buttons? See if ee does owt?'

As soon as Gordon spoke up she spoke over him.

I listened, but felt like I needed to walk it off.

'A couple o fuckin sambos from that Bob Marley crew round Hulme will come into this famly pub at three ter kill me usband.' She took out a cig and Simon hovered. 'Stan'll be behind the bar, mindin is own, probly watchin snooker up on telly.' She paused and

Simon gave her a light. 'Ah know this cos av arranged it. Av arranged fer um to murder me usband through one o Thin's fuckin lieutenants. Least ee were up until las week. Now thev got a new boss wiv a new daft name n now ee's shiftin gear n shiftin shooters, only ee's bin keepin tight old o the lot.'

'Thin did business with the Barkers?' I said.

'That Thin were mixed race. Ee were arf black, arf bright.'

'You're missin both halves already.'

'Never mind that, ay? Least this job's still on. Now this lieutenant, im what works fer us – ee's found two new recruits fer this afternoon's job. Still wet behind the ears. Spose to be dyin fer a rep. Dyin fer one. But when they come fuckin blazin in ere, gunnin after our Stanley, it's not gunna go ter plan. Shall ah tell yer why?'

'Tell me why.'

'They're firing blanks, babe.'

This was a game. This was a tantrum.

'Why risk it?' I said.

'There ee is again. Soft cunt, you.'

'Still do a right nasty job with a blank.'

'Oh ah bet yer could, babes.'

'Ow much?' Gordon said.

'Anuva large,' she said. 'Fer each o yers. N al chuck in a party bag if yer fancy a sniff. Thas sixty a throw right there.'

'We gettin tools?' Gordon said.

She clicked those teeth together, grinding a smile:

'Ah like um dumb n ah like um keen.' She opened a desk drawer and rooted. She slapped two Stanley knives on the desk. 'No shooters. Am not askin yer ter tek anyone's life ere – thell do that fer us when we send um back, our Stanley still breathin. Jus cut these black bastards proper. Ear us? Ah were a Sunday-school girl. Ah like a bit o blood, me.'

I said: 'Pigs'll shut this place for good before you've mopped it up.'

'Thed av ter shut every pub in Salford if they think they can get us. N the pissin brewery.' She gave us the machine gun till it sounded cartoon-wicked. Then she nodded to Simon and he took some more wads out of the safe and gave them Gordon. Gordon held mine out to me but I waved it off.

'You tryna start a war cos they won't do business?'

She fiddled with a blouse button, tapping with those claws. 'Ad give the new cunt in charge a bit o fuckin time to find is previous's phone book if this were jus about pride.'

I laughed and it threw her.

She rambled: 'They come, they fuck off, they come back. Roundnround we go. Their kiddies've ad kiddies n we're still steppin on their toes when they're not steppin on each uvas. Bin like this forever. When they want what's ours, they're good at gettin it. Only nowa-days yuv fuckin got white lads tryna act like um. Sad really.' She rubbed her cig out.

Gordon fingered his second lot of notes.

Come on, son – tell her to shove it up her bony arse.

'Go downstairs,' Kara said, all teeth. 'Av a think. Both o yers. Drinks on the ouse.'

'It's still bollocks,' I said at the bar, keeping my voice down. 'We're the ones gettin rinsed, mate.'

Kara trotted past our stools in a cloud of cig smoke.

Gordon downed his fourth shot. 'Reckon?'

A feller on the pool table stopped playing to ask after her sons. Other punters sipped and smoked, watching her or pretending not to.

'You've just got out,' I said. 'Wanna go back in? Slashin two kids? It's bollocks.'

'It's a grand.'

'Fuck the fuckin cash. She's more than a few pennies short where it counts.'

'Ad shag the fuckin arse off it n all.'

I sighed, then drum-rolled on the bar.

The pool player hard-knocked a red.

'I'm gunna go for a piss, mate. When I get back, you're leavin with us.'

Gordon downed his sixth and got a gin in. He wouldn't look at me.

The men's was empty except for us.

She snapped my belt loose in a blink and dipped into my boxers, her face right up in mine.

'Think ah owe yer n apology.' She pushed me between sinks. Acrylic nails scraping my tackle.

'What for?' I said.

Weighing me like market fruit.

'Not jumpy a'yer, babe? Might be some ope yet.'

She gripped tight.

'What for?' I said again.

She walked me to a stall and backed me inside.

I put my hand on the cistern for balance. Her needle heels were in a piss puddle, scratching the floor tiles.

'Not soft, this one,' she said, wanking me – claws in deep. 'Ah could fuckin drink yer like milk.'

Milk.

Roisin's shopping.

I laughed and Kara did and all.

I pushed her off, zipped up, and went back out.

I tapped Gordon at the bar.

I waited but he stared into his gin.

I left the pub – a proper blizzard outside, slanting thick.

I got the motor going – wipers doing their best to catch up.

I spotted a corner shop and bought two litres of skimmed.

I got back in the car.

I put the carrier bag on the passenger seat.

I made a crack in the dash.

I couldn't see the steering wheel.

I rubbed my eyes half out.

I stamped knuckle blood on my cheeks.

I cleaned myself up in the rear-view.

20

IGLOO STICKS

JAN TOOK TRENTON to her mam's last night. She was still up when I got back from the safe flat: in the front room, in the dark, watching horror pornos that Trenton borrowed from his mates.

Gangbangs, coffins, raspberry blood.

He labelled them *wrestling* and hid them behind the wardrobe. Jan found the stash looking for his school Rockports, which he claimed had been robbed. She first showed me one when he was out. She commentated right through and had me in stitches. She put it back and acted none the wiser. Nobody ever left one in the VCR.

Jan came to bed naked, gone five. Her breath was Bensons-stale. I felt her shin stubble on my hip, her goosebumps. She was teary, pissed, shaking me for a shag, and she bit my collarbone till I swore and pushed her off to get my boxers down.

Bodies clapping. A hard graft fuck. Scratching sticks together to make a fire.

She blathered even as she came: '. . . ah can't lose yer. Ah got yer. Ah can't now. Ah can't . . .'

Princess Parkway. Biggie on loud but I'd tuned out. I'd been driving round for two hours with a milk bottle on the seat, and it was already getting dark.

I went through Whalley Range, through Moss Side, unlucky with every set of lights, queuing for the third time. I checked my phone while waiting.

One missed call and three messages.

Our Jan's text: Wen u home?

Our Jan's text: U mad busy?

Our Jan's text: *Worryed love*

I sent her one back saying *Home soon* and got an X back in a snap.

I wound my window down to get the snow off it, felt a blast of ice wind and rolled it back up. There were kids on BMXs on the long island between the lanes – mud tracks in the snow. A tatty Fiesta was in front of me, clouds over the brake lights from the drippy exhaust. I read the registration slowly. It wasn't our Roisin's.

Biggie sewed up the holes in the beat, tied it in knots, put it in his pocket and left the building, my door speakers throbbing till the fade-out.

The traffic lights were still fucking red.

Snow kept falling.

I felt my suspension twitch and it woke me up. The

motor rocked from side to side, two hands out there, pushing at the top of the passenger doorframe, a scarfed face up at the window. Another sound made me look round – a second lad was on my side – a black kid on a bike, a phone to his ear, scarf under his chin so he could speak. He tapped the glass with the barrel of a .22. I recognised him as was one of Hagfish's boys. Gordon had tried running him over two nights ago.

My foot was down before I'd taken the handbrake off. It knocked him off his bike and they both fell, no gunshots over the screaming revs.

It was amber on the junction and I made a half-donut left, steering wheel useless. I skated until it locked and stayed in second gear, managed to point the bonnet where I was going.

I straightened up the back and gunned it in third. The kids kept sliding in and out of the rear-view, giving chase on bikes.

I overtook on the inside, a blare of horn – gone.

The kids were just specks now, a quarter-mile behind.

By the time I reached Store Street every pavement shadow was after me. Street lamps gave them faces, and every face seemed to clock me drive past. I was sure that somebody was following in a motor.

Bus traffic flashed under the bridge and all the window-seat eyes were on me. They were Halloween monsters. They were animals butting the glass, snarling like Perry boys on the terraces come Derby day.

*　　*　　*

I left the engine running in the roofed car park for a quarter of an hour – waiting – just to be sure. Dead quiet. Monday evening. Only a few white collars nipping back from work.

My mobile rang in my pocket and I left it, thinking it was our Jan, but answered the second buzz. It was a message from Rana, Maz's missus. Maz was still in his coma. She sounded knackered but together. No tears left.

Hagfish was still at large after another run-in, thanks to me.

I got out of the car, locked it, made sure, then took the lift up to the flat.

Roisin was coming up the stairwell as I stepped out. We both halted at opposite ends of the hall like we were about to quick-draw. A red bottle cap poked out of a Spar bag in her hand and her kagool was shiny with snow. She looked drowned.

'Milk,' I said, holding up my carrier bag.

'We gave up on you,' she said.

'You risked pissin off Abrafo for a pint o skimmed?'

'I fancied a brew.'

'You offerin?'

'No.'

She walked forward, stopped at the door with the key ready – water dripping around her feet.

'Dan still in?' I said.

Flat line: 'No, he went for a jog.'

I hooped my carrier bag over her wrist and took the key from her fingers. She let me.

I whispered in her ear – cold water on my lips from the ends of her hair.

'Bane—'

I held the door open for her.

Roisin shook her coat off and hooked it on the inside of the door. She wiped her hair, pressing it behind her ears – Morticia-pale.

'Dan!' she shouted through. 'Company.'

No answer.

A trickle on the hard floor – underneath the coat was already a puddle.

She stood on one untied boot with the other and lifted her small feet out of them. 'Dan?'

No answer.

She poked her head round the kitchen/living room, turned back round to face me – hands out, clueless, panic brewing.

I passed her and went further into the flat, smelling it before I opened the bedroom door. I kicked the door wide.

A blanket of ganja. Nothing but haze.

A rabbit-punch turned me into a ball and I saw the fist grow in the corner of my eye. Another half a second and it'd blocked out the light.

A silencer in my gob – cold – it hadn't fed a bullet.

'Dis mon again. He be Mister Mention.' He patted me down with his free hand and took my wallet out. I was still on the floor. He squinted at my driving licence like the name was tricky, like he was reading fucking Shakespeare.

'Henry Baayne?' he said, head up as another feller brought Roisin into the bedroom. 'Igloo Sticks, mon. Koo-deh! No kya – dat da right ooman!'

'Every ting cook an curry,' this one said.

He was dripping with diamonds. Ice on every finger: Igloo Sticks. He squeezed Roisin's arms, pushed her on the unmade bed and shook her till he was happy. She slapped his face.

There were just two of them. Proper Kingston Yardies, over here for a working holiday. Ashley's killers.

'Where's Dan?' Roisin said.

Maybe they'd done him first. Maybe he'd fucked off before they'd got here.

The other feller dropped my wallet, rattled the silencer against my teeth – extracted gun from gob. I sat up slowly.

Igloo Sticks reached into his coat and pulled out his own Glock. He held Roisin's face to the pillow. He put the silencer to her temple. 'Skeltah, mon – sure dis one? Time tough. Nuh time fi dog-heart cutlass.' He split her tear tracks with a ringed finger, then traced them south, under her chin. He drew an imaginary slash across her throat.

I tried to get up but Skeltah jumped on my chest – ribs turned to springs – emptied my lungs.

'Leave her,' I said without sound. 'I know where Dan is.'

I sucked in some air and said it again, holding my chest.

'A lie,' Skeltah said.

They both watched me try to stand.

'Whatever the Lundon crew've paid you. I'll match it,' I said. 'Five grand a piece. I can take you to the safe n I can take you to Dan. Then you lot can settle whatever's between him n your don.'

Skeltah trapped his Glock under his cowboy belt. He was skinny, his ragged summer pants falling off his waist. 'Fuckery,' he said.

Igloo Sticks glared at me. I could see the cogs turning. 'Come tess me. Eff yah nuh tell bloodclat troot yah be hearin chamber music, mon. Me nuh lie.' He took the gun away from Roisin and waved it at me, a diamond ring tapping the trigger guard.

21
MARY

IT WAS THE kid that had shown me the shooter. The
one from the traffic lights. He was slashing my front
tyres in the car park with a blade – a brick by his foot,
ready for the windscreen.

Igloo Sticks put his Glock on the back of the lad's
skull and sprayed the concrete red. The silencer
smoked. Roisin screamed. Skeltah made her stop.

Other kids ran, echoes chasing them.

I knelt over the body like I knew this lad, like I was
mourning – and my hand searched under his hoodie,
lifting his little .22, my back to Igloo. There was brain
on my wheel arch.

'Ga-lang,' Igloo said.

'Y'what?'

'Move.'

With my motor a no-go, we piled into theirs. A

scratched brown Vectra, snow on the wipers. Skeltah
and Roisin got in the back, and I was designated driver.

'How we doin, love?' I said to her in the rear-view.
'We right?'

Roisin nodded, dead-eyed.

Skeltah patted her thigh, kept a hand there.

'You two fly into Manchester or what?' I was driving
fast, wipers on slow. 'Did you two stop off at Lundon
so boss could give you a briefin?'

Skeltah took his hand off Roisin and jabbed the space
between the front seats for me to slow down. 'Tek time.
Yah waan tess me?'

Portland Street. Trams out of action. Snowstorm in
the dark. A couple of cars were going twenty, tops –
headlights, full beam. I twisted round to look at Skeltah
and put my foot to the floor. His head snapped back
against the headrest and I talked loud over the engine:
'Reckon you come straight here. Swapped sunshine n
Lilt Ladies for a decent chippy. Judgin by the cock-ups
– the boss must o told you what's what from the phone
box – pips runnin out fast. If brains were fuckin dyna-
mite—'

A hand grabbed the wheel and I sat round and used
the brakes. Roisin's seat belt locked.

Igloo Sticks put a Glock to my belly: 'Nuff chatty.'

Hollywood Butchers, Hulme. All of us still in one piece.
Desmond's fishmonger was shut next door since it was
after five.

I said: 'Safe's in there. Ten large n some change.'

The rear car park was almost snowed in, nobody about. We all got out: Roisin walking ahead, me next, Skeltah behind – pointing the shooter through his pocket, just like in the pictures.

Igloo Sticks hung back, gabbing into a mobile. I heard him say where we were.

Roisin was in socks, no time to put her boots back on. She snatched a look at the bottom of her feet but Skeltah pushed her forward.

'Piggyback?' I said.

She squinted with the wind and wiped the snowflakes off her nose.

We walked past Desmond's back door – the shutters locked on Hollywood Butchers. I knelt down and rattled a frozen padlock. 'Look, I haven't got the k—'

Sparks grazed my hands as Skeltah shot the padlock off.

'Nice one,' I said, counting my fingers.

'Fahward.'

I lifted the shutter halfway and ducked under. The lights were already on inside.

'Weh ih deh?' Igloo caught up with us. He swapped his mobile for his Glock, then pulled the shutter back down.

'Y'what?' I said.

'Weh is it?' he said.

The bolts were off the inner doors separating Des's shop from this one. The metal plate and the cutters they'd used rested against the wall by the bottom bracket.

Everything else here was the same.

'This way,' I said.

Igloo picked Roisin for a dancing partner, shuffling her along at gunpoint.

A sound stopped us. Skeltah went over to the shared doors.

'Im a samfi-mon.' He looked back at me.

'Coo!' Igloo waved Skeltah through the doors to check what the racket was. God help Des.

I said: 'Chiller's out o commission. We use it for a safe.'

I took the three of us round. Igloo wasn't having any of it. The silencer kissed Roisin's temple – her head tilted, coy.

I dragged the chiller door along its tracks and we all peered inside.

It was still broken, still room temperature. The light switch worked. Maz's blood and Thin's blood were just cheap stains. Somebody had tidied up. The shelves running down both walls were stacked with old paint tubs and crushed cardboard was heaped at the far end.

I listened, sweating, but there was fuck all there. Roisin was breathing the hardest.

I stepped inside and picked a paint tub, frantic, curious. The lid came off easy, the tub overflowing. With my feet on the other side of the door tracks, I emptied the paint out with a throw. A fat kilo flew and went splat on the chiller floor, bowling down the river of paint. I opened another paint tub – another hidden brick of White Wife, wrapped tight.

Me, laughing: 'All that fuckin gear.'

Igloo, laughing: 'Good bwoy.'

The cardboard stack twitched.

Hagfish.

How had he managed to stash that much in a week? The Barkers had reasons to worry. He must've been raiding local dealers left and right, pinching off other crews.

Igloo took Roisin in with him, his back to me for the first time.

I put a couple in his arse with the .22. The cylinder ticked round, emptied. Flash-flash-smoke. Too easy. It felt like a toy.

Igloo screamed. He hopped once, snapped round, hopped twice, took aim at me and then lost his legs, firing wild, mid-fall.

Roisin chanced it. She leapt back out before his knees had reached the floor.

Something moved in the back. She was still there, guarding all this new gear. Mary scrabbled out from under the cardboard stack: tail shuffle, claw-clicks, gob wide – ready for some tea.

Igloo howled and switched targets. I shut the chiller door and locked it.

We heard nothing.

I grabbed Roisin, squeezing her too hard.

'What the fuck was that?' she said.

'A Komodo dragon.'

'Sorry?'

'Bit of a story.'

She waited for it.

'Don't know it,' I said.

Flutter. Birdsong.

A dock-off hawk landed on the meat table, three feet away, half a salmon in its feet.

Roisin: 'Are we dreaming?'

White face specked brown – a dark strip over its eyes like a bank robber. It folded its wings again and eyed us both like dirt, then started stripping the fish.

'Hide,' I said.

I came closer and it flew away without the salmon – wings beating with no sound.

Roisin stayed put.

'Henry.'

'Said hide.'

'Come with me.'

'Go.'

'Come with me.'

'Fuck off. Now.'

The double doors were open. I stepped through into the back of Desmond's shop and kept low – holding another empty shooter like it would keep my heart ticking.

Des's chiller was open as well. This one was up and running – clouds of cold under the see-thru strips. Coat hooks empty on the wall outside – no thermals. I spread the curtains and saw Skeltah belly down on the chiller floor, using a bag of ice for a pillow. His eye wore frost mascara. He was stiff already and it was a job to turn him over. The blood-spill shone like stained glass. He was minus a shooter, minus the whole hand.

There were fillets iced into blue pallets, stacked floor to ceiling, and a bucket of fake plants for the counter decoration. No gear, just Des's marker-pen signs, swearing at his staff for putting out fresh kipper before old kipper.

My teeth rattled. I heard patois echoing from out front.

The hawk peered down and I peered up. We were beak to nose. It blinked cleverness. This was no town pigeon. It hooked its toes over the counter edge and spread its wings till it was wider than I could see all at once. It snatched the top cod from the ice counter, took off – lost it mid-flight along with some feathers, then swooped back to pinch another.

I kept my arse on the floor and stayed behind the till – the drawer open, emptied.

The shop lights were off. It would be hard to see in through the bricked windows anyway. Hagfish was ranting about who'd been feeding his dragon. He had a couple of local lads with him, playing fetch-n-carry. One came back from Hollywood Butchers, empty-handed, and he laughed and sent the other round to check again. Neither of them looked my way.

What the fuck were they doing here?

His feller tried to speak – said something about open shutters, footprints in the snow. Hagfish talked over him.

'Me know tis you, mon! Bayyyyyne. Abrafo's white bwoy. Me know yah now. Hagfish have eyes an earz everywhere. Me gwan pay yah fi whatta happen wit Berta Mambo. Now yah fren wit batty Kingston mandem? Bwoy? Tink dat go save yah? We kill dem. Hagfish hungan. Hagfish a go dead all dem.'

I shifted and spied through a gap at the end of the counter. He hadn't gone upmarket, forked out for a three-piece Versace now he was raking it in. Some fucking don. He was still decked in his tatty army coat – vest on under it, chest scarred, but enough jewellery to give him a stiff neck. Skeltah's Glock was in his hand. I watched him roam about, flap his coat collar down. He wasn't feeling the cold.

'Bayyyyyne.'

I thought he'd flog me a *Big Issue*.

Maybe the boys were scared of him, and that's how'd he'd done it. Maybe he'd showed them a bit of voodoo, danced on water, let them pet his dragon. It worked on the lost girls stopping at Church Place, Apostles' Warning. Maybe that and snuffing ex-boss, Thin, gained him enough respect.

Flutter. Birdsong.

His lad was mithering the hawk. He was trying to get it to eat out of his hand but the hawk wasn't having it. Hagfish kicked up a fuss and the lad started mouthing off. The second lad reappeared and everybody squawked at once – bird and all.

I made tracks and ducked into the back again. The doors through to the butchers were locked now and I gave them a shoulder and got a loud rattle. A gap under the door showed me two fucking slide bolts in the drill holes.

I heard a scuffle, then Hagfish laughing, then a gunshot – the bullet humming through a silencer. Skeltah's Glock.

Back in the chiller with Skeltah himself – I stepped over him and kicked him by accident. He was frozen solid.

I towed a split sack of ice from the far corner, twisting a stack of pallets to block myself in for some cover.

The see-thru curtains flapped before I could bob down.

Someone: 'Fuckin . . . ell.' It sounded like our Gordon benching his weight on the Olympic bar after a night on the sambuca.

He stopped what he was doing, had a breather, gave it another go.

I squinted through a crack between two pallets. The body fell on top of Skeltah's. It was one of Hagfish's lads – the other bloke had dragged the body in.

He dumped it there, rubbed his hands and shot back out, closing the door. The door smacked the seal and I listened to him lock it.

My teeth rattled. Lips burned. Toes numb.

I kicked the pallets away and stripped this lad of his Adidas, pushing a finger through the bullet hole in the back for a fraction of heat. I put the jacket on over my Harrington and started worrying – tried the door for the fuck of it. No joy.

I dug out my mobile, breathing ice on the display. No signal. I rinsed through two dead blokes' pockets and found theirs. No signal.

I looked at my phone again, keeping track of time. I spent five minutes thinking how rank the smell of fish was. Ten minutes and I was melting on a white beach – palm trees, coconuts.

Fifteen minutes and I was doing star-jumps, shadow-boxing, anything to keep the blood flowing.

Twenty-five. Having a lie-down seemed like a grand idea.

Thirty and I didn't feel a shiver. I was sleeping sound.

22

KISSING FOR BALANCE

SCOTCH BONNET WAS burning my nose. I sneezed. Eyes open.

This cow with giant Deirdre specs, a blue make-up smudge behind them. Fifty-odd, bad perm, lipstick in her teeth, Littlewoods catalogue pullover – deep V-neck, never-ending knockers. Deirdre took her hand off my forehead and I punched the blanket away and gave her a fright. She jumped back, tits bobbing.

I was above the shop – feet up on a loud leather couch in Des's flat – a fluffy hot-water bottle on my chest. It was a big room with peeling sunflower wall-paper, shelves crammed with holiday knick-knacks – golliwogs lined up on one, kissing for balance. Porcelain hot dogs, ships in bottles, carvings of African ladies with jugs on their heads. There was a photo on top of the telly. The little boy in it might've been Abrafo, but I couldn't tell from here.

I swung my feet round to the floor. 'She the missus?' I said, swapping a leather cushion for the water bottle. 'She's—'

'White?' Desmond was in a basket-weave chair, folding up an *Evening News* in his lap.

'*Lovely.*' I looked at Deirdre. 'How'd y'do? Bane.'

She stood up. 'Mildred. Milly,' – then waddled over to a gas cooker – the kitchen units were squashed into one corner of the room. I could hear the scran bubbling in the pot.

'Where's—'

'I'm here.' Roisin sat on a dining chair behind me – legs crossed, feet inside borrowed slippers. The tears made it to her mouth.

'Soppy cow,' I said.

Grinning: *Fuck you.*

A dominoes set was laid out on the coffee table, a leather flat cap hiding a couple of the pieces. Des sat forward, slapped the cap on and angled it down his brow.

'Des has been teaching me to play,' Roisin said.

Des flicked the top of his ears out from under his cap. 'Now she winning.'

Roisin: 'It was best of three.'

'We should be keepin lights off,' I said, checking to see if the curtains were drawn.

'They gone now,' Des said.

'Time is it?'

'After two.'

'In the mornin?'

'Yes.'

'We're all doin alright?'

'Yes.' He patted the *Evening News* creased on the arm of his chair.

'They robbed your till,' I said.

'Me know. They come axin for money this afternoon. Wanting to collect every month. I say I already pay nephew security and they vex. They break window and they go next door and make noise. They come back with their boss man.'

'Abrafo know? You rang him?'

'Yes. I tell him we aright.'

'We'll get this sorted, mate. They're not gunna be mitherin again.'

'Bane, there be dead men in me freezer.'

Milly at the stove: 'Yer was nearly one of um.'

Roisin – still grinning tears.

Milly dished out the hot stuff and Des got up and brought it over.

'This warm you.'

Milly to Roisin: 'Yavin some, love?'

'I'm alright, thank you.'

'She so maga.' Des pointed at her flat tum, then patted his own belly. 'Me hungry *for* you.'

Roisin laughed.

Des put hers on the table and passed me a steaming bowl. Asbestos fingers.

'Ta.' I dropped it in my lap and caught the fork before it fell on the zigzag carpet.

'Taste,' he said. 'Taste!'

I did.

Fire. 'She the chef? This is the good stuff, love.'

Roisin picked her bowl up with her sleeves and had a dainty pick around the edges.

'Thumbs-up?'

She was coughing, her throat flushing with the heat. 'It's . . .' Her big eyes went bigger – she said sorry as the red climbed her face like a thermometer.

Milly fetched Roisin a glass of water and Des patted her arse on the trot past.

'She love what she make,' he said.

She laughed and offered me a water as well. I thanked her while I could still speak.

'You used to be worse than me with spicy food,' Roisin said – voice down, croak missing.

An alarm clock on the bed table, underneath a bowl of seashells: 03:25 – the red glow reflecting off her bare legs. It was a spare box-room, single bed, square window, lights off. Roisin had put her socks over the mucky radiator. I should've been kipping on the loud leather couch in the front room.

She rocked on the diet mattress, sat hunched, bug-eyed, choking a pillow under her chin.

'You hated trying new things.' She watched me pace.

'I never.'

Fixed-frown: 'Yes you bloody did. I made you that Thai. You said you didn't do fancy food.'

'What's it matter, love?'

'You should be dead.'

Dan.

'What bout Knobhead?' I said.

'Where is he?'

'*You* don't know?'

'No,' she said.

'Must've stepped out the flat before the dread squad knocked on for him.'

'. . .'

'He knew they'd pay him a visit.'

'. . .'

'Love, you're tellin us you don't know nowt? Right now he's hoppin around Manny in the snow? Minus six. No chance.'

'Look, he's been playing it up. He can walk a bit.'

'Fuckin *Knobhead*. I knew it.' We should have snipped his toes off with the bolt cutters while we still had him.

'Anyway.' She rubbed her eyes. 'He took my car.'

'What?'

'The Fiesta.'

'Thought Gordon still had it?' I said.

'No.'

'It was in the car park?'

'Yes.'

'Fuck me.'

'I didn't notice on the way up. But when we went into the flat, I saw the car keys were gone.'

'What the fuck were you still doin with car keys?'

'When they took us back out – it wasn't there – I looked . . . before they killed that lad.'

I said: 'So Dan's just done one? Not too arsed about you then?'

'Don't.' She raised her voice. Croak on the mend.

Even if he was putting some of it on, somebody had to have been driving him.

'I'll kill him,' I said.

Her toes scrunched duvet, hands mauling thighs – about to explode.

It was painful to look at her.

I said: 'When they come for him – n they will – I'm gunna be there, lightin the barbie.'

'You're pathetic.'

'You're blind as fuck.'

Roisin launched the pillow at me, ripped the duvet and got under it, her back to me.

'Bet Knobhead reckons you're a right tough bird. He's left you fendin for yourself. N y'don't need us, do you? Never should've asked for our help.'

'You're driving me mad,' she said, fingers in her hair.

'A tough bird. That's you, love. A tough bird.'

She rolled over, her face stiff: 'Are you after a shag?' Her lips just about moved. 'We had about a week together. Eight years ago. A week. It wasn't the summer of love. It wasn't even love. Now are you after a shag or not?'

'I'm after some shut-eye.' I picked a seashell from the bowl on top of the alarm clock – cracked, no colour, still gritty with sand – and put it against my ear. 'Ever do this when you were a kiddie? Hearin the seaside?'

A hand popped out from under the sheet and I gave it to her. She said: 'I didn't mean that.'

I sat on the bed.

'I'm scared,' she said, having a listen.

'They've gone, love.'

'Of you.'

She sniffed, holding the shell like a phone. I took it back and got into bed. There was sand on the covers.

'Feet,' she said, curling away.

'Remember that one time I made you tea?'

'Freezing.'

'Remember?'

'I do.'

Bra-strap grooves, backbone – I found the moles on her waist, everything where it belonged.

'What did I make?'

23

INDEPENDENT THINKER

July 1990

HOT MORNING. A lazy madam next to me, refusing duvet. Tits suckered to the mattress, face in pillow.

She stirred.

'You awake, love?' I said.

'. . . No.'

'It's gone noon.'

'Too early.'

'Spose to be meetin a mate at ah-past.'

'Good luck.'

I poked a finger into her side and she complained, went *oi* for ages on one breath – it sounded like I'd given her a puncture.

'God, love, you are pale.' I rode her spine with the same finger – journeyed neck down, admiring the goods.

She kneed me in the arse, blind. 'Tickles.'

'Shame there's not time for round two.'

'Three.'

'Oh aye.'

'Henry?'

'Yeah?'

'I had this dream. I was a punk-princess and all my hair fell out.'

I shoved up next to her. Even with the covers off, she was oven-warm. 'Thought you were a raver?'

Daylight was coming in through the middle of the curtains. I rubbed her short hair the wrong way – shiny flick-flick. Roisin lifted her face out of the pillow and kept her eyes shut. 'Do you still like it?'

I said: 'You're not out o bed yet. Give it a quick comb n you'll be decent.'

A hand went down me and grabbed my cock. Her eyes were growing, getting used to the light. 'I try not to look too well kept,' she said.

'We've noticed.'

'You fucking love it.'

I grabbed her waist and she squealed, lashed out – swearing at the top of her voice. She gave me a kiss, crawled on top of me, straightened her arms and looked down. Both of us were panting. Her nails dug into my shoulders.

'Will you ring me?' she said. If looks could burn.

'Will I bollocks.'

'Bastard.'

Another scrap – both of us going mad for it. Roisin was laughing and laughing.

One thud through the wall made us freeze. Her elbow was in my cheek, and I had her in a headlock. I heard bedsprings bounce from the next room.

'What was that?' She ducked out from under my arm.

'Me dad's back.'

She put a hand over her gob. 'We were being dead loud.'

'Don't worry bout it. He'll have been well out of it.'

She shifted onto her back and rubbed her face. 'I'd better go.'

'Not want breakfast?'

A kiss: 'I thought it was dinnertime.'

'Toast soldiers goin if you want um?'

'Tempted.' She stuck her head over the edge of the bed, scanning the floor. 'Knickers?'

'Bathroom, love.'

'Shit.' Mucky grin: 'Be a prince and fetch them for me.'

We heard the loo flush down the hall.

'Shit.' She tried to kick me out of bed. 'Retrieve my dignity.'

'Y'what?'

'Henry. Go!'

I rolled off my side and the floor rushed up – palms touched-down.

Twenty press-ups.

Roisin looked down. 'I hope that's just for my benefit.'

Thirty press-ups.

'God, what do you look like?'

Forty press-ups.

'If you end up like my brother I'll feel sorry for you.'

'Say . . . what you like . . . I've . . . had you now.' I finished, stood up, made a meal out of a yawn and a stretch.

She watched me – gob sulky. 'Are you being serious?'

'Don't be daft.'

She was acrossways on the bed, belly down, her legs scissor-kicked.

I said: 'Last night was grand.'

Sunshine grin: 'Shoo then!'

The hallway was all clear – the old man downstairs in the kitchen. I could hear a teaspoon rattling in a mug.

I stepped onto the landing and shut my door to. Knickers were dangling from the doorknob.

'Ee-ah.' I tossed them over to the bed, back inside.

Pouty: 'That was quick.'

She jumped off the bed and pulled them up as she walked.

'I'll ring you,' I said.

'You better had do.'

'Gordon'll answer.'

'He's never answered the phone in his short, angry life.'

'He'd clue it was us.'

'I'd make out it's Auntie Viv.'

'Might stop round for a brew later, anyway. You be in?'

'Might be. I've got these books to give back to the library.'

'She reads. Listen to you. The intellectual bird.'

'I thought I was just a raver?' Roisin did a slow twirl – clocking my room for the first time.

James Brown on my wall – 1963, still lean, sweat-spray, candyfloss 'fro, knees sinking with the mic stand – mid-scream.

I said: *'That's* a raver.'

Hearts on her head, feet in cherry Docs – laces untied. The bracelets went on last. She wriggled her hands through the tangle and put them on all together.

I kissed her before I let her out, feeling daft – a bit shy now. She waved at the gate. It was a gorgeous day – blinding – she tipped the hearts over her face.

Front room. He turned the paper over – skimming the classified, cut-outs from *Loot* piled up on a coaster, a tea ring on the top ad.

'Michael Jackson,' he said. 'Bloody ell.'

'What?'

'Some bugger's sellin is bloody Michael Jackson vinyls. Japanese singles. Be wurf a few bob if there wan't s'many.'

'One day,' I said. I blew on the top of my brew, got the *Radio Times* under it and sat opposite the old man.

'She were a goer wan't she?' He didn't look up.

'Here we go.'

'She's not fer you, son. Wunt get involved.'

'What – cos she's your Vic's little girl? Give over.'

'Them were nice knickers,' he said.

'Alright, mouth.'

'Think er ladyship were the mouf. Bloody ell.'

'Time d'you get in?' I said.

'Never mind that. Time yer opened yer eyes.' He looked across at me. Hangover stare, three-day tash stubble.

'What's this about?'

'Like er, d'yer?'

I gave my brew another go. 'She's alright, yeah.'

'She's cut from different cloth now, lad. She's moved on from us bloody workers.'

I laughed. '"Work", he says. You rolled out o bed gone noon n all.'

'It's Monday, smartarse. Stall's dead. Anyway, that one – she's jus back after a bit o rough.'

'She is a bit o rough.'

'She reckons she's not.'

'That enough to hate her – is it?'

'She ates what she comes from.'

I nearly spilt my brew. 'Does she eck, Dad.'

'Oi. She dunt speak to Vic, yer know. Is own daughter. Not a word. Gordon's not got time fer er – yer know that yerself. She comes back, stops under Vic's roof when er bloody fellers get rid of er. N she dunt talk to er own father. Too good fer im.'

'Never used to stick y'nose in like this, Dad.'

'Better off wivout, son. All am sayin.' He tore a page out and put it with the rest.

'We keep you up?' I said.

He coughed and fist-slapped his chest. 'Mek us anuva brew, will yer, lad.'

Civic. 2 p.m. A scorcher. Kiddies in pushchairs licking ice-rockets, tired mams – roasted cleavage.

I went in the hardware shop next to the bookies and the door buzzed open, buzzed shut.

'Iya, gorgeous,' I said.

Noreen was behind the counter, minding her dad's shop. She sucked her thumb through a smile, shaking her head as I walked up. 'Unbelievable.'

'Didn't know you were still workin here.'

'Yeah yer did.'

'Part-time?'

She crossed her arms. 'Mornins.'

I leaned in and tapped her watch. 'Time n a half?'

'Ah bloody wish.' She slapped my hand away.

I said: 'What? Y'dad about?'

'Nah.'

'Well then?'

Guinness eyes, fluttering: 'Don't distract us when am workin, enry.'

I looked around. Spirit levels, WD-40, drill bits. 'There's no customers, love.'

Noreen pressed a few buttons on the till. She started humming a nice tune. Her long locks were glimmer-black and dead straight, and a lightning-bolt hairband made her ears stick out. She was twenty-one, a dark princess in gold Lycra shorts, size six. I'd had her out of them just once, but this was years ago.

'Where's our Maz?' I said.

'Avin is dinner.'

'You had your dinner?'

'Nah.'

'Wanna get summat?'

'Pends,' she said. 'What we avin?'

'Ee's avin a black eye in a minute.' Maz came out of the back and dropped a hand on his sister's shoulder.

I said sorry for being late.

Maz bumbled up the stairs and I followed. I said hello to his nana in the top room. She was threading sequins on a fancy frock. She was singing another nice tune.

He unlocked his bedroom – Page Three blondes on the inside door, ready with welcome smiles, darts keeping them up.

Maz was in a City away shirt, David White's number, his belly stretching it out. Forty-four-inch jeans, bunched above his knock-off Reeboks: one less pair I had to get rid of.

'What yer want on?' he said.

'You give *Road to the Riches* a play?'

'Yeah. Not bad.'

'"Not bad"?'

Maz went through his cassette pile. 'What bout the Mondays?'

'Behave.'

He banged on 'Wrote for Luck' anyway, to mask the chat, pigeon-nodding to the beat.

A combination box came out from under the bed

and I watched him raid his piggy bank, counting some twenties. 'Two ton. Ee-ah.'

'Sound.'

'Can yer get it all?' he said.

'You worryin again?'

Our Maz was clubbing in with me and Gordon to try and make an extra few quid. More capital meant we could buy bigger – not that we were getting daft. He'd said he might even help us shift some of it this weekend.

'Yer gunna get um off the usual lad?' he said.

Blue Monday.

'No. Another one. This lad from Chorlton. Student. You've not met him.'

Eyes to the stereo: 'There's spose to be a fuckin rave, Friday night. Some mega DJs comin down n all that. Avin it, like.' His feet were tapping to the Mondays. Shaun Ryder – the bugger sang like he was deaf. No Jackie Wilson but the message was crystal. *You form the queue, try anything hard.*

'Where there's dancin, there's dealin,' I said.

'They're avin it in a couple o knocked-through flats in Charles Barry.'

'Hulme?' I said. 'There yesterday. Some posse wants Stan Barker's clubtrade now he's put away. The Jamaicans rinsed this bird's flat n some student wallets n gave us a scare.'

'Fuckin ell.' He sat on his bed and nearly sank it. 'Jamaicans? Stan oo?'

'Barker.'

'Paki-bashers is lot.'

'Heard of him?'

'Erd enough.'

'These Yardies were top lads, n all.'

Our Maz, grinding his teeth with worry. 'Maybe not Friday then, ay?'

'If it's gunna kick off, it'll be in the Barker clubs. We might be alright down there.'

'The Charles Barry do's called the Surgery. Be plenny goin. Free entry.' Maz tried convincing himself.

'Those nights never end up free.'

'They do for us.'

I said: 'Now who wants trouble?'

'Could be a laugh, though. Decent tunes, bitofanny. We'd get rid o the lot fore midnight. Could bring yer new bird.'

'What bird?'

'Oo is she?'

'Who's who?'

He said: 'Mate, you're never late fer nowt.'

'Fuck off.'

'You av ad a busy weekend, ant yer, mate?'

'Fuck off.'

Maz gave up. 'Still a bit risky trekkin down, init?'

'Shouldn't be.'

His carp mouth ballooned, mono-brow doing a McDonald's arch. 'Come back wiv a black eye the uva week, dint yer?'

It wasn't a black eye. And I wasn't about to go into details over the trouble since, with Horace and Dudley.

I said: 'You n black eyes. Old news, mate. We sorted all that out the other day.'

'What – wiv that mate o yours? Gordon?'

'Yeah.'

Maz sniffed. 'Needs a fuckin chill pill, im. Should tek um not sell um.'

Ryder, tuneless: *There's more than one sign.*

'The Surgery,' I said. 'This Friday.'

'If ah elp yer flog um?'

'Yes or no?'

A dart dropped out of the door while he had a think. The blonde's smile bent. The rest of her peeled off too.

Roisin was padding around barefoot, dodging the tea drips on the lino in a Jane's Addiction vest and red cut-off shorts. Beyond gorgeous. She made us both a brew while I perved for England.

It was gone nine and still light out.

Vic banging down the stairs: 'Bloody great big spider in that tub!'

Gordon in the front room: 'D'yer get rid of it?!'

'Ah give it summat ter drink!'

'Oi – seen what she's done to er air. Fuckin daft cow!'

'Am not sayin a word!' Vic made it to the front room and the double act quieted down.

Roisin handed me a mug in the kitchen. 'See why I don't do this often?'

'You mean come home?'

'I'm off again soon.'

'How soon?'

'Another couple of days. Then London.'

'Lundon?' I said. 'What you wanna go there for?'

She put the milk away. Carlsbergs rattled on top of the fridge. 'Now you sound like those two. I'm staying with a friend.'

'A feller?'

'Might be.'

'Don't fancy stoppin a bit longer?'

Hand on hip: 'Why?'

'Why not?' I had a taste – perfect brew.

'Convince me,' she said.

Her thighs were bed-bruised.

First kiss since this morning. We were both ready for it. More tea-spill on the lino. I copped a feel – she tugged her vest back down and just showed me her teeth.

'Maybe I can stay another week.'

'What's this "maybe"?' I said.

'There's something good on Friday. I've got friends organising the Surgery again. They're hosting this flat rave. It could be the last one before the Crescents get knocked down.'

Good fucking riddance.

I said: 'Y'know everyone, you do.'

'Fancy taking me?'

I put my mug on the worktop.

She watched, waited, giggled. 'You're supposed to say *yes*.'

'Hulme?'

Nod.

'Think that's wise, love?'

'I need to see Sally. Give her some of that money. I need to see all that lot before I go.'

'See um durin the day,' I said.

'We tried that yesterday, remember?'

'You can remember it?'

Another kiss – softer. I was counting the breaths. 'Why don't you drink?' she said – lips still up close, making like she didn't know.

'Ta for the brew,' I said.

She stiffened up, stepped back. 'You're going?'

'I'm nippin in there for a bit. Wanit to be alright between me n him.'

'Gordon won't give a shit.'

'Yeah he will.'

'I'll be upstairs.' Roisin picked up her brew and I watched her walk.

Vic was in the chair, a filled ashtray on one arm – fabric burns like moth holes. Gordon had the sofa. Steven Seagal was breaking noses on the telly. *Nico: Above the Law*. I'd seen it two summers ago at the pictures with feather-cut Debs, a Poundswick bird I'd pinched off our Gordon because I could.

'How yer doin, enry?' Vic shook a twenty-pack upside down, holding it up to his face after every three shakes, muttering *bugger*.

'Not bad,' I said.

'Where's yer dad?'

'Said he's stayin in. Checkin stock for scratches. He'll play um all night.'

'Now Lola's buggered off again ee can.' Eyes went from the box to me. 'Sorry, lad.'

'Forget it.'

'Reckon ah can get im out. Ee'll be on them fruit machines fore av got the first ones in.' Vic put the empty box in the ashtray and squinted at the clock on the mantle.

Gordon, watching *Nico*: 'Dad, fetch us anuva one.'

'Lord above, fetch me anuva son.' Vic got up, pulled the cushion off the chair, ran his fingers down the sides and rescued a green Bic lighter but no fallen cigs.

I sat down next to Gordon. He hadn't looked at me once.

Seagal put this one feller through a window. The rest of them queued up for a kicking.

'We're good for Friday, mate,' I said.

Vic wiped his hat hair down in the mirror over the mantle. 'You're all bloody villains,' he said. 'Ooligan, this one.'

Gordon: 'Thought yer was goin pub?'

Vic: 'Al go n give yer a crack in a minute. Thinks ee's a big lad now, enry.'

'He is a big lad,' I said.

'A bloody big girl's blouse. Ay – what's the story wiv er? What's she done to er air?'

'She's had it cut,' I said.

'Can see that. What's she done that fer? Looks a right state.'

'Ask her.'

Vic sighed. 'She's what yer might call an independent

thinker, is our Roisin. Always thinkin. Too much bloody thinkin. Worse than doin no thinkin at all, that is.'

Gordon belched on cue.

Vic slammed the door on his way out to the pub.

Nico played possum. The bent CIA fucker was about to do him in. Adverts cut halfway through.

'Shaggin er, then?' Gordon said, flicking channels.

'I'm not gunna mess her about,' I said.

'Can do, mate. Do what yer like. Not arsed, me.'

'She loves you, mate. She's your fuckin big sister.'

'Don't fuckin start wiv that.'

'You hear what I said before? Bout Friday.'

'What's the plan?'

'Hulme. There's a do in one of the flats in Charles Barry. Ravers' last stand.'

'We tekin er?' he said. 'Our kid?'

'She was up for goin anyway.'

Gordon switched Seagal back on. Nico hit the baddie so hard his nose went into his brain. 'Don't give er owt fer free.'

24

SNOWBALL SHIELD

17 February 1998
Tuesday

DESMOND WAS OPENING the curtains with his free hand, a cup of Ovaltine in the other. I could smell the malt milk. 'City of no sun,' he said.

I went: 'Oi, we're not decent.'

Roisin pulled the duvet up to her eyes and said: 'Oh god.'

Something sharp dug into my back. I sat up, had a feel around under the sheet and found a broken seashell.

'Clear off, Des.'

He left us to it.

It had just gone seven – nearly light out. I got up, bones clicking, everything sore. The window was drippy. I scrubbed a circle, squeaked it clear and saw another lot of fresh snow untouched. Skeltah and Igloo's Vectra was still in the car park. At eyeline: spotty old brickwork, iced rooftop chains, chimney smoke, mangled satellite dishes, a tabby scaling the drains, high-rises off in the distance. No sun.

I looked back in the room and Roisin stuck an arm out, snatched a pair of woolly socks off the radiator and put them on under the covers.

The cabbie twisted round, his breath stank of Fisherman's Friends. I gave him a twenty and got out – pavement side – ankle deep in snow.

The drapes twitched as I unhooked the front gate.

Jan had left her keys in the inside lock. I rang the bell, snapped the letter box, then pointed for the taxi to go. It moved off the kerb, Roisin watching me as it drove her away.

Mouth to the letter box: 'Jan, love. Freezin out here.'

The key twisted inside.

'Trenton at school?' I said.

Jan sucked on a fag, finished it, sat down, took another out of the pack on the kitchen table and lit it – fifth spark. She wasn't dressed yet.

My takeout note from Saturday night was ripped up in the ashtray, the corners glowing. The Nescafé jar was out, lid off, mug empty.

I put the kettle on and pulled two slices of Warburtons out of the bag. The crusts were green.

'Bread's manky,' she said. 'Need a fresh loaf.'

I chucked it and pulled up a chair.

'Where've yer bin?' she said.

Her hand was warm. She didn't let me keep it.

'What's she got that I ant got?'

The kettle boiled. I took the jar and her mug.

Tears: 'D'yer not fancy us?'

I made her another one and sat back down with it.

She wiped her face. 'D'yer not love us?' Another drag, ash growing long. 'Say summat, then. She any good?' Her shakes broke the ash-finger into the fresh mug. 'Found this upstairs.' Jan took Thin's semi-automatic out of her dressing-gown pocket. She turned her wrist over and the diamonds sparkled. 'Evvy, init?'

I said: 'That one is.'

'Yuv ad that skinny fuckin trollop ant yer? Yuv bin wiv er all night. Ah saw er in cab. Al kill er. Al fuckin kill er. That fuckin tart – oo does she think she is?' Jan threw the gun at the fridge and stood up quickly, lifting the table an inch with her. Coffee splashed the floor. She pointed at me with her fag hand, stabbing it back and forth like she was taking aim. Ash flew over me. 'Yer come to see us right out the blue. After ten years. Ten years. See, ah knew yer fore she did. Ah were in school wiv yer. N ah wanted yer n not jus cos yer was Alice's. Now ah know they all ad *me* back then. Me mam laughed when ah told er. Knocked up by some gorgeous nigger down Whalley Range. Stupid cunt, she said. They all did. But sod um. Yer fuckin mine now. They still don't understand. Yer mine!'

'Jan—'

'Say sorry. Say sorry.'

'I'm sorry.'

'Not sorry. Not even listenin'.'

I changed clothes upstairs. I pinched the car keys off the phone table in the hall.

'Meant nowt, did she?!' Jan yelled through, still in the kitchen.

'I'm borrowin y'car, love.'

'Yours anyway.'

10 a.m., radio off. Thin's empty gun was in the glovebox. A snowball thumped the windscreen. This mob of kids outside Cornishway off-licence was pelting traffic. I was going to see Maz and wanted chocolates and a card for Rana, so I pulled in for the newsagent on the end. They opened fire before I got out. The driver door became a shield. I yelled *oi* while the cocky bastards reloaded – speed-packing fresh rounds – growing another pyramid of ammo by the bin.

'That's me mam's car, that,' Trenton said. He broke ranks and did one.

25

CURSED

GORDON REACHED UP, opened the airing cupboard and I saw the stretch-rips under the arms of his Everlast hoodie. He took out something wrapped in a towel. 'Anuva prezzie, this were.'

'For doin what?' I said.

'Lookin after their Keith inside.'

'Not for stabbin those lads?'

'Dint turn up. Wan't menna appen, ah said. Yer were right, Bane.'

'Let's have a look.'

I kept it in the towel and put my eye down the sight.

Gordon said: 'A fuckin stopper that, init? Plenny o shot in the box. Might come in andy if launch night kicks off.'

'Fuck me. Should be a law against you havin one o these.' I handed it back. 'Oh wait, there is.'

He put the gun away and we went in the front room. The mantle clock said half-two. Roisin was asleep upstairs, Vic and all – he said he was too old now to be on nights.

Gordon pressed the telly and we sat down. Sound off, Teletext subtitles, a snooker repeat.

'Be nowt on,' he said.

The remote worked, then didn't.

I watched the bloke stalk the table, pot one, pot two, stalk again, after his next.

Gordon bashed the remote awake on his knee.

The bloke found his angle and went for it.

Gordon changed over.

I'd lied to Rana this morning, when she asked me if I'd been there when it happened. Maz had still been telling her it was a Staffie that bit him. Doctors knew different now.

There was an oldie on the other side – Lana Turner, or someone – and *Blockbusters* after that. Gordon put three seconds of snooker on – brow-sweat showing in the close-up, every option getting a dress rehearsal in the bloke's eyes. 'Told yer,' Gordon said. 'Fuck all.'

Thin had been business-friendly with Abrafo. Thin's murder split his lads from ours. Hagfish was using Abrafo's Hulme property for a zoo pen. It was a Fuck You, and if there was more to it than that, I didn't know it. Stashing his gear in Hollywood Butchers was the same Fuck You. And all that gear was getting the Barkers' blood up.

Abrafo had listened.

I'd told him Dan was missing. I'd told him about Skeltah and Igloo – his wife's killers.

Whatever Dan's mess was, it had taken his Ashley, while Hagfish had almost taken his Uncle Des.

Abs looked after family, even when he couldn't. He absolved his mam's death in a woman's blood. He eyed for an eye, and this would end the same way. Even if Ashley's killers were dead, there was plenty more to settle, from Hagfish's corner, and Danny boy's.

Abrafo, today: 'Cheers for savin me Uncle Des.'

I said: 'Think he saved us.'

We stood inside his empty new club, behind his empty new bar. Billyclub stank of cheap paint and wood polish. Builders, decorators wandered about – sipping afternoon brews, whistling to chart radio, local reception like a hornets' nest.

I asked him if plans had changed.

'Never know what yer thinkin, Bane. But ah do trust yer. So ah fuckin let it be. But al av a guess at what's goin on up there now. Ee's thinkin pride before a fall.'

'This for Ashley?'

'Fer us all. We open Friday as planned,' he said. 'End of.'

Back on the TV: Lana Turner minced for her life in pencil skirt and heels. Shadows chased hers. Boxhat netting made a spider's web. Everywhere led to black.

'Am lookin after er,' Gordon said out of nowhere,

watching Lana get the chop. 'Our Roisin. Shiz me sister, end o the day, init?'

Smoking guns. Somebody died in style.

'You two made up?' I said.

'Good as.'

'Any news bout her Dan?'

'Ant come back. Ee timed it well by sounds of it. Fuckin off from that flat. She's bin tekin it well n all.'

'Least she's not gone after him,' I said.

'Even she's not that daft.'

If the London Yardies didn't have him, Dan couldn't stay missing. Roisin was still at risk. There'd be fallout over Skeltah and Igloo when they didn't check in with their don. If Danny boy was worth this much grief already, they'd fly someone else over to get the job done. Maybe they'd sod the outsourcing – come up themselves and sort it.

I said: 'He take his mobile with him?'

'She's bin tryin it. Nowt.' Gordon yawned, watching the snooker again. 'Ay, yer kippin ere, mate, or what?'

Too knackered to fib: 'Jan's kicked us out.'

'As she?' He rubbed his giant hands together. 'Ee's back in the game.'

'Calm down.'

'Won't she tek yer back?'

'How can she?'

'Bin playin away?'

I looked at the ceiling. 'She reckons.'

'Our kid – she were assle before, now shiz fuckin cursed.'

'Our fault,' I said.

'Ay, your Jan – she forgot ooz ouse it is? Tell er ter fuck off.'

'Helpful,' I said.

'Could stop at yer dad's fer a bit.' Gordon winced. 'Shit. Ah jus forgot. Am dead sorry. God bless im, ay? Enry senior.' He changed the record back and we were both relieved: 'Your Jan. She the one yer knew from donkey's back? Got in a right state when we went fer that Chinese on Charlotte Street? Jus fore ah went inside.'

'Messy do.'

'She were fuckin ammered. Ad a right laugh.'

I said: 'Till I put her in a taxi before nine.'

Sly grin: 'Wiv all bin there, mate. Cept you.'

I changed it again: 'So how'd you leave it with Kara's clowns at the pub?'

'Kara said ee-ah, ere's a fuckin shotgun. Ah said ta very much n did one. That Simon give us lift back.'

'N the club? Her lads doin the doors for cheap or what?'

'It's sorted. Boss not say? They're comin Friday, meetin at Billyclub.' He stood and slapped the dust off his crushed seat, leaned back – second yawn, King Kong chest-beat. 'New leaf fer us, this is. What wiv the club. Afro Man, ee's alright – goin frew a rough time of it wiv his bird n that, fuck me. But this Billyclub – it's lookin good, init?'

'Good? There's allsorts goin on. We're up to here in grief.'

He looked up and laughed. 'N someow, our kid's right bang in middle. Er fuckin ladyship. See. Shiz cursed.'

Third yawn.

I caught it this time when I tried to speak.

26
THE SURGERY

July 1990

'WHAT DOES YOUR dad think of me?' Roisin croaked, shaking her water bottle, body pressing against me as we walked. My pockets were too fat for me to feel her.

'Thinks you're smashin,' I said. 'Why?'

'Liar.'

Friday. Half-eleven. A hot night filled with acid tunes. White lads were coming off the decks – lost in baggies, knee-length round-collar shirts, haircuts to mop the floor with. Gordon clipped one of them as they passed us, just for the fuck of it – a brick shoulder and the poor lad spun 360.

Roisin broke off, not impressed: 'You're such a bastard, you are.'

'What av ah done?' Gordon said – arms out wide, mad grin.

Still walking: 'Don't be you tonight.'

'Erd this, mate?'

I kept quiet.

She said: 'Be cuddly instead.'

We reached the Surgery – a throb-throb rattling the door out of its frame. There was a posse in a row, each one with a leg up on the outer wall, head-nods to the bassline. I didn't spot Horace or Dudley, or anyone else, but one of them tapped Roisin and offered her an eighth, buttering her up. They were trying to shift weed to the wrong crowd.

Roisin took my hand and we waltzed in.

The place was already rammed. It stank of sweat. It was two ground-floor flats, the main wall knocked through. A couple of fairies were dotted about like sore thumbs, half a dozen birds by the DJ booth. The DJ: a little black feller in a leather beret. The booth: decks set up on a shiny moon bedsheet draped over a kitchen table – speaker stacks on either side. The birds were leaning over in mini-dresses, big hair, tiger-stripe tights and rainbow heels.

It was mostly just the usual offenders up for it – harmless twats – pasty lads shedding pounds to the beat. Gordon went off, swallowed by the traffic of dancers. They were too high to be afraid of him, and there wasn't enough space to give him right of way.

Our Maz was already there, a big blonde on her tiptoes was gabbing into his ear. He gave me the eye from across the room but he couldn't get away.

We clocked Sally going for the kitchen with a cider in her hand. Roisin kissed my cheek and shoved off – the two of them hugged, shouting over the noise. I lipread the start of it –

Sally: *Looks gorgeous.*

Roisin: *Guess who cut it?*

– but faces got in the way and I lost my line of sight. I decided to go rescue Maz.

The KLF – 'What Time is Love?' didn't go down a treat, the DJ swapped it for something funkier, something fresher. It was hard to hear anything over the racket.

I said: 'How we doin, mate?'

Maz wiped a sweat-drip off his temple, watching fat arse sail away in slashed leggings. 'Not too bad. Ah was in there.'

'You were in trouble.'

'Ah was workin.'

'Had any grief?'

Maz reached into his pockets for a quiet stock check. 'Could be summat brewin, but it's bin alright. No sign o dibble.'

'That's not what you've gotta worry bout,' I said.

'Ay, oo's that bird yer come in wiv?'

'She's our Gordon's sister.'

Back-slap: 'Oh, aye. She yours ter look after fer the night?'

I was grinning. 'For as long as I can.'

Two birds danced in matching baseball caps and army camouflage pants – donkey jackets round their waists.

Roisin pointed them out – hopping on the spot in her purple Keds, Docs getting a rest. We watched their routine. Roisin squeezed my arm, dying to join in. We'd been necking it against a wall for half an hour and now she felt guilty, like she'd been neglecting the tunes.

Her eyes were crystal. 'Come on. Let's have a dance,' she said.

'*You* can, love.'

She laughed at me. 'You're a mover. You can't deny it, Henry – I've seen you.'

Watching the Detectives.

A cannonball hit my shoulder. Gordon kept his hand there. 'Cav a quick word?' His face was dry – there were no sweat patches on his Lonsdale.

'What do you want?' Roisin said to him.

'Same as you. Our enry.'

'Leave him alone,' she said.

I said to her: 'You have a dance, love. I'll be there in a bit.'

One kiss. Tight lips.

We muscled through the bodies and found a spare patch of carpet to stand on. 'You're still alright with me n her, aren't you?' I said.

Gordon: 'Said ah was, dint ah?'

'Think I'm just slackin off?'

'Sold owt?'

A feller pushed himself between us. He was tugging at his damp T-shirt collar. 'Got any pills, mate?' Long greasy hair – student scum. Gordon passed him two without blinking and I took the money – a screwed-up twenty, always soggy notes. The feller pogo'd back into the crowd.

Gordon itched his bum chin. 'That cunt we sorted out las Saturday down ere – one oo sold yer wormin tablets—'

Blue Monday.

'*You* sorted him out,' I said.

'—Ee's knockin about. Bandage over is eye. Got a few queers round im fer support.'

'He seen you?'

'Aye.'

'Where's he now?'

'Fuck knows.'

We watched another lad flapping about, legless, a drawstring hoodie tight over his head. He fell into Gordon and asked if he had any charlie.

'Ee-ah, mong,' Gordon said.

The lad took an E instead of a gram and got his wallet rinsed.

An hour later. It was fucking sweltering. Roisin's face was shiny – her arms felt sticky round my neck. She tripped, tried to kiss me but missed, giggled and tried again. I turned my face away.

'What's wrong?' Her voice was light and slow, her lips smiling. 'Henry?'

'Nowt.'

'I'm not with you so I can get gear cheap.'

'I know,' I said.

Her head lolled. 'What?'

Louder: 'Said I know.'

Pure bliss: 'Well then?'

Roisin had scored off a local lad, one of Blue
Monday's fairies – I'd just got back in time to see him
take her money. I'd seen him twenty minutes earlier,
mooching about outside the flat, getting friendly with
the Jamaicans. He knew we were in the same racket,
and he knew about last Saturday – but he'd still kept
his distance.

Roisin popped another and downed the rest of her
water. She took her arms off me and waved them to
the bass-drop. Some bird dancing too close knocked
the plastic bottle out of Roisin's hand and it sailed over
heads, bounced on a couple and then disappeared.

27

PATIENCE

20 February 1998
Friday

BUZZ SOON GOT round. Our street team had been a few decent-looking birds tossing flyers down Market Street – posh flyers, printed on the cheap – a contact that used to do the menus for the Britton, Frank Holland's old restaurant.

I was outside Billyclub with Gordon, polished shoes on red carpet – toes numb. He was looking the business – leather gloves, earpiece, a black Crombie from Abrafo's shop, the one below his old digs.

Head up: a sharp night, crystal cold, a nerve-cutter. Half-moon out, stars missing – nowhere to hide.

Head down: sirens blaring. Bobbies skidded down Deansgate – two Pandas, the trouble elsewhere.

Gordon whistled, ice-breath: 'Competition's fuckin kickin umselves.'

'What competition?' I said.

'Aye.' He tapped my arm, leaned out and pointed at the queue: endless totty lighting up, feet-stamping to keep warm – stalk heels, dicey – the last of the snow was still caked around the grids.

'Gunna be rammed,' I said. 'Pay off, son.'

'Fuck me, if ah don't cop off tonight, mate—'

Simon came out behind us and shut the main doors again. 'Oi, Kara said ter give yer this, lad.' He winked and pushed something into my hand on the sly – Crombie sleeves covering his swallow tats.

'We fuckin ready or what?' Gordon said.

'Five min,' Simon said. He went inside again and Gordon shined his ID torch into my hand – his back to the line of punters.

It was a Beanie Baby with its belly cut open, a tight roll of fifties inside instead of stuffing. Gordon steadied the beam as I rolled off the outer note – red marker pen over Her Majesty's mug:

SOFT CUNT X

They fancied a long-term bargain with Abrafo, with Billyclub, with me.

Two dressy meatheads from the Firm haunted the line, harrassing lads they knew, harrassing lads they didn't. Stanley and Kara hadn't thrown us amateurs.

'Remember Jamie?' I said.

Gordon put the torch away. 'Oo?'

'Big Jamie. Doorman.'

The DJ fired up inside – bass cracking the new paintwork.

The line got fidgety, keen. 'Urry up!' one bird went.

'Patience, love,' I said.

'Sez you. Ah forgot me fuckin tights.'

Gordon said to me: 'Went gym wiv im once, that Jamie. Where'd ee fuck off to?'

'Knocked up his bird. Twins. Heard he was inside for summat.'

'Never saw im in there.'

A bloke over the road wolf-whistled a tall bird clopping along on our side. She was a push-up bra – all tits, after a queue-jump. We let her try her luck and she grabbed our Gordon, gave his cheek a peck and slipped in behind the red rope.

'Time yer openin?' she said – half-caste, fluffy open jacket, crayoned beauty spot. There was an Asian lad next to her who'd been there awhile and kept trying to show me his watch. Instead, I pulled Gordon's sleeve up to check the time – his watch made it half-ten already. 'Bout now, love,' I said to her.

Gordon unhooked the rope, buzzing – lippy smudge on his face. 'Let's av um then.'

The two Barker boys started checking handbags – another three inside with Simon, making sure everything went sound. They were dealing their own gear tonight, cutting Abrafo twenty per cent. Cash hopped from pocket to pocket to safe, all in the same building.

Decent innings and we'd all get a bonus tomorrow. But that would've been old Abs, the one that still had a bubbly missus.

I nodded to a black feller in a daft fur-trimmed coat who was next in line. He had diamond studs in his ears. I waved for Gordon to pat him down.

He reached inside his coat and pulled out a money clip – his hands were long and bony – carved skull rings on every other finger. Not quite bling – juju bollocks. He put a twenty inside my top pocket and sorted Gordon out with another. I gave Gordon the eye and he showed some brains.

'Nice one,' Gordon said. 'Now, arms out fuckin straight, there's a good lad.'

Skull Rings squared up, his face a couple of inches away from mine. His eyes went beamy until he gave me some room, smiling with his gob shut. He did as he was told and Gordon opened his fur coat.

Clean.

We stepped aside and he strutted up to the flyer girl behind the door. He touched her chin, spoke to her, and she gave him a giggle. His bony hand got stamped.

It was one-in-one-out by half-eleven. By midnight, we were turning buggers away.

Roisin was upstairs with Abrafo. Not my idea – hers, but at least we could keep an eye on her. It was safer than leaving her on her own.

Lauryn Hill was on fade-out for the divas – the DJ playing it a bit safe. Then Noreaga – 'Superthug' had the lads shuffling – a jaw-rattler.

I had a walk round and saw the cloakroom queue. We were making a mint.

I checked the Gents – wet floor tiles – piss-ripples from the bass kick out in the main room. Our toilet attendant was a white feller flogging knock-off CK One sprays for a quid. 'Alright?' I said.

Thumbs-up.

There were tenners already in his collection hat. The stalls were locked – gasping, sneezing – blokes hoovering the Firm's nose candy. Eyeing the second stall on the right, I thought about foreign birds with birthmarks – grubby shags and more loose ends. I went back out.

The main room: Asian lads not dancing, just playing the wall. They chain-smoked in a line – every now and then one would step out and snatch a bird's arm on the way to the bar.

Abs had made sure we'd have a few Premiership lads in the VIP. I walked over. They were all sat down – legs on strike, plenty of tagalongs – slimy sods. The birds were perched on the sofa arms, arses squirming for room, frocks riding high.

I lifted the rope and asked the fellers if everything was alright.

One player raised a tall glass, his drink half empty.

The bird closest touched my leg and smiled up at me. Twenty-one – maybe not even that, plunge cardi – plenty to see, red lips smacking chuddy.

I said: 'Another bottle for the table?'

The ladies squealed.

*   *   *

I watched from up high, behind the DJ booth. These happy clubbers – a sea of heads. Sweat and cigs and perfume. Lights tripping silver, then blue. Tunes thumping. Temperature rising.

There were flashes of ugly wherever I wasn't looking. Pockets of nightmare between my blinks. Next time the lights changed I missed wings and claws. I missed bear-pit noises – animals yammering over the drum-claps. I thought I saw girls working blood into their hair, rubbing it all over, dyeing their frocks while they danced.

My tongue was dry-stuck to my cheeks – teeth grinding it free.

A barmaid ducked under the VIP rope with the ice bucket of Moët. The first girl stuck her chuddy under the table and held her empty glass in the air for a top-up.

More birds poured in through the main entrance. Gordon was being a soft touch. A couple headed for the loos, the rest trotted straight onto the dance floor, singing along to 'Hard Knock Life', pissed lads swarming like flies.

It was twelve deep at the bar, a tough gig on the first night for new staff, and most of them were fucking clueless. I'd swiped a Kaliber and poured it myself.

I looked down and pointed to a torn sleeve in the record box. The DJ lifted a headphone ear and I mouthed: *bang this on next*. He took the record out but acted like a non-believer.

I stepped off the DJ platform with my drink and clocked Gordon pushing through the mob.

'Sup wiv yer?' he said.

'Nothin,' I said.

He flapped his Crombie. 'Am meltin in this, me.'

'Any trouble?'

He pinched an arse on the move – a damp face, slicked-back hair – she was too hammered to notice. 'Cunt tekin the piss outside. Nowt though – jus ad a few. Ah give im one kick n ee'd ad enough.'

That qualified as our Gordon reining it in.

A hand brushed mine. It was the girl from VIP, waving a Nokia in my face.

'Iya,' she went.

'After me number?' I said.

'Might be.'

I kissed her cheek, whispering in her ear. She walked by. The DJ dropped Busta's 'Turn It Up', and Willie Mitchell horn-stabs made the birds slow down and show off.

Gordon said: 'Av it on a plate n yer send it back? Bin chucked, ant yer? What yer fuckin playin at? Oo said am the one wiv problems?'

'You did, mate.' There was a tiny feather floating in my drink. I thumbed it up the glass, and it stayed on my thumb but fell before I could show our Gordon.

Heads turned.

There was something going on in the Ladies. The queue scrambled – ankle-wobbles – the last one out swearing, hoop earrings flapping wild.

I got in her way. 'What's scared you, love?'

Her eyes were sober, spooked. 'In there! Crawlin out the sink! Ah nearly died.'

'What?'

'Av a look.'

I told Gordon to radio Abrafo. He looked at me like I was daft.

'Tell him,' I said.

Off he went.

28

OPAL FRUITS

THE LADIES LOOKED empty – the cold taps still running in two of the chrome sinks. They were overflowing – a waterfall splashing a ditched Gucci handbag – tampons, mascara brush, a pocket mirror sailing the floor tiles.

I squeaked both taps off and saw it.

A fucking scorpion in the middle sink.

Grabby hands, curly tail, ribs up its back, little black legs trying to scale the wet porcelain, and slipping every time.

I drowned it.

My fingers twitched under the blow-dryer.

A door squeaked open. There was a girl in the last cubicle. She was well underage. She sat on the seat. Her heels were off. She lifted her legs to roll down her tights. She slow-flashed me without a care. She balled the tights round her fist and put them in her handbag. She put her heels on and blew me a kiss, walking out.

Something spread like Chinese whispers. The crowd thinned in no time – strobes clicking over empty space, dead drinks on every banister.

A door code led to a fresh carpet stairwell, and a gate lift took me up to Abrafo's flat.

The big light was off in the open plan – corner lamps dim, ripped packaging next to them, boxes all over the show.

There were fancy paintings on the floor, tipped against the far wall. But the biggest was mounted – stick-men chasing stick-animals, symbols over the top in spray-can. Abs had taken Ashley to an auction last year, and she'd mithered him for it.

'Shame your Dan's not seen these,' I said.

Roisin was scoffing something.

'Look tired,' I said.

Her eyes were red and massive, milk hands holding a brew. 'You kept me awake.'

'Gordon's fault.'

Her arse was on the breakfast bar, feet dangling in flats. She said: 'No. After that. You were shouting in your sleep.'

'Dreamin?'

'Dreaming of what?'

'You tell me.'

Gordon gave me a nod. He stood over Abrafo's shoulder, who sat in his plush chesterfield, desk to the wall, watching CCTV monitors.

A few brawlers were scrapping outside. I saw Simon behind one of his own for safety and remembered they were our lot. A Barker boy headbutted a black lad. More came to the rescue. The old Perrys took the posse down.

'Am fuckin missin this,' Gordon said.

White flashed on the black and white monitor. No sound.

I couldn't see who did what.

A gunshot.

Scatter.

People leapt out of the frame.

'Shit.'

'Shit.'

Roisin scraped her mug on the breakfast bar and tipped sweet wrappers into it. She hopped down and came forward, our Gordon making room. 'Do they have Dan? Are they here for me?'

'It's the other lot,' I said. 'From round here. Their feller's got a Komodo dragon n a screw lose. He's what happened to Maz.'

'He's what could've happened to you.' Roisin touched my arm. 'What does he want?'

'Grief.'

Gordon said: 'Let's go give it im.'

Abs looked up and gave him the lion stare. Abs tapped a screen with a finger. 'Bane, that im?'

Hagfish rolled up looking the usual scruff: dreads down, torn coat. He had a little army behind him, funnelling through the main doors.

'Call the fucking police,' Roisin said.

Abrafo twisted in his chesterfield. His cornrows needed a touch-up. 'Ring um if yer want, love. Now let's go down n see if ah know this cunt.'

Our Gordon: 'Fuckin aye.'

Abs killed the monitor and said to Roisin: 'Ow old d'yer reckon I am?'

We watched him disconnect the feed and stop the recorder. He asked her again.

Roisin croaked: 'Thirty. Five.'

'Mystic Meg,' he said. 'Ah were born January tenf, sixty-three. Now open that safe on the wall.'

It was behind Ashley's painting.

Roisin keyed in: 10–01–63.

She had her back to us for half a minute and Gordon went over and pulled her away. She went strange. She tiptoed on the spot as if to keep warm, summoning tears. Gordon opened the safe wider and held up his gift of a gun.

Roisin pointed at me like she was expecting lightning bolts. 'You told me you weren't fucking Al Capone.' She walked into my chest and tried to go through it. I trapped her and held her at arm's length – pink face, gulping tears, rainbow tongue.

29

BEST SERVED COLD

GORDON OPENED HIS Crombie and dumped it on the bar. He cracked his back and forward-marched, flexing the starch out of his shirt as he went.

Flashing lights – techno stutter – an empty dance floor – no music. The bar staff had fucked off, but three doormen, and none of them Simon, were still sparring with maybe seven Moss Side lads. Kara's lot were doing the footie chants, monkey sounds – all coke-courage. Both sides cleared tables of glasses, chucking bottles like snowballs.

One of the kids flashed a six-shooter, and the old Perrys gave it a rest. They booted the fire exit and scarpered. Two lads chased them off – the gunman first.

There was no sign of Hagfish.

Gordon battered two to one – his guard up,

heavyweight slaps, plenty of cell practice since his last street fight. One of them came at him with a tin baseball bat, swinging wild. He whacked Gordon on the arm. Gordon took it and fed him the end quarter.

I locked the fire door. The biggest feller threw a punch my way but threw it wide.

'Back off,' I said.

A loose jaw, about to give me shit.

Gordon packed a bomb and turned him into a baby giraffe. Another black meathead coughing teeth. Gordon pushed him over and stamped the fight out of him.

I'd seen him throw slicker but never this hard. He dragged one down by the scruff of his hoodie and showed him his Rockport tread – steel toecaps kissing ribs.

Some fucker glassed him from behind and left his ear gushing rivers. I got hold of the lad. The rest of the glass smashed on the dance floor and Gordon emptied his gob. Gordon spat in the lad's face, wiped the goz from his own chin, panting, swearing.

Gordon blotted his ear with his cuff, the collar soaked red, worms of blood already down to his belt.

We were the last buggers standing.

Breathing on every word he said: 'Where's fuckin pigs?'

'Can hear sirens,' I said. 'Just about.'

'Fuckin Friday night, mate. Thez always fuckin sirens. These cunts don't wanna go anywhere. Bet thev fuckin locked us in.'

One lad got up, hissing, holding his broken head

with two hands like Humpty Dumpty waiting for the glue to set. He limped a bigger space between us while the rest found their feet.

More lads came in through the main-room doors, with one or two familiar faces, but most weren't on show. This was a right mob: a good seven or eight lads, dressed for war.

I looked at our Gordon. He was grinning, knackered.

They acted like we weren't there.

They used baseball bats on the booze shelves.

They smashed the tills with a hatchet and rinsed the takings.

They tore out the new sound system.

They washed the bar with paraffin and broken spirits.

Somebody threw the fuel can, cartwheel-spraying the room. It landed on a couch in the VIP.

This was fire for fire – for what had happened in Hulme Hippodrome with Berta, and for all the grief before and since.

My pocket buzzed warnings, but I didn't check to see if it was Abrafo or Roisin. The pigs must've been out front by now. Maybe our Gordon was right.

I went up to the platform behind the DJ booth for a golden vantage. My legs were solid. Blood sat in my feet.

Attention, gents.

I yelled *oi* till my throat ribboned.

Some feller at the back lit the match, dropped it and came forward as if to listen. He was just a smile, the rest covered up.

One last *oi*.

They all grouped as one.

The flames were low-key – they spread quietly in the background, melting the sofas, popping the dead drinks.

I said: 'HAGFISH. THIS TWAT? HE'S NOWT. FUCKIN CHEAP TRICKS. DIDN'T EVEN SNUFF THIN. I DID.'

They talked over me, swarming our Gordon.

I pulled out Thin's gun and waved it high.

'I did Thin.'

They looked.

I said it again like it wasn't suicide. 'You lads deaf? I killed Thin.'

Flutter. Birdsong.

The hawk swooped my way – disco lights stretching shadows. It flew above heads in slo-mo making the hairs needle the back of my neck. Somebody was kicking over my grave.

Boom.

The hawk exploded in feathers.

Everybody dived except for Hagfish.

Gordon went for the tables, away from the fires.

Abrafo aimed down at Hagfish, barrel-to-face, his back on the staff door, close to a corner.

'Oi, Marley. What can ah do yer fer?'

Hagfish had his hands cupped. 'Hush, mon. Ya mussi Abrafo. Me bin earin yah bin troo mayja sufferation.'

'Fuck off. Now.'

Stiff grin. Sweat-glow. Drug-stare. 'Bad mon no flee.'

I'd seen him flee. Legs like Linford.

'Mus be fuckin mental. What's all this for?'

He scarecrowed his arms. 'Disya belong to mi. Lang time mi wait fa dis. City nuh change.'

The heat stung now, and I tipped the broken DJ kit onto the floor, ripped out nests of wire till I found the mini fire extinguisher. The nose was fucked and the pin stayed.

'All cyan rope een cept im.' Eyes on me. 'Him a go dead, mon.'

Billyclub was bright and cooking – Hagfish's crew shuffled low, watching the place fall. He was still looking at me when one of his boys spoke up.

'Nobody gwan nowhere,' Hagfish said. 'Dev-als inna me brain. Dis bloodfire yahso. Dis no brukout – dem tink wi cyan tek dis. Me vank dem! Me tief all dat. Wi mek dem pay fi Berta burnin.' He got down on one knee, his gloves together, knuckles to the floor, whispering gibberish. He'd rescued it from the Ladies. The scorpion twitched and stepped off his palms.

Abs pulled the trigger and put holes in his new dance floor. Hagfish flicked his dreads. Hagfish tugged out a small piece, passed it to a big feller next to him, tugged out another and opened fire.

Gordon tipped a table. Abrafo got himself round that corner and sprayed blind, a wide blast catching stray kneecaps. Hagfish stumbled through flames, big bullets eating the wall, chewing plaster and paint.

The shooting stopped, and my eyes watered watching the blaze feed one fat cloud. Then the flames met and there was only smoke. I could hear shuffling and yelling and one lad begged.

Metal thumped metal, but I couldn't tell from where.

I tripped down from behind the broken decks and saw shapes flashing – empty guns playing pass the parcel.

The ramrod opened the fire escape and the bobbies poured in – firemen and the rest of it.

Bedlam.

Everybody heaved smoke.

Abs fled through the staff door, back to the lift, and somebody big enough to be Gordon had the same idea.

I saw Hagfish only when he was a punch away – strutting with his hands behind his head, singing the pigs to him. He didn't see me. They cuffed him flat, while I butted my way through the smoke – pigs barking, lads howling – legs full of glass and shot. Hagfish laughed over it all on his way out.

Upstairs, Roisin was waiting outside the lift with a dozen Kendals bags, good to burst. She looked a ghost.

Abrafo got out, ignoring her.

Gordon retched again and set me off.

Roisin raised the bags to me in a car-crash daze, veins popping the backs of her fists.

Still spitting, I said: 'That our dinner money, love?'

30

IT'S DARK AND HELL IS HOT

A GAUZE BALCONY behind Deansgate. Slippy mesh steps – ice making the old paint job shine. I crunched the ice out of the holes with my shoes and the whole thing shook as we went down it. Gordon gozzed a huge one over the railing. Roisin was a flight up, the next behind me, and her feet knocked the ice out of the steps too, and made it snow again.

The night was loud – plenty of pisshead echoes, blokes mouthing off, birds laughing. The bacon wagons kept the sirens on.

Lenny rolled the driver's window down, DMX blasting inside.

'Where's this fuckin Lexus?' Gordon said.

'Be bit of a squeeze round ere.'

The alley had restaurant kitchens with glow-in-the-dark

back doors, strays clawing bin bags. The sirens were so close we had to shout.

I said: 'Dibble'll be on the lookout for it, any road.'

'Don't piss about – get in,' Abrafo said.

Roisin scooped a clump of ice off a railing and pressed it to Gordon's ear while he was filling the boot.

He hissed.

'Don't be mard,' she said, reaching on her tiptoes.

He laughed. 'Fuck me. Almost sounded Manc then, dint she?'

Roisin got in the car first, her knees together.

'Budge up,' I said.

She pulled me inside – small wet hands.

I said: 'Good job there's nowt of you, after all.'

We crammed into the Micra – Abs in the front, Gordon and me in the back.

Lenny, glove hands spinning the wheel: 'Cosy, this.'

Abs thumped the stereo quiet and the faceplate fell off.

Deansgate was like Blackpool illuminations – just one giant Christmas tree. We zipped past St Ann's Square to avoid the diversion – windows up, the heater broken, more of Abrafo's cash in the footwells, Roisin clutching the last Kendals bag on her lap.

We turned onto South King Street, exhaust rattling.

Lenny scraped the gearbox and we bounced potholes. 'Fucksake.'

'I'll get our Maz to have a look at this,' I said.

Roisin: 'Is he—'

'When he gets out.'

Sirens blared and more pigs passed us, heading the wrong way.

Lenny clipped the kerb.

Gordon: 'Think ah should do fuckin drivin.'

'No chance,' I said.

'Back to the ol digs?' Lenny said.

Abrafo stewed.

Roisin squeezed the money bag. 'But the police know that club's yours. Be the first place they'll go.'

I said: 'Least someone's switched on.'

Lenny gave her a once-over in the rear-view. 'Not jus a pretty face, this one. Shame bout er feller.'

Gordon: 'Shiz always ad a bit o sense, our kid.'

Roisin squeezed forward and looked past Gordon at her reflection in the passenger window. She touched the sleep rings over her eyes like she was somebody new. She croaked: 'Since when did you think that?'

4 a.m. A terrace off Platt Lane. Six empty brews on the table and two crammed sofas.

Rana wore Maz's City shirt for bed. It reached her knees.

She stood up and said *night*.

We all said it back to her – shattered, a round of yawns.

Abrafo thanked her with cold-cash sympathy, but she wouldn't take anything. Rana thanked him for Maz's card and told him she'd seen the papers. She said how sorry she was and left us in her front room – sleeping bags and spare linen heaped in the corner away from the gas fire. We all watched the ceiling, listening to her go upstairs.

Lenny muttered: 'She should o said nowt.'

I shut him up with a look.

Abrafo paced.

Gordon rubbed his hands together, sat on the second sofa. 'Get that thing up. Nippy in ere.' He pointed at the fire – his knuckles were blood crusts.

Roisin flopped sideways, drew her feet up and put her head in my lap. I needed pinching.

After playing with the gas fire for an awkward minute, Lenny cranked the heat.

'Clockwise,' I said.

Gordon: 'There's a good lad.'

Roisin stirred.

'Comfy?' I said.

'You'll do.'

I touched her hair, pretended to snip it with finger scissors.

'Back in business,' Gordon said.

I let it go.

Lenny baked his hands by the fire.

'Big ands, them are,' Gordon said, inspecting his own, which were twice the size. 'Yer done a bit o boxin, mate?'

'Now n then,' Lenny said.

'Licensed?'

'Nah.'

Gordon whistled. 'Inside, ah got pally wiv this coloured, right. Black as bloody midnight ee were. Like you.'

First warning: 'Gordon—' Roisin said.

'Said ee did bit o boxin. Little feller ee were. Must av bin only flyweight. Reckon ee still could've ad yer.'

Second warning: Abrafo clipped Gordon's bad ear, just like Vic would've. Roisin flinched liked he'd hit her instead.

'Don't push yer luck, big lad.' Abrafo cocked another backhander. 'Ee saved our bacon.'

Gordon: 'Ee nearly got us stopped by fuckin bacon,' hand to ear, blood seeping through his fingers. He went out to clean up.

'Got problems ee as,' Lenny said.

'He's fine,' I said. He just hadn't copped off.

Abs said to Lenny: 'Go check on the motor.'

'Now?'

'Keep it quiet.'

He left.

Abs went to make phone calls.

Roisin kept still, she wouldn't look at me.

I wanted the fire off – too hot already.

She stretched an arm down to thumb through Maz's cassettes and CDs – floor stacks by the sofa ends – anything to take her mind off the circus.

'Half o them are ours,' I said.

I moved my hand down her back and found a bruise.

'Anythin good?' I said.

She flinched again and looked up. 'Nothing.'

I had earache. Eyes closed I saw flames and tasted smoke.

I heard our Gordon on the second couch, winning the snoring contest.

Roisin breathed in and out. *We* breathed in and out. Her heart lapped mine three beats to one.

A nudge opened my eyes and I was jittery as fuck. Abrafo stood over me.

Roisin stayed curled, her face under my chin. I got up without waking her and she stretched to fill the settee, and then crunched tight again, talking her dreams.

31

PAID IN FULL

July 1990

GORDON HAD LEFT Blue Monday more black than blue. He had a pad taped over one eye, and Dudley was talking in his ear, by the decks, circle sunglasses on inside. Neither of them looked my way. There was no sign of Horace.

The Surgery, gone half-one but the night hadn't peaked.

Roisin was away with the fairies.

'Listen, love – what did your Sally have to say?' I had to roar.

She kept dancing on me – slave to the beat.

'Did Sally say owt bout what happened after we went?'

Nothing. Extra bug-eyed – pupils a total eclipse.

'What was the fallout with them Yardies?'

Two hundred weekend druggies were burning up around us, boxing us in. It might as well have been the end of the world.

'Oi.' I shook her back to earth.

'Don't do that,' Roisin said.

'Well wake the fuck up then.'

'Henry? Henry?'

'Go n dance,' I said.

She stepped back from me, drenched in sweat, not dancing, not doing anything. She looked paper-thin, absolutely gone. 'Have you just been pretending this?' she said.

'Pretendin what?'

'This!' She filled up.

I said: 'What do y'want us to say, love?'

She snatched a tear before it got past her nose.

'Fuck off,' she said. 'Fuck you.'

The sea of twats parted for a split second.

I let her disappear.

A white bloke I recognised from Sally's flat danced his way over and said: 'Do ah know yer?'

'No,' I said.

Acid grin: 'Yer sure?'

I roughed my arm around his neck and pointed across the way, fixing his gaze on Dudley and Blue Monday. I wondered how those two were pally.

'Who's that? The black feller,' I said.

'The coloured? Dudley, that init? Dick ed nicked our telly uva week. Ay, yer was there wan't yer?'

'What happened to that other one?' I said. 'Gold teeth. Dreads. Adidas tracksuit.'

'Yer mean Horace? Dibble nabbed im again, dint they? Ee did over Stan Barker's club. Ome office flew im back ter Jamaica. Thank fuck.'

'How'd you know all this?'

The next record took him and he clapped the DJ, lost in it.

I gripped his neck harder, pointing again. 'See the white feller with the bruises?'

'They're comin fer im n all. N Dudley. All them lot.'

'Pigs?' I said.

'Tonight.'

'What they gunna do – pinch everybody?'

Laughing: 'Nah. Dealers, mate. They got names n faces. Gettin too greedy nowadays.'

It was a bit late in the show for a raid. Every dealer had got rid of his gear by now.

I said again: 'How'd you know all this?'

Still laughing, sweat tears: 'Me cousin's a PC.'

'Then what you doin here?'

He swayed. 'Wunt miss it fer the world, mate.'

Headachy, I went outside for the stale breeze: ganja smoke, open bins, barbecued tyres. I touched the wall and felt tunes coming through it – tags and cocks were keyed at eye level, Rakim lyrics scribbled above in permanent marker. The music echoed over Charles Barry. I shut my eyes and opened them again.

I climbed the grass bank to look over the courtyard

and saw pissed gypos giving the top dibble a rough time of it for blocking their caravans in. Caravans minus wheels. The gypos were slowing the whole operation down.

I turned back, found a stairwell and climbed two flights onto the lower deck to get a decent view.

They had the sirens off, lights whipping the courtyard, vans ready to be filled.

I heard gasping in the shadows to the left of me – maybe thirty feet along the walkway, and thought it was shaggers in the next stairwell.

Looking down again, my fingers drumming the guard wall, I played perspective as heads flocked outside the Surgery.

They raided it. A couple of them stayed to mind the motors, keeping the peace with the gypos.

There was more racket from across the way, and it sounded too rough for a shag. The tunes in the Surgery were unplugged just as a silhouette backtracked onto the deck. The Crescents fell quiet.

Then coughing, yelping – it could've been a bloke but it was hard to tell. The silhouette was kicking but when the yelps stopped the boot kept on.

I locked my jaw and went over. It was Gordon on the deck, standing at the top of the stairwell.

I tackled Gordon, all questions: 'Who is he? What's he fuckin done?'

He shrugged me off, shaky breaths, eyes glazed – I had to say his name twice just to get him to see it was me.

I asked him why.

He said: 'Ah come out fer a slash n this cunt tries to get a grab o me knob. Fuckin Marys. Told yer bout this fuckin place, dint ah? Queers n nig-nogs, the fuckin lot.'

He'd battered him to a stain. Bones tented through his leg where Gordon had stamped him between stairs. It wasn't dark enough to hide it all.

'Copshop's just down there,' I said. 'He could be dead.'

'Oo gives a fuck?'

'Why y'like this? What's gone on?'

He spat between his feet. 'Yer can fuck off n all.'

'What've I done?'

He hit the side wall of the stairwell and the loose banister rail shook out rust.

'Fuckin Christ.'

Gordon paced on the spot, palming his eyes. His knuckles dribbled to his elbows.

The battered feller choked and I bent down and tried to find his face.

'This is you, this is!' Gordon said.

'Me?'

Gordon stepped out of the light and some of the shadow lifted. There wasn't much left of his face. He was lying with an arm bent the wrong way, his head on the top stair. It was a white lad, one of Blue Monday's dealers. I recognised his shirt.

He was the one who'd sold gear to our Roisin.

'Shit. Was he carryin?' I said.

'Nowt on im,' Gordon said.

'Checked his socks?'

'Aye.'

'Got anythin on you?' I said.

'Bitocash. Coupleoton.'

We heard voices below, somebody yelled *black bastard*, then torch beams crossed, lighting up the gloom. It was dibble climbing the stairwells.

'Give it,' I said.

They were chasing Dudley. He rushed towards us, leaping four steps at a time – good work considering the belly on him. We stepped out of the way as he tripped on Gordon's handiwork and went flying, hands out just in time to stop him from going over the low guard wall. His Kangol cap went off the deck instead. He turned and bolted along the walkway – dog-pants, flat-footed.

I took off after him with Gordon's notes and half a button bag of gear in my fist.

A quick look back:

Gordon managed to keep up, and the pigs gave chase – two or three uniforms.

Eyes ahead:

A white feller was stood on the ledge, taking a piss over the balcony, watering the bacon wagons. His jacket flapped when Dudley shot past. I passed him next. One nudge and he'd be fucked.

This place was a rabbit warren – plod's worst nightmare. Bombed-out flats, trick doors, a thousand dark corners, a maze of stairwells, escape routes – the deck access connected the lot in a giant horseshoe. Boots followed us – I could hear the issue rattling. They soon tired, wasting their breath calling us names. We gave them the full tour.

'Oi, whippet!' Gordon was still behind me and I had another look back – flat out – a freight train.

I pointed at myself and then pointed up at the next deck with no clue whether Gordon would twig it.

Gaining on Dudley, I followed the rivers of sweat in reverse – from the back of his head to his eyebrows. I few more strides and I overtook him, psycho-grinning. He glanced at me out of the corner of his eye. He was holding a stitch.

'. . . Wa di . . . bumboclat—'

I banked at the next stairwell and went up a level just to make it interesting, hoping our Gordon would carry straight on. Dudley followed me. Up another flight, and another – there was a dodgy bulb mounted on the wall, flickering over the graffiti. I could hear voices ahead and bottles clinked – junkies cruising for handbags.

'STOP. POLICE.'

Darkness. Glass smashed. Somebody must've lobbed a bottle.

I pushed through, blind, reached the top and came up on the next branch of decks.

A hot black sky, tons more city lights winking at this height. It was a massive drop down but I didn't look – gasping, already dizzy.

Dudley staggered out next and I watched him duck

into a flat, twitching the key into the lock after dropping it twice.

Two uniforms on the horizon. They reached the flat door.

A gunshot stopped them dead – fucking Dudley, the outlaw, playing it like the Wild West.

They weren't an armed squad.

I turned to keep watching, jogging backwards, already far enough away. Dudley gave them another warning round. They dived back into the stairwell and he ran out waving a Glock, back on the move. Dudley went one way, I went the other.

Ground level. I lapped back to the Surgery and slowed to a strut – dusted myself off, home and dry. I was still breathing hard, just as sweaty as every pillhead coming out of there – some of them still bouncing.

More plod were outside the door, herding sheep, their radios barking.

Purple hair bobbed with the flock – lanky Sally getting roughed about by the current.

I pushed through to her. 'It's Henry,' I said. 'Remember us?'

Ironed-on grin.

'Where's Roisin?' I said.

Sally latched on for a hug. 'She loves you, yer know? She really does!'

Some student-type with a fringe instead of eyes pulled her off me and said he'd walk her home.

Maz found me next.

'Where's Roisin?' I said.

'Oo?'

'Roisin.'

'Yer bird? Dunno. She not gone ome?' Maz tensed up but his fat cheeks still wobbled. 'Dodgy do, this, enry. Where's yer mate, Gordon?'

'He's about.'

'Let's jus get off,' he said.

The chubby bird from earlier in the night came up and took his arm. She was a smiler – guaranteed shag.

'Get a taxi back,' I said to him. 'Stay clear o the last bus. I'll come shop tomorrow mornin.'

'Steady.' He got lost in her rack and everything changed. 'Bes mek it afternoon.'

Gordon swanned up, greasing his short bowl cut back down. He nodded at Maz, he only knew him through me. 'Where's our kid?' Gordon said.

I said: 'That's what I wanna know.'

'Ah, fuck it. Leave er. We busin it back or what?'

We were stood still in the moving crowd. A bobby gave us an earful: 'There's just bin a shootin. We need to keep this area clear . . .'

Maz glared.

Gordon winked. 'Anyone dead?'

He passed us and opened the back of a van and three others chucked Blue Monday in.

Some twat jumped on a bonnet and shouted *rave* this *rave* that. The chubby bird said: 'Ay, look at im!' and started to lead Maz away, giggling. Gordon huffed and went with them.

'Henry?' That soft croak.

I looked round and there she was.

I said: 'How we doin?' instead of *I'm sorry*, instead of *I love you*, instead of, instead of . . .

She smiled and wobbled. 'Not. So. Good.'

I had her face in both hands.

I watched her eyes roll back.

I caught her mid-fall.

I yelled for Gordon, Maz, a bobby, an ambulance.

I held her for as long as I could.

32

FULL ENGLISH

21 February 1998
Saturday

7 A.M. BLACKBIRD tweets. New detached monsters north of Timperley – flat-pack posh, pattern brick driveways, CCTV towers, heaven gates, every curtain shut, every ponce tucked in bed.

I left the motor on a fresh tarmac road, sparkle-white with frost. My desert-boot soles were sticky.

I found the right gaff and pushed the gate buzzer.

'Top night, mate?' It was Simon playing butler.

'If you hadn't o fucked off early you might've found out.'

'Step back, mate.'

The gate hummed.

Two mastiffs were sniffing the frozen lawn in straight

laps like mowers. They both looked up at the same time. One put its back leg up, piss steaming in the cold. It barked once as a warning when I crossed the threshold.

The gate hummed shut behind me.

More woofs, just echoes.

One came up to meet me on the driveway and the other circled – huge square faces, ears shaking after every attack bark. They kept close, making a right din.

Arms up in surrender: 'Easy, boys. Come on now.' I lost my nerve and got ready to sprint back and vault the gate.

Simon opened the front door but the dogs took no notice until Kara stuck her head out of a first-floor window. 'WENDY. PETER. FUCKIN SHUT UP!' She hissed the rest through her teeth: 'Thell wake the fuckin neighbours again.'

Wendy and Peter dropped down and their gums disappeared – jowls back over fangs, snapping the gozz bungee ropes.

Kara: 'AWAY.'

They mooched back onto the lawn. Wendy had a tackle. Both mastiffs were dogs.

Kara grinned down at me. 'Jus growly cos thev not bin fed. Simon, love – feed them doggies inabit.' Her fingers wiggle-waved and then slammed the window shut.

Simon breathed on his hands – he was wearing an Italian sports top – too long on the arms, and no coat. He whistled for the mastiffs to follow us in.

I said: 'What d'they have for breakfast – postmen?'

Before he'd spoken –

– 'CYANIDE! You ought to feed those beasts cyanide!'
Next door's well-to-do yelled it over the ivy wall – voice
like a sergeant major.

Simon gave me a pat down in the hall. Silver stubble.
He turned the headbutt glare up a notch as he got all
touchy-feely.

'What's this for?' I said.

'Tough times, mate. Nowt personal. Rough do, was
it? Las night?'

His hand went in my Harrington.

'We missed you,' I said.

'Steady on, cunt. Fuck's this?' He took out Thin's
shooter, pushed the slide back and it popped forward
again.

'Empty,' I said.

'Still, best fuckin tek it, ay?'

'Course, mate.'

Stainless-steel kitchen. Bacon sizzle. Stanley Barker
was in a striped pinny, tossing fry-up, arm tats on show.
Kara Barker was setting the breakfast bar in a purple
bruise velour hoodie – half zipped, one leopard-skin
bra strap showing – and matching velour pants. She
put bony arse on chrome stool, moved a newspaper and
told me where to sit.

'Brew?' she said.

'Ta.'

The antique teapot on the breakfast bar had a

hare-coursing picture running round it. Kara poured herself one first.

There was a row of Union Jack egg cups next to the bread bin but Stan was bashing up some scrambled. Holiday snaps on the fridge showed three gap-toothed kiddies climbing Daddy.

I knew Stan was an old pal of the late Terence Formby. Both borstal boys, Salford tearaways, wog-bashers, armed robbers. Formby was the flash, Stanley was the smash. Stan spent the early 90s inside, while Formby looked after his clubs. Stan was the one with ties to the old Firm, the one still pushing muscle and charlie, the one still alive. Formby had been a grubby nightclub entrepreneur with three ex-wives, and the best part was: Kara had been wife number two.

I said: 'Thought you lived above that pub?'

'We did once. Dint we, Stanley?'

Flipping bacon: 'Aye.'

'Wiv got a few little places, ant we, Stanley?'

Toast popped: 'Aye.'

Her tits spilled forward. 'Sup, love?'

'No sleep.' I cleared my throat.

Kara tutted. 'Our Simon told us what appened t'yer disco las night.' She held up yesterday's crushed *Evening News*. 'Thell be full of it today – thev said on radio this mornin that alf o Deansgate were shut off. Still, nobody dead this time, were there?'

'No.'

'Maybe nex time. Full English?'

Stan had his back to us. 'There's plenny goin, lad.'

Kara let the hoodie drop off her shoulder – oily tan cleavage, sunbed moles, more leopard-skin bra strap. 'Go on, love. Av a bacon butty.'

'I'm alright,' I said. 'Honest.'

Stanley: 'Fuck off. Yavin scrambled.'

'Go on,' I said.

'Good lad.' He scraped eggs onto the plate and gave me some toast with it, then carried on cooking.

Kara sipped her brew and watched me eat. 'Cah show yer summat?' she said.

Chew. Swallow. 'Whatever you like.'

She gave me that machine-gun laugh and then took something out of her hoodie pocket. She kept her hand over it and slid it down the breakfast bar, still making me reach. When I did, her nails raked my hand – ice-blue acrylics cut square and tapping the teacup again by the time her Stan looked round.

Kara said: 'Found it on doorstep, Thursday, nex ter the fuckin Avon catalogue.'

Inside the small envelope was a Polaroid of a young lad's head. Just his head. Dizzy gruesome – a black ring of blood.

I put my knife and fork together, pushed the plate away and thanked the chef.

'Know oo that is?' Kara said.

'He was your informant,' I said, giving her the Polaroid back.

'Ear that, Stanley?'

'Well done, lad.'

Kara had too many teeth. 'N oo did im?'

'Hagfish,' I said.

Stan turned round, pointing at us both with the spatula. 'Ee's a fuckin chancer. Thinks ee can get away wiv tekin—'

Kara shushed him and took over: 'Few nights ago, two of our employees' ouses got robbed.'

Stanley banged the frying pan over the sink.

Kara's false lashes blinked with the noise.

'Shot um in the legs,' Stan said. 'Niggers done um like IRA.'

'What they take?' I said.

Kara: 'Av a guess.'

Stanley: 'Summat valuable'

Kara nodded at me like a horse. 'Forty fuckin grand's worf o valuable.'

I said: 'Don't worry, I can't whistle.'

She held the teacup to her lips. No machine-gun laugh.

Forty grand's worth of White Wife, and I knew where it'd be.

Abrafo hadn't told them anything. He wanted to use them to do Hagfish, leaving the gear out of it if we could, until there was money to be made.

Stanley said: 'Thev forgot where the jungle ends. Ee's not jus pinchin off all them ee's gone after our lot. Bin more murders las fortnight than there as bin round ere fer fuckin years.'

'Is real name's orace,' Kara said.

'Horace?' I said.

'Ring any bells?'

It did. I told her it didn't.

'Stanley's ad run-ins wiv im before. Ant yer, love?'

'Years ago. Tried to tek me club when ah got sent down. Thought ee were the man, yer know? Well they all do, don't they?'

I didn't nod.

'Erd ee were fuckin deported, though. Ow do they get back in the country?'

'Suggestions welcome,' Kara said.

'As ee got brave?' Stan said.

'No,' I said.

'Bright spark?'

'No.'

Kara chipped in: 'What then? Ow's ee organised it?'

I looked at both of them. 'Said it yourself. He's a fuckin chancer. Mad as a March hare. Pigs nicked him last night at the club durin the fire.'

Kara turned Medusa: 'Ee's bein released this afternoon. Ee wan't witnessed resistin arrest n ee dint av anthin on im. Investigation's gunna be a bit fucked cos o the barbie. Said ee's bin deported twice, dint they? But they can't keep im in a cell till they send im back.'

'Fuckin why not?' Stan said.

Stanley made himself a bacon and sausage butty with the rest on the side. He took a bite and stayed standing by the cooker.

'What can I do to help?' I said.

'Magic words, them are,' Kara said, zipping her hoodie all the way back up. 'Said ah like this one, Stanley, dint ah?'

He said something with his mouth full.

She leaned over the breakfast bar again and trapped my stare. 'Find out ow ee's bin movin this much this quick. N which beds ee keeps it under.'

'I'll do me best.'

'Yer jus tell us where our gear is n we might club in proper – nex time yer boss fancies runnin a discotheque.'

'Abs wants you to buy in?' I said.

'Ee's loaned yer out to us, ant ee? What – yer think we're prejudice? Stanley, love, ee reckons we're preju-dice.'

Gob full: 'We're not a'we?'

'Cheers for the scrambled,' I said.

Simon showed me out.

'Ee-ah,' he said, tucking Thin's shooter back into my Harrington. 'Yuv five ollow points in there now, mate. Let's see what yer fuckin made of.'

33
SENSIBLE FOOTWEAR

10 A.M. I thumbed the doorbell for a minute straight. My front-room curtains were drawn, breath-spots on the inside pane, smears up and down it.

She'd left her key in the lock.

I gave the bell a rest and flapped the letter box.

Teary: 'Fuck off!'

I pushed my face up to the diamond window and squinted through the wavy glass.

'Jan.' I could see a shape crouched on the stairs.

Next door's feller came out of his house. He coughed with the cold – ice-breath, patting his head to double-check his bobby hat was on. I could hear their Staffie barking inside until he shut the door to. The feller nodded to me. Smug bastard.

'Alright,' I said.

'Bitter.'

There was black ice on our front steps.

'Sun's out,' I said.

'Aye. Can't fuckin feel it, can yer?'

I watched him go, leaving his gate open.

Round the back. Weeds surviving the frost. Cheap tat rotting away – all of it our Jan's. The newest recruits were a garden gnome, two plastic penguins and a ceramic frog. The washing had been left out – Wonderbras flapping on the wet line – clear skies above, cold sunshine drying nobody's knickers. She'd lost the plot.

I saw her come into the kitchen through the back window and I watched her at the sink for a couple of seconds before going in.

The bedroom radio was on loud in the kitchen, the toaster unplugged. 'Lucky Man' on fade-out. Classic Kylie coming up next.

Jan washed pots, ashtrays in the drying rack, her back to me.

'Jan—'

She jumped out of her skin and knocked the Fairy Liquid over – green guck bleeding down the sink cupboard.

'Who's it gunna be?' I said.

Deep breaths – 'Ah bolted that back door.' Her eyes looked sore and wouldn't blink. Towel dressing gown belted loose, make-up stains on the wet cuffs. 'Sorry av not ad a tidy-up.' Deadpan.

'Y'been in this week?' I said.

'Off sick.'

There were coffee rings on the breakfast table. Dead cigs in a Kit-Kat mug. Everything was glued to the cloth. The laundry bucket had keeled over by the washing machine, twice full. Persil powder trailing the kitchen from end to end.

'Trenton out with his mates?' I said.

'Me mam's.'

'Kettle on?'

Jan went back to the pots.

'Had breakfast?' I said.

'No.'

'I'll make some.'

'Yud be lucky. Ant bin shoppin.'

Her feet were in a pair of my socks – elastic slack under her calves. I saw the tiny surprise above her left ankle where she'd had my initials tattooed last year. The red *H* looked burned on. A thorny rose stem curled to make the *B*.

'How bout a brew?' I said.

'Milk's off.'

'How off?'

'D'yer still love us?' Same breath.

Kylie finished, Gary Barlow next – DJ gabbing dedications.

I said: 'Can we turn this shite off?'

'Leave it,' she said.

'Why?'

'Cos ah fuckin like it. Thas why.'

'Sorry.'

'Sorry?'

Sod the pots – splash, bubbles – Jan turned round again.

'What av ah done?' She didn't wait for an answer. 'Is it cos she knows bout songs n that? Like you n yer dad?'

'No.'

'Can't be better in the sack. No way. Is she fuck.'

'You pissed?' I said.

'Bin shaggin er?'

'No.'

'Av yer?'

'Said no. You pissed?'

'Pissed? We know you're fuckin not, don't we?'

'Give it a rest, Jan.'

'D'yer love er?'

'Give it a rest.'

'Fuckin answer then.'

'It's not that. It's just history.'

'Ow can it be fuckin istry? Istry's what we av. Us. Togever. Av known yer longer. Thas istry. Av wanted yer longer. Thas istry. N now av got yer she reckons she can av yer.'

'Jan—'

'Wiv er again las night, was yer?'

'Jan—'

'Ow can yer fuckin stand there n fuckin speak tuz? The nerve.'

'Cos nothin happened.'

*   *   *

Dead air: smell the booze. Duvet over the floor, fag ash striped the sheet.

Jan sat on the bare bed and crossed her legs, half dressed. Slurping black coffee, she said: 'Av never bin wiv anyone since ah bin wiv you.'

'Even when it was touch n go?' I said, changing clothes.

Sobered: 'Even then.'

'Y'told us you did when we called it off for a month, last year. Lyin cow.'

She laughed and nearly spilt her Nescaf. 'Only so yud be jealous.'

'It worked.'

Jan put the coffee on the floor since the bed table was a mess and then she showed me the top of her bob – roots growing out thick. 'What we doin?' she said.

'Need you so I can get in somewhere.'

'Why me?'

'Y'have to bring a bird.'

'Why not tek er?'

'Truth?'

Jan folded her arms, quick-nodding.

'Cos I don't trust meself.'

'Finally.'

I knelt down and held her wrists, letting go so she could wipe her face.

Thirty seconds of quiet.

She broke it.

'Ta.'

'For what?'

'Fer sayin yer was sorry before.'

She stood up and went to the window and cracked the curtains. 'Still icy?'

'A bit.' I took her new boots out of the wardrobe and dropped them on the bed. 'Might have to hold onto us. Case you slip.'

Jan watched them bounce, laughed at me, naught to hysterical in five seconds. I was frightened to touch her. I hadn't seen her like this since she'd quit smoking weed.

34

LICK

JAN SLAPPED THE passenger sunblind and checked her make-up inside the mirror. 'D'yer murder people, enry?'

I missed a gear change – leather gloves on. 'Ywhat?'

'Ah never ask yer nowt. That gun. There's bin uvers. Yer bad as me bruver. Ah turn blind eye. Ah know enough.'

'Well then?' I turned the stereo down a notch.

Her knees kept bouncing – we had her shite on.

Hulme was dead on the way through.

HAGFISH: tagged on the boarded-up pub opposite – a little gathering outside it, just women. They'd started repainting the front – this local journo totty doing interviews.

I parked on the kerb outside Church Place even though the car park was nearly empty. Jan got out with a fresh fag in her gob, handbag under her arm. She zipped her tight funnel-neck jacket up to her chin, earrings twisting in the wind.

I looked across at Church Place.

I didn't even know if she was still alive.

Finger-taps on the passenger window – Jan mimed a lighter. I found a disposable in the glovebox, got out on my side and chucked it to her over the roof.

A white girl, no older than ten, biked past slowly in the middle of the road, a Kwik Save bag hooked on the handlebars. Her plaits poked out from under her bobble-hat. She gave me the shifty eye and rode off towards the pub.

The birds painted over *HAGFISH*.

Jan trotted round the car, cupping a flame. 'What they doin?'

The traffic roar from town seemed miles away.

The journo totty picked a face and pointed the Dictaphone. 'How has the news of so many local arrests last night affected the community?'

The bird sucked her fag to the filter, blew smoke on the Dictaphone and played with her jewellery.

It was an Apostles' Warning fund-raiser.

The journalist tried: 'Tell me about today.'

She stamped the cig out with a pink Tim. '. . . Our Soph's cousin, right, was im what got killed in ere las year. N now they're openin it up nex munf. So right, we fought we'd do it up – in time fer it – show everyone we can make it good n move on n that . . .'

Another bird asked Jan if she wanted to help. Jan took a spare paint roller off her and had a go.

The journalist tried again: 'This is the forth facelift a local building has received—' She had a hair strand in her gob thanks to the breeze, and she spat it back out, lippy-stained.

The paint tubs were stacked on the entrance steps, no brand labels – the same kind that had been given to a dragon to mind.

I wondered who was in on it.

Jan did her bit – a lick of white covered up some bad words. She looked over and nearly smiled.

I dropped a copper into the collection bucket and said: 'Don't break a nail.'

35

RETURN TO THE FLOCK

CHURCH PLACE, FLAT 39 – the real Apostles' Warning. The two of us waited in the corridor. It was the same routine, a different bird at the door, keeping the chain on.

'What's yer name, love?' Greasy skin. A yellow shiner round her eye. Smackhead glare.

'Jan. Jan Dodds.'

'Oo's ee? Yer fuckin feller?'

'Yeah.'

'Why'd yer bring im?'

Jan: 'We wanna see—'

'—Berta,' I said. 'We wanna see Berta.'

'She's not seein anybody.'

I rolled off Kara's notes. 'Ten minutes,' I said.

'Berta's avin a sleep.'

Ninety, a ton, a ton-ten.

The bird snatched it – grey fingers through the door crack. She shut the door and rattled the chain off.

The little bedroom was clammy with body heat. It stank of blood, sweat, sickness.

I saw the same naff shite on the wonky shelves: prayer wheels, pentagrams, naff miniatures of animals and gods. There were black charms, dead things.

Jan sneezed with the dust.

The bed was now laid flat and a crowd of women fussed around it, hiding her. One white girl was rinsing a dishcloth in a plastic mop bucket – lezzer hairdo, tribal tats, a laced spliff burning long in the corner of her lip.

I didn't recognise any of them except Sorrel.

She was in the corner behind me, sat very still on a spinny desk chair, the sides of the seat spilling foam. I said hello and knew I was fucked, knew she'd give me away. But she didn't.

Not a glimmer.

Tight white vest, sovereigns on a thin necklace, goose-bumps down her arms, black shell popper-pants, scuffed Tims. Eyes gloomy like before – the rest of her was monged out, missing.

She was back in the flock.

'Who deh?' Berta said.

I coughed.

The other girls kept fussing, slowly.

'Tis yah, yeh?'

'I'm sorry bout last time,' I said. 'Nearly burnin your hands.'

Jan put hers over her gob. I walked to the foot of the mattress, looked down and saw the state of her.

There was another dishcloth over Berta's eyes. A few surviving freckles went up as she smiled. 'Tanks. Dat was dev-al's warnin. Mek me know dat dis a gwan appen.'

Her skin had stripped from her chin to her chest. Mummy bandages shoddy over one arm to the elbow.

'She needs a hospital,' I said.

The girls ignored me – tended her burns.

Berta didn't know that I was the man in the stalls that broke up the congregation, put wounded animals out of their misery. Her candles. Her tonics. Up in fucking flames. She didn't know I was the man who'd left her like this.

'Yah neba fine Hagfish?' Berta said.

'No,' I said.

'Me nah see dat mon since Chewsday gone. Time tough. But he gwine come today.'

Berta was out of the loop.

Jan touched my waist and mouthed: *What happened to her?*

I said I didn't know.

'Who deh?'

'Me name's Jan.'

Berta laughed – spit-bubbles. 'Dawta Jan. Dis mon get mad atch-yah fa be chaka-chaka inna di house?'

'What's that?' Jan said.

'Bein untidy,' went the bird who'd let us in.

Jan bent down. 'Bloody ell. Should charge summat, she should.'

'She does,' I said.

Another bird patted the dishcloth over her eyes to cool the skin. It didn't stop Berta's motormouth:

'Yah love-love dis mon. Wah fa? Yah nah gwine be is baby mudda? Berta know dis. Berta see troot ting inside yah. Yah likkle bwoy no fadda? Bwoy jacket. An now dis mon yah bring wit today mek yeyewater?'

The lezzer mimed tears.

Daft Jan, shock-impressed: 'Sometimes.'

Burned Berta, preaching drivel: 'Yah a come wit wi. Apostles' Warnin. Dat nah wicked mon but me see pyur crosses inna future an inna pass. Good mon is hard t'fine. Yah haffi mek him respek. Dis Science fi you. Not fi him. Not fi dem. Fi Sistren. Oomon! Yah get fi realise. Check it. Yah muss waan dis. Mek him i-sire.'

Three loud bangs on the front door stopped her spouting. Sorrel nearly blinked. Another fist-knock. The other birds ignored it.

Berta: 'An you mon . . .'

I said: 'What?'

'Is yah still go kill Hagfish weh yah fine him?'

I answered during another round of bangs, the noise swallowed my voice. Then one of the birds broke off to get the door and I followed her out.

No Hagfish. A tubby West Indian feller came into the front room holding a tennis bag. Bald head and raisin eyes. A string vest was showing under his brown safari shirt.

He gave me a cagey nod. 'How sis?' he said.

I didn't answer.

The bird who'd let him in hugged herself.

Silence.

He belly-laughed. He walked over to the fish tank, patted the glass and spooked the goldfish, still laughing.

He grinned down at Berta like she wasn't in her deathbed, still carrying his tennis bag – mystery gifts.

Berta sent everyone out.

The smackhead took Sorrel's hands and led her to the door.

Jan was out last. I stayed put, kicked the door shut, pulled Thin's gun out and wiped his grin away. I cocked the hammer, manual, and held it to his temple. Tick-tock. A face, stretch-reflected along the top of the chrome slide.

He looked at Berta again – eyes dancing, head still – saw her dishcloth blindfold.

I shook my head, a finger to my lips: *carry on your business*.

He wheezed, shit-scared.

I pointed my chin to the tennis bag and he knelt down to unzip it, chatting with Berta.

She called him Dudley enough times to make me remember.

In the bag was a glass box with a screw-down lid, a handle on the top to lift it around, battery lights incubating four eggs inside. He left it by the bed.

Berta told him to get the money. It was in a jewellery tin on the top shelf.

Dudley looked round.

I twitched the shooter for him to get a move on.

He counted Berta's notes and watched me as he put the jewellery tin back.

A door squeak.

Jan's voice said my name, screamed *fuck* and I turned, saw the suprise fear, saw the horror-film flinch.

Sound.

Heartbeat.

The muzzle flash stayed forever – made time crawl.

Heartbeat.

Air whipped my cheek.

Heartbeat.

I fired back at Dudley without aiming and dropped to my arse.

Jan tripped into the room – arms out for me. I caught her – the two of us floor-tangled as Dudley did a runner, belly first, a Glock in his fist.

Screams.

I covered Jan's ears.

Dudley shot up both rooms until he was empty.

Jan was punching my chest, hissing Catholic prayers.

Splinters from the door panel were arrowed in my glove hand. I took the hand from her face and checked she was still in one piece.

Crouching, one eye shut – I looked through a bullet hole in the bedroom door: the front door of the flat was open wide. Shouts echoed from the corridor.

I said to Jan: 'Wait till I go, then get out before copshop come knockin. Walk. No runnin.'

Cig breath. Dusty fringe.

I stood up and fumbled the cashbox off the shelf, heaps of tat smashing onto the floor. Inside the box was a Yale key on a ring with Dudley's sweaty thumb-print. I snatched the key and went into the front room.

Goldfish on the rug – flapping over crack crumbs.

'Who's hurt?' I said.

Sobs behind the torn couch.

There were two of them bleeding in a huddle on the kitchenette floor, their backs against the cooker, their eyes shut. I took a step closer. Sorrel opened her eyes and said: 'Jus go.'

Every flat door was open an inch in the corridor but nobody was daft enough to come out.

Dudley had made three flights down the stairwell. He didn't look up. I chased after him and gave an old biddy on the landing a fright as I leapt over her wheelie cart. She shouted abuse – plenty of go left in her.

By the time I was out of the entrance doors, Dudley was on the other side of the car park. I saw him get in a small blue van and reverse out. He fucked his tyres, skidded off down Epping Street – met traffic – a left onto Stretford Road – horn instead of indicator.

36

TEETH

I FOUND HIM heading across Trafford and gave him room.

Driving flushed the adrenaline. I had the radio up to keep me focused but my eyes were still dipping.

They played the local news bulletin just after one – the bloke spewing it at a million miles per hour over a Casio jingle: Weekend gang violence . . . fifteen clubland arrests . . . three being treated for gunshot injuries . . . Longsight father of four poisoned by wife said to be in critical condition . . . temperatures rising to nine degrees Celsius by Monday . . . enjoy your weekend.

Dudley's blue van was doing forty-five in the bus lane. This Mondeo pulled out between us and I braked hard, so knackered I missed a turning and lost him.

* * *

I ghosted down another tight road, wide awake again – looking, looking – red bricks on each side, the kerbs full of Escorts, bronze Cortinas, Volvo 940s.

The three end terraces had been refitted into shops with homes above: an exotic pet shop, a tiny greengrocer's, an off-licence to let. All of them shut. Dudley's van was parked outside the pet shop, its bumper touching Roisin's Fiesta – the bin bag still over her passenger window.

A disused garage lot ran down the back of his road on a narrow accessway – lost footballs, glass, johnnies, frozen nettles.

I hopped over his rear fence and tried the back door – no joy.

The first-floor windows were open an inch.

There was music playing inside, I could hear it and feel it – no double glazing. My elbows were sore on the top windowsill which was about to go any second. The seal was cracking up loose flakes.

Don't look down.

I looked down and saw a toddler tripping over a bouncy ball in next door's garden plot. He looked up at me and pointed. I was inside before his mam came out.

Dudley's box room smelled of wet fur, cat piss. There were chewed bags of animal feed, a faded poster of John Wayne on the wall wearing a left eyepatch, *True Grit*. Dudley didn't look old enough. But then neither was I.

I'd landed on a cardboard box underneath the window and crushed it flat. Inside the box were hundreds of Beefeater-shaped car fresheners. I picked one out – it said TOWER OF LONDON in gold over his uniform, *Made in Taiwan* over his boots. There was plenty more imported trash knocking about – foreign booze, all sorts.

Reggae was blasting from the next room. I went onto the landing – the whole gaff stank of pet shop. Dudley was downstairs, barking patois, half drowned out by the tune.

I took out Thin's shooter – relaxed, calm – aimed it through the banisters. Eyes bleary again – no sleep. Dudley appeared and crossed the shop threshold, crossed my sight and went back in. He was on the phone, oblivious.

I mooched about in the flat, tried the bedroom opposite.

There was a starved *Indiana Jones* monkey in a little cage on the carpet – sad eyes, patches of missing fur. It didn't make a peep when I shut the door.

Creepie-crawlies up next. Scorpions in a sealed tank with a hot lamp and fake desert floor. Next to it was a Tupperware brimming with dead crickets.

By the bed was a chest of canvas drawers – inside the top two: string vests, pullovers, a falconry glove, Y-fronts, a dull ratchet blade with its handle worn. Bullets, hash, crack rocks, were all stuffed down the back of his sock drawer.

The reggae tunes still played and the monkey tested the bars, dopey with the bass-buzz. I went over and he slapped his cage, rocked it and stuck an arm through the bars, hoping for scran. I tried my pockets but couldn't find a Polo mint. 'Got nowt, pal.'

Spying through the bedroom door, I saw Dudley come upstairs – sweaty, shaking, clueless. He ducked into the bathroom and I walked out the other way.

Kitchen: empty, a state.

I looked in on the pantry room.

There was a feller crushed inside – duct-taped overkill to the piping on the wall. Hands bound, legs sprawled out, one foot in a Fila trainer with no laces. The sack on the shelf above had covered him in dogbiscuit crumbs.

I swallowed the smell, ripped the fresh duct tape off his eyes and left the strip over his gob.

Danny boy.

He started hum-howling through the tape but I shook him quiet.

The reggae stopped.

Dudley tramped downstairs.

We heard the back door slam, keys locking up.

'Where's he goin?' I said.

Knobhead shook his head like he didn't know.

I went out into the kitchen and grabbed a dirty steak knife from the drying rack. I gave the knife to Dan, trapping it in his hands.

'Best not drop it,' I said.

Teeth snagged the tape but his fingers could only twitch to saw.

37

THE LAUGHING STOCK

DUDLEY WAS BACK in his blue van, just two motors in front of me – no time lost.

Trafford Park Euroterminal. Mid-afternoon traffic – lorries hissing down Westinghouse Road, a few hardhats working Saturday shifts in the container yards, a mile stretch of P&Os through the tall steel gates.

Dudley joined the queue to enter one of the yards.

There was a security post checking IDs, letting the barriers up one vehicle at a time.

I drove on and parked up the road, in the same car park I collected gear in with our Maz.

I rang Gordon's mobile and got answerphone. Abrafo wasn't picking up either. There was a missed call from our Jan, but she hadn't left a message.

My dashboard clock bled 14:30. I felt drained, collapsing, like I could breathe out but not in.

An ancient Vauxhall was parked on the left, with an empty space between us. When I woke up, Dudley's blue van had filled the spot, his engine still running.

14:59.

It felt like I'd blinked.

Another motor left the car park and I waited for the all-clear.

Dudley had swapped vehicles and was busy counting money inside the old Vauxhall. The windows hummed – more dub tunes on the go. I booted the driver's glass into a Charlotte's web and dragged him out onto the tarmac. His Glock shone in the footwell. I pushed it inside my Harrington and throttled him on his knees, crushing neck flab through gloves. When he'd had enough, I bashed him temple-first into the door – deep breaths, Gordon-possessed, panel dents still wobbling the sun.

I rolled Dudley underneath the Vauxhall and wedged him belly-up against the petrol tank.

The back doors of his blue van were padlocked, but I tried the Yale key he'd left with Berta and it did the job.

I checked the stock and nearly spewed.

They had their fangs out, mouths broken wide and drawn up like they were laughing. It was hard to tell how many were coiled round each other in the back of the van. Fat things, jungle-size, gaping holes instead of bellies. They'd been carrying parcels inside them and it looked like they'd burst digesting their dinner. The snakes were still, frosted in charlie or smack. Then a sprinkle of drug dust floated through van and one of them came alive.

I thought about chucking Dudley in.

38

ROBBED

GORDON RANG WHILE I was driving.

I said: 'Where you now, mate?'

'Outside ollywood Butchers. Agfish still ant showed is face.'

'What you doin?'

'Readin the *Mirror*.'

'Roisin there?'

'Sat ere wiv us, loadin shooter.'

'Fuck off.'

'She's at our ouse. Yer dint even get a shag, did yer?'

'What y'on about?'

'Ee's back.'

'Who is?'

'Dan. Danny boy.' Gordon sang it.

'What's he said?'

'Nowt. Fuck knows where ee were. Our kid jus rang us ter say ee'd come back.'

So Dan had crawled to Wythie. 'Must be walkin alright,' I said.

Gordon laughed. 'Bet ee's fuckin tap dancin.'

I put the mobile back over the dash.

It was late afternoon and everybody had their head-lights on – a storm sky brewing, clouds from nowhere, practically night.

I fed Jan's stereo my only tape, fast-forwarding 'Victory' to Biggie's bars.

The mobile lit up again, skimming the dash-top when I turned, and dropping our Jan into my hand.

'You alright?'

'Where a'yer?'

'Work.'

'Yin car. Ah can ear.'

'Where are you?'

'Me mam's. Am wiv Trenton. We're gunna go ome inabit.'

'Don't. Stay there. Hear me?'

'Right.'

'Stay there.'

'Right.'

'I'm sorry.'

'Am sorry.'

'No. I am.'

'Love?'

'What?'

'Love, did any ov um get—'

My battery died.

Victor Payne was in his chair in the front room with the lights off, trilby tipped over his face, chest still, gas fire glowing through the ashtray on the arm. I lifted the trilby up and put my finger under his bugle. He was breathing lightly – fast asleep, just pissed.

Vic must've been sixty-odd but he looked about ninety-five. The anorexic Father Christmas. Even my old man looked in better shape before he went, and he only shaved once a week.

His Twiglet fingers held a cig he'd let burn out. There was a green groove where his wedding band lived. Just once, I'd seen him out with some bingo bird, donkey's back, not long after the late Mrs Payne – the pale Irish Proddy – our Gordon's mam. I'd wondered if Vic used to knock her about. Gordon and I had never talked about that shite, not even when it mattered.

I heard feet on the stairs.

Roisin pushed the door open – gas flames instead of eyes. 'How the bloody hell did you get in? I thought we were getting robbed.'

'Like a cat, me.'

She put the big light on. It didn't wake Vic. 'Why didn't you ring the bell?'

'Why tip Knobhead off?'

'You frightened the life out of me.'

'You've had bigger scares this week.'

'Is Dad asleep?' she said.

I nodded. 'Looks like he's had a few.'

Roisin came into the room and crouched by his chair – inspecting the damage. 'How does he drive for a living?'

'Sammy Jnr keeps him awake.'

Smiling, she touched Vic's hand, pulled out the cig and dropped it in the ashtray. 'He's been wearing this shirt since I got here.'

'Remember that yellow coat you used to have?'

She looked up with a puzzled grin. 'I do. I wore it that day Gordon and I went to Arndale Market. First time we met.'

That wasn't the first time. 'Oh aye,' I said.

Vic shifted in his sleep and the telly came on – footie highlights, the sound off. He must've been sat on the remote.

'Sally reckoned you were gorgeous,' Roisin said.

'She reckoned everythin was gorgeous. Shame *she* wasn't.'

Fake-frowning, she wiped ash off Vic's cuff and put her nose up at the footie results.

'You were dead clever,' I said. 'Cleverer than us. I was proud o that. Had more brains than all our lot put together. So when you got in a state, the gap shut. Felt robbed.'

'I took philosophy for a year and dropped out,' she said.

'I took you for a snooty cow.'

Roisin stood up and said: 'Did you cry when your dad died?'

'Fuck you, love.'

She shrank. 'Henry. I'm fucking sorry.'

'Yeah, well.'

'I am.'

'Where's Knobhead?' I said.

'He's in the bath.'

We heard feet on the stairs.

39
MYTHS

ROISIN JUMPED ON the spot, shrieking after I threw the first one at Dan.

Vic burped to life. 'Bloody ell, that enry? Ee's lost the plot.'

'Go back to sleep, Vic,' I said.

Dan got up for more. Boy-band haircut, fresh gel holding strong. I gave him a boxer's nose.

'You saw what was comin n left her for dead at the flat.'

I cocked another – putting in work on the same eye.

Roisin was hysterical. Her nails carved my neck, but I couldn't feel much. 'They took him!' she said. 'They kidnapped him!'

I saw my spit-spray land on Dan's face: 'You rang Dudley. You told him where you were cos you reckoned he could protect you better than us lot. You *knew* him.

You'd both fucked off the same someone down south. But Dudley fucked you over. He locked you in his gaff n kept you there to bargain with – since he knew if you'd made it up here, the posse was gunna follow. Maybe Duds could hand you over. Maybe a chance for him to get back in their good books.'

Dan said to Roisin: 'What's he on about?'

I choked him till he gagged – lips pink, white, blue. 'Don't. Fuckin. Lie.'

Roisin screamed one long note.

Vic tried to get up but his legs were still asleep. He shifted again and the volume maxed on the telly.

Roisin let go of me but kept screaming – drowned out by the telly now, her mouth an O.

I dropped Dan.

I flung Vic's glass ashtray at the telly and it bounced off the screen, left a crack and killed the set.

Quiet.

Just the mantle clock ticking.

Then Dan coughed and sucked for air – Roisin helping him to the couch.

I thought my ears were ringing until I realised it was a phone.

Vic stood up – groggy, gobsmacked, still pissed: 'Fuck's that?'

I went into the hall and answered it.

'Gordon sez yer phone's off.'

'Dead battery,' I said.

'Come down ollywood Butchers,' Abrafo said. 'Right fuckin now.'

'Hagfish showed?'

'Ee's goin nowhere. Let Barker know. N offer im what ah told yer.'

'Dan's here,' I said.

'And?'

I rang Stanley on Vic's landline.

'Weather's gone bad, ant it?'

'Kara,' I said.

'What's nex forecast?'

'There's a church cult round Hulme paintin up derelict pubs n buildins. It's spose to be for charity. They're usin some o the paint tins to move it for him.'

'Aren't yer good? Where's ee got it now?'

'A butchers to let, nearby.'

'Ow much yer after? Twenny-five?'

'Abs wants half.'

Kara hung up.

Roisin sat on the stairs holding her elbows, and she came over when I put the receiver down.

'Wait,' I said.

'You can just switch it off, can't you?'

The quiet dragged. Kara redialled.

I twisted to see the state of my neck in the hall mirror, and answered on the fifth ring.

'Where's agfish?'

'He's there now,' I said. 'Behind the High Street.'

Kara hung up again.

* * *

Gordon was still on stakeout when we got there. The Micra lights flashed from a side street opposite Hollywood Butchers.

I left the motor and the three of us walked across.

Gordon wound the driver's window down, his other hand over the little heater fan. He looked past me, winked at limping Danny boy. 'Nice shiner. Ay, Bane – what yer bring the lovebirds fer?'

I said: 'Smiler fancied the ride out.'

'Alright, our kid?' Gordon said.

Little big sister Roisin. Foot against the BT box, face buried in scarf, owl eyes – daggers weren't the word.

Gordon locked up the motor, popped the collar on his leather coat and tickled the bandage over his ear. 'It's a right fuckin do in there, mate.'

'Pigs not showed?'

'Av they fuck.'

He shouldered Dan as we crossed the main road – phony apology before impact – a bully comedian.

I got between them and Gordon gave me a back-slap, giddy. 'Temper, temper.'

An estate pulled up near us, carrying too much weight. Barker boys were twinned front and back – slapheads shining in the door light when Simon got out. Behind the wheel, I saw the Sharston brickie they'd used for the Halifax job.

'This fuckin it?' Simon said.

'Just you for now,' I said.

Simon shut the door and told them to drive round.

*   *   *

Lenny lifted the shutter from inside, watching us all closely as we came in, as if he was doing a headcount.

'Round the corner,' he said – then to Roisin in last: 'Cept you, love. Yer stay ere wiv us. Ah wanna practise me pub jokes.'

I made sure Dan followed me.

Abs was opening a fresh pack of Wrigley's – glove fingers making a meal of it, his back against the chiller door. He was tall, nearly our Gordon-tall, and looked taller when everybody else was lying down.

Four bodies.

Dan: 'Dear God . . .' He turned green, except his puffed-up eye, which was purple and closed.

Gordon started whistling 'No Woman No Cry' – an impressive performance.

The party was over – paint and blood, paint and blood – everywhere. I walked the concrete floor – so cold it could've been an ice rink – mindful of puddles.

One lad was on his back with a broken sawn-off nearby. There were fresh shells in a torn Superdrug bag hooped round his wrist. Eyes wide open. He could've been twenty.

The Wailers lost their melody, and I told Gordon to pack it in.

Another bloke was slumped against a meat-table leg, still holding a paint tub from the chiller. The rounds had gone through the tub and splashed his face white.

Hagfish had outdone the rest of them – covered most of the floor – exit splatter – made ten metres before giving up the ghost. Buckshot had cost him an arm and most of a leg. Blood had drained along the gutter trays and put the old butchers back in action.

Gordon said: 'Thought ee got nicked?'

Abrafo: 'Ee's bin out two hours n dead fer some o that. What d'yer think, Bane?'

I said: 'I think you could do with his brief.'

Hagfish had come back to cut and run, but his lads had found out. Maybe my speech at Billyclub had helped turn them against him sooner. The nutter only had a fortnight wearing the crown.

Abrafo: 'Anythin else?'

I said: 'I think you should move Des's shop.'

There was a silenced Glock in Hagfish's severed left hand – Skeltah's last tool. I knelt down and put Thin's gun into his right, closed his fingers around the engraved grip. Dudley's shooter was the only burden left in my Harrington.

Abs shouted for Lenny.

Lenny came round and did as he was told – fitted Skeltah's silencer onto Thin's gun and squeezed Hagfish's finger through the fancy trigger guard.

Simon stepped back.

Bullets fed the wall.

Abrafo chewed.

'Been in the chiller?' I said.

'It's wedged shut,' he said. 'Give us and.'

There was spilled paint drying in the seal, but the two of us snapped the door open, tracks crusty with it.

The light was on inside and the shelf stock still there – half a dozen ki's, easy. One of the ceiling fluorescents had blown but Mary was out in the open, no shadow – tail stiff and curled short.

She came forward, dopey, ill as anything. This bloated dinosaur, ready to keel over, gashes on her head, red gauze scales – neck flap like Shredded Wheat. Her head drooped and the tongue came out, lizard flick – bottom jaw scuffing the chiller floor.

She was an animal locked in a room to scare off drug dealers, to make a fucking myth out of a crackhead Johnny Too Bad.

She should never have been there in the first place.

I shut us inside and gave Abs Dudley's shooter. He thumbed a round in the chamber and finished her off. Abs looked at me, still chewing his spearmint. 'Fer Maz.'

Gordon let us back out. 'Wan't alf kiddin, was yer? Fuck me . . .'

Then I saw Dan hopping about like a nine-year-old on Sports Day. He clipped a meat table and fell over – no finish line.

Lenny and Simon had arms in the air.

A black bloke was stood on the other side of the room. Six-four, no neck, short comb twist dreads and a cable-knit pullover that said *MOSCHINO* in big white letters. Gold chains, white Prada trainers – an inch away from a blown-off hand.

Moschino was holding Roisin by the wrist, a MAC-10

beaded on the rest of us. He stepped over the dead and didn't look down once.

'Y'know um?' I said to her.

'No.' Soft croak.

I told her to shut her eyes.

40

NO PROTESTS

ANOTHER ONE TOOK over guard watch and Moschino led Abs and me out back to a stretched silver Range Rover with giant wheels and daft sparkly rims. Next to it: Skeltah and Igloo's battered Vectra, still there in the car park. The fucking idiots we were.

Moschino knocked on the Rover's tinted glass. There was a tacky mermaid stitched down the leg of his baggy denims.

Doors unlocked and Abrafo climbed in first.

The Range Rover smelled like new car leather. I'd been expecting ganja smoke.

Moschino shut the door and waited outside.

We both sat on a bench seat facing a feller in a creased double-breasted suit with long straight hair – lacquered hard. I turned to see up front. A Beefeater-shaped air freshener was dangling from the rear-view. The driver didn't look round.

'Do you know who I am?' said the don.

He could've been forty – ancient by real Yardie standards.

Abs: 'You're them lot from Lundon.'

A ratchet blade lay on the seat next to him – decorative handle, point-end against the door, piercing the beige leather.

'My name is Kim.'

'Abrafo.'

'Bane.'

Slow handshakes.

'I am a business owner and I am looking for this man.' Kim leaned forward and a diamanté tiepin winked. He showed us Dan's airport ID – Abs took it, passed it to me.

'What's he done?' I said.

'He's inside,' Abrafo said, before he could answer.

Kim gave a nod and buzzed the window down. Ice-cold air made me realise how warm it was. Kim spoke to Moschino in a patois so thick it didn't seem worth the mither.

The coke was the peace offering. They loaded the tubs in the boot – no room left for Knobhead. Simon didn't protest. He kept his hands over his head instead of helping.

Roisin was the one who'd got it out of Dan – getting more truth in five minutes than our game of little miss piggy with the bolt cutters could ever manage to. Better too late than never.

Dan came out, punch-drunk: 'I didn't. I didn't. I didn't.' He snapped awake when he saw the motor and Moschino had to drag him in by his haircut. They let him ride in the back with Kim.

Roisin stood next to me, dead tears striping her face, just watching it happen.

I said: 'What did he really do?'

Quick blinks – she kept watching.

Gordon stood behind the silver Range Rover as it backed out, waving them out of the space. 'THAS IT, MATE . . . The day the fuckin sambos . . . KEEP GOIN . . . fucked off wiv all that pinched gear . . . THAS IT . . .' He looked round for me, about to say something for my benefit: 'Oo's gaspin fer a pint after this?'

They drove off with Dan.

Lenny suckered Gordon in the gob.

He took it, laughing blood.

41

HAPPY ENDIN

DAN'S BOUNTY WAS over a drug mule from Kingston. The mule was a woman calling herself Fye. Kim had used Fye regularly because it was her that Kim was after, not the home-grown she sometimes carried with her. Fye was one of Kim's baby mothers – the mam of his latest kiddie back in Kingston.

So Fye was special. I imagined her being easy on the eye, not like the desperate cows risking it – the ones forced to shit pellets of smack not even to make ends meet. Their luck lasted about as long as an AA battery off the market.

Dan was already on the posse's payroll and had been for a year, which was why he was marked.

He'd let her bring it in every once in a while, and make sure she got through – hard work these days, not just a nod and a wink. And over time, the two of them became friendly.

An educated guess:

July: Groping more than luggage.

September: Broom-closet shags.

November: Hotel rooms, meet-ups outside the airport. Fuck it, you only live once.

Then Dudley found them out.

Dan must've thought he was a dead man.

Maybe Dudley had been working for Kim's posse in London since the Bullring fiasco and wanted to start running his own import scams.

So Duds offered to keep it shut in exchange for Dan's help in getting his own gear through.

Knobhead couldn't say no.

Business as usual for all parties concerned.

But by December, Kim had found out Dudley was bringing in a bit on the side – that one of his own lads had been going solo.

Dudley did one before Kim could snuff him. He didn't even have time to grass on Dan – he disappeared on the posse and went back up north.

A fucking sigh of relief. Maybe Dan started sleeping at night now that Dudley was out of the picture.

I reckoned Dan was sparing Roisin the gory details. He swore to Roisin that he'd stopped it, which meant that Fye had wanted to quit while they were ahead but he was having none of it. So then he warned Fye she'd have to stop taking her holidays.

Fye called his bluff.

She strutted off the plane for her January visit. Random passport check. No Come To Bed Eyes. Not even a look-in.

Dan called hers.

12 February. Half a kilo found. He probably thought he could square it with posse since they knew it wasn't an exact science – too many variables, too many buggers checking this and that, even if the smart ones were all shit-scared.

Nobody got away with it forever.

Somewhere down line Fye blabbed and owned up to Kim with a version of the facts.

Maybe Kim found out first – if it had been going on that long, chances are Kim already knew and was about to step in. That would explain why the posse were ready to snuff Dan when he clocked off work.

Up north: Hagfish and Dudley. Mates reunited.

Down south: Dan and Fye. The real lovebirds.

Kim: a personal vendetta worth oceans of grief.

I didn't. I didn't. I didn't.

Dan might have raped her. Maybe one last courtesy shag and he'd got rough with her. It would've stopped her holding back at confession. Make that white bwoy suffer.

Kim's methods were extreme.

Find Dan.

Butcher Dan's missus.

A botched job: *Poor Ashley*.

I wondered what had happened to Fye. Whatever

she'd got Kim to swallow, I doubt it would've made much of a difference.

Fye grassed. Danny boy did one.

The posse had taken a shot at him but he'd escaped thanks to our Roisin.

I wondered about their car trip north: Roisin doing eighty-five in a shot-up Fiesta heading home – Dan bleeding all over the seats.

He'd been shagging some gangster's missus.

What did he say to her right then? Roisin wasn't daft. What could Knobhead tell her that would do the job?

'Did you know?' I said.

Roisin pushed her glass away – still full, nursed till flat. 'No.'

'I'm goin up in a minute. Want another?'

'I'm fine,' she said.

The Red Beret, gone eleven, quiet for a Saturday. It was wild outside – the rain packing up the grids. Only true believers were in tonight, everybody else had stayed home with the wife.

Abrafo was AWOL. Simon had gone to the Barkers' to deliver the good and bad news. Gordon and Lenny were arm wrestling in the next booth.

I asked Roisin about that ride up from London to Manchester. 'What did he say to you?'

She stared away. 'Hmm?'

'What did he say to make you believe him?'

'He told me that he loved me.'

That was it. His biggest porky.

'That cleared it up, did it? "Listen love, the Yardies are gunna fuckin mither us to death but I love you."'

'Don't,' she said.

'Dead now, anyway.'

'I said don't.'

I touched her hand. 'Not like anybody had a choice. He went or we all went. N no, it doesn't make it right.'

We sat there and listened to Gordon and Lenny getting chummy, naff Elvis on the jukebox – a slush ballad, the jumpsuit years. The rest of the pub was quiet.

'What's going to happen with you and that Jan?' Roisin said.

'Probly blown it, love.'

'Thanks to me?'

'Thanks to me.'

I wanted our Jan to walk in then and there.

Presley reached for Priscilla.

Roisin leaned out of the booth and eyed the jukebox. 'Who do you think put this on?'

'Could've been any o these soft sods.'

'You mean it wasn't you?'

'Or you,' I said. 'No, it's the wrong Elvis.'

'Do you love her?' Roisin said.

There was a lull at the bar.

'Sure you don't want a glass o red?'

'Have you ever been in love?'

'Time ago. She made champion brews.'

'But it didn't work out?'

'Had a happy endin. Sort of.'

'What was her name?'

'Began with an "A".'

'Do you ever see her?'

Summer '96. Down Pomona Docks.

'Now n then,' I said.

A bang – empty glasses rattled from the next booth. Lenny was cheering – it was our Gordon's next round.

We both got up together.

'Dandelion n Burdock?' he said to me – a ripe fat lip.

42

IF SOMEBODY
TOLD YOU

July 1990

4 A.M. MANCHESTER Royal Infirmary. Faint music on the tannoy to soothe the pissheads.

I waited.

The bloke on the desk called me *Sosorry* whenever I mithered for an update. A coffee drinker. Phone glued to his cheek. Half a uniform. Watery eyes. Razor rash.

I said: 'Can I go see her now, or what?'

He was by himself – graveyard staff. Even the nurses had stopped toing and froing – bad perms, seen-it-all stares – no one rushed. Dopey night security did the rounds, the squad spread thin. I'd seen nobody with a clue for twenty minutes.

'Sosorry.'

'It's Henry,' I said.

'Sosorry.'

I paced. Through the glass entrance doors – a taxi beeped and pulled away. In came a dozy cow with a snapped stiletto heel and a sprained ankle – giggling, still too pissed to feel it. Another bird was walking barefoot, holding her steady. Teary grins. Make-up smears. Matching Yazz hairdos. Classic Cyndi Lauper serenade.

'This it?' Barefoot said to me, after the chorus. Her toenail polish was dirt.

'Hope not,' I said.

'What's yer name?' the other said, before she'd even made the desk.

'Sunshine.'

'. . . THEY JUS A-WANNA . . .' She screeched the high notes long and loud enough to break windows. Big arse found spare chair. Short-short skirt – stonewash denim, peace-symbol patches sewn on the pockets, smiley logos. '. . . OOOOH GIRLS—'

'Will yer shud up!' a skinhead went. He was sat on his bill at the back, needing stitches.

'Oh, get fucked!' she shouted round, popeyed.

Barefoot padded up to the reception desk: 'D'yer usually work nights, love?' One hand scrubbed her hair, shaking the dried-out mousse.

He said: 'No.'

'D'yer not?'

'No.'

'Yer dead new or summat?'

'Days I do.'

'Where yer from?'

'I'm sorry?' He put the phone down.

'Got accent n that.'

'England this, mate!' the skinhead was on his feet, bladdered.

I said: 'Hospital this, mate. Sit the fuck down.'

He took a step forward, pinching bloody cotton wool round his bugle. 'Fuckin what?'

'You heard.' I went over to the end of his chair aisle.

He spewed curry on his bovver boots and sat down again.

I patted his back, breathing through my mouth.

'Ta.'

The receptionist stood up and leaned over the desk at the sick puddles.

'Go get someone,' I said.

He lifted the phone, dialled and then hung up, panicking. He ran off.

'—GIRLS. THEY WANNA. THEY WANNA HAVE . . .'

I walked through.

Henry Bane was nodding off on a corridor bench, his Harrington on his lap with a crumpled *Mirror*.

'. . . if somebody told yer that they dint love yer, n later they told you, they said, the ole world loved yer . . .'

'Fuck are you doin here?' I said.

'. . . Lola . . .?'

'It's us.'

He snapped awake, coughing. His eyes were red.

'Said what you doin here?'

'Was wiv Vic when yer rang im. Give us lift in the taxi. Ee'd only ad a few.' He belched. 'Was ah singin?'

'Aye.'

'Jackie Wilson?'

'Anna King. Did you not see us?'

'We must o come in uva end,' he said.

'I was the one who fuckin brought her in. They made us wait out there. Family only.'

He shrugged.

'Where's Vic?' I said.

'Smokin room.'

'How is she?'

'She's got one o them Paki doctors. Ee's ad a word wiv Vic. Thev not got er in the ward yet. Yer wanna shite brew from the machine?'

'No.'

'Yer wanna go ome?'

'You can,' I said.

He rubbed his eyes, making them worse. 'Ee can't be doin wiv all this again, Vic.'

'What?'

'Er puttin im through all this. After is missus goin? Poor sod's ad enough.' He sniffed. 'Bloody druggy, this one – is she? Tekin this, tekin that. Daft cow. Bin a bloody week n she's got yer wrapped round er finger. Ah said she were trouble –'

'Get out me fuckin sight,' I said.

Up and squaring off: 'Am yer father. Don't YOU
dare—'

There was a hand the size of a dinner plate on my
chest – knuckles skinned to fuck. It was Gordon, out
of nowhere, holding me back.

'Cheers, mate,' I said.

Gordon: 'Fer what?'

We walked it off – hospital corridors, useless signs,
windows looking out on brick walls, the two of us getting
lost.

'What yer done wiv the money?' Gordon said. He
was more mithered about pay day.

'Gave it Maz,' I said.

'Wiv the leftover gear?'

'He's got the lot. How is she?'

Gordon yawned. 'Av not seen er. Me dad as.'

'She awake?'

'Thev got er whatsit . . .'

'Sedated,' I said.

'Oo give er the dodgy biscuit?' he said.

The bloke you might've killed.

'Dunno,' I said.

On the ground floor we went through two sets of
double doors and ended up outside. The night was cold
now, and getting light. I could see the start of the
ambulance rank across the staff car park, the backs of
more buildings. Everything dead. Everything about to
glow.

Two white nurses were sharing a fag by the wall next

to us. One checked her watch – two guilty faces. They took a last drag, then headed back inside. I held the door for them.

Gordon said: 'Bit quiet, init?'

My ears were ringing.

43

GIFTS

1 April 1998
Wednesday

'LOVEY!' – SHE kissed me *thank you*, hugging the new frock.

Mirror dash.

I followed her into the bedroom.

'It's gunna need new shoes,' she said.

I'd tucked it in the stair cupboard last night, and kept the price tag on.

Left. Right. Left. Straight on. I pinched her arse mid-spin.

'Come ere,' she said. Tickle kisses went fierce. Her skin smelled grand. Her hair was still hot from the dryer. I found her ear and whispered muck.

Jan dropped the new frock – butter fingers. 'Yer filthy, you are.' She gave me another kiss.

I started on her work uniform – stiff fabric, tiny buttons. 'Time you in?' I said.

Bra hooks. Skirt zipper. I peeled her tights and she lifted her feet.

'Alf-nine.'

'Only ten to.' I sat her on the bed and she lay back, eyes shut, touching it. 'Yer droppin us off.'

'Might do,' I said.

Jan spread it and giggled, three-knuckles deep. 'Say yer will.'

The cathedral bell rang. Just gone ten. The traffic in town was as bad as rush hour. I crawled up Store Street, wipers catching drizzle.

Roisin was stood outside the old caff under a brolly. She wore a navy jumper for a dress, woolly tights over pencil legs. Her new boots kicked a puddle my way.

I dodged the splashes.

Roisin was grinning.

'Could o gone in, love.'

'It's shut,' she croaked.

There was a handwritten sign in the caff window: *CLOSSED DOWN*.

'They sure?' I covered the extra S with a finger to the glass. 'We'll go Arndale,' I said.

'You're taller.' She nudged my arm and passed me the brolly to share.

Hardhats were working in the rain, fitting steel and concrete for the rebuilds. Cranes poked the clouds. Pulleys squeaked over the drill noise. There were towers of scaffold 360 – eighteen months' worth – no sign of it finishing soon. We had posters of brand-new investments going up from scratch and the future still looked a lot like it was pissing it down.

'That's a lovebite,' she said.

'A bruise,' I said.

'Twenty-nine going on twelve.'

'Twenny-*eight*. N says you, thirty-bloody-one n splashin us with puddles.'

We went inside. I put the brolly down but held onto it.

Roisin said: 'How is it with you two?'

'What, me n Jan? Gettin there.'

'Told you it would.'

We found a hot-drinks stand in the little food court. I gave Roisin a Styrofoam cup of tea and the feller gave me a fist full of shrapnel with mine.

'Got no fivers, mate. Soz.'

I still had Kara's cash to rinse. I wondered how she'd taken the news that Stanley's and her gear was London-bound. At any rate, I hadn't heard from Simon.

Roisin thanked the bloke and we went back out towards Market Street. Young lads were window-shopping nicked handsets outside the trade-in shop. Asian mams pushed prams with rain covers, their own faces hidden. A few of them were at the make-up stand as we walked past Boots, picking out eyeshadow.

I said: 'Where to, smiler?'

Roisin cupped her brew in both hands. 'Piccadilly Records? They've moved it up the road.'

'Me n you? In that place? No chance. Spose to be meetin Maz n that in an hour.'

I didn't want her at the do.

'How is he?'

'Gettin there,' I said.

'Henry, I spoke to her, you know.'

'Who?'

'Your Jan. She rang yesterday. Did she not tell you?'

'She called Vic's?'

'Last night when you were out.'

'Shit, I'm sorry. She pissed?'

'No. She wants to come round tonight to talk. Dad's working till ten, you'll be with Gordon. We'll have some quiet.'

'Christ. Why didn't she say owt this mornin?'

Roisin smirked, tried for a staring contest. 'Maybe you didn't give her a chance.'

'It's a bruise, love,' I said.

'I told her I wasn't after you.'

'She ask if you were?'

Roisin blinked and then tried her tea. 'She did.'

'Fuckin hell, Jan. What's she playin at?'

I watched her snap the lid to blow on the surface. 'I think she reckons I'm sticking around up here.'

'Aren't you?'

Roisin looked away, pouty lips still cooling her brew.

I said: 'Oi, love – watch it tonight, our Jan packs a right wallop. She could have you.'

'Don't worry, I'm a tough bird.' She gave it another go but it was still piping hot.

'Yeah – not Jan Dodds tough, you're not.'

Her face went hard to read. 'What's she going to do? She seemed alright on the phone.'

'That's a bad sign.'

We were outside again – brolly up, shoulders touching.

There was a beggar sat down outside the old Marks & Sparks with a ferret asleep in his lap – a piece of string tied round its neck for a lead. He was keeping dry under the scaffold planks.

I took a swig of my brew and gave it him.

I said to Roisin: 'Let us find out what Jan wants. If you still wanna have a chat, I can pick her up from yours after, bout nine.'

'We know what she wants. Peace of mind.'

We walked back up Market Street, Roisin a step ahead, Piccadilly Records drawing her like a magnet.

I said: 'What was that Siouxsie/Mozza tune they did together?'

'"Interlude".'

'You're inter-shite.'

She wiped her hair back to show off her funky earrings. 'And you're picking fights.'

'Could be,' I said.

Playful: 'Are you worried about me or her?'

'Askin who me money's on?'

Henry Bane: 1931–1998. Heart attack outside Ladbrokes – small winnings still to collect.

'No. That's not what I meant.'

I said: 'Good job I'm not a bettin man.'

Roisin started to say something but didn't finish it.

Town was thick with shoppers – busy for no reason. Heads down, hoods up – marching from door to door. C&A had a sale on. Old Lewis's needed a facelift.

Piccadilly Records was two fucking streets away.

I stopped walking after the tramlines but Roisin kept going, and it was a second before she clocked she was getting soaked.

'Bastard.' She dived back under the brolly. I gave it her, my fingers brushing hers – cold milk.

I kissed her hair.

'. . . Come on,' she said. 'Just a quick browse.'

'You go,' I said. 'See if they've got owt by Bettye LaVette. I better get off.'

'Wish me luck for tonight.'

'Our Jan drinks coffee,' I said. 'Plenny o skimmed. Two sugars.' I popped my Harrington collar up and started to go back.

I waved ta-ra. Roisin kept still and watched me – her brolly pointing at the ground.

44

GIFTS PART 2

I P.M. A three-storey terrace off Platt Lane, blue party streamers in the front room, helium balloon tails in my face.

Rana wheeled him in like the Asian Ironside.

Somebody yelled *SURPRISE*.

'Fuck off!' our Maz shouted, an arm over his face, sausage fingers giving us all the V. Then he looked up at Rana. 'Soz fer swearin.'

She handed him the crutches.

'Steady, love.' He was up and wobbling about, his belly more than his legs.

Abrafo clapped, sarcastic slow – hard to tell. He'd shaved his head the other day. I noticed he wasn't wearing his wedding band.

Maz just missed the coffee table – dancing for balance.

I said: 'He's had all bloody week to practise. Spent it on his arse.'

Gordon opened a Carlsberg can with his teeth. 'Ee-ah, dickhead.'

Maz took it and nearly dropped his crutch. He was eyeing the beer like he'd never seen one before. Rana plucked it away.

Gordon shook Maz's hand.

Maz: 'When'd yer get out, big lad?'

Gordon: 'Uva munf, mate.'

'How's it goin?'

'Bin non-stop, mate.'

'So av erd.' Maz looked over at me and said: 'Ay, Bane – sort out some tunes.'

I took some dead drinks into the kitchen to save Rana a job. She wouldn't agree to a do in the evening because she thought Maz needed his rest. I was sure they both did.

Abs was stood by the fridge with his coat on. 'A word,' he said, chucking the rest of his can in the sink, splashing the dirty plates. I nodded to the front door.

It'd stopped raining. We stood on the step and I looked up the road and spied the Lexus on the kerb outside the 7-11. Lenny was turning it round.

Abrafo said: 'Bane – Billyclub, it's yours. Am givin it yers.'

'There isn't a Billyclub to give,' I said.

'Will be.'

'Name only?'

'Listen, am fucked. The taxman, the policeman – am fucked. Am a proper shady bastard. We're not payin all these twats off this time. We're gunna do it above board. N you're gunna run the show.'

'N you run me.'

'Jus try n say no.'

I laughed a beat too late.

'We'll work it out,' he said.

'That the plan?'

'Thas the plan.'

'What's the timescale?'

'A year ter fifteen munf. Fuckin council finished guttin it las week. Am still footin the rent bill. Got anuva meetin wiv the accountant tomorra. There's ways.'

Stanley and Kara Barker.

I said: 'I'm sure there is, mate.'

'Well then?'

'Why here?' I said. 'Why do y'wanna try again?'

Abs took a stick of chuddy out of his coat pocket and popped it in his gob. 'Cos ah want a fuckin nightclub,' he said.

'Scarface?'

'Nah. Am luckier than Tony.'

The Lexus stopped in front of the house, blocking the road.

'It was touch n go for a bit,' I said.

Abs squeaked the front gate open and let me out first.

Wythie. Evening. Nobody home. There was a note on the kitchen table from our Jan saying she'd fed Trenton and my tea was in the oven – gas mark 6. She asked me to put a wash on.

I did the rounds upstairs.

Big light on bombsite: the bedroom was still a state from this morning. I grabbed a load of tights and knickers and stuffed them in the wash basket along with a couple of going-out shirts. Jan's foundation was smudged on the collars.

Trenton's room wasn't as bad as expected – he was tidier than our Jan. I shut the door and had a root around.

No mucky mags at the bottom of his wardrobe, just a tobacco tin under his Rockports. The boots were last year's style but looked brand new – the lad kept his gear in decent nick. One of Jan's old lighters was inside the tin – no Rizlas, a small stash – three more of his mam's Bics in the toe of one of his trainers.

I put the lot back where I found it.

A school shirt was creased up on his homework chair, a Nike coat on the floor with mud splashes. I checked the tag.

Washable.

I checked the pockets.

Cold metal.

A stiff spring handle – there was a pop when I pressed the catch.

It was a double-edge – lethal – a good seven inches.

He'd turned thirteen last September. Jan would have a fit.

I checked under his bed and my fingers skimmed

something but knocked it further away. I stood up and tried from the other end.

A bottle had rolled out on the window side. It was small with a handwritten label.

Berta's War Tonic.

I shook the liquid, holding the top to make sure the cap stayed on. The bottle wasn't full.

I heard the key in the front door.

'Jan?'

'Mam?' It was Trenton. Since when did he have a house key?

I said: 'Come up here for a sec, mate.'

He tramped slowly up the stairs and opened his bedroom door. 'Where'd you get it?' I said.

We locked eyes – Trenton giving me his fight or flight face. His little trackie legs were bent at the knees and then he rocked in the doorway like he'd made up his mind to bolt.

I asked him again.

Nothing.

I grabbed him and gave him a slap round the ear.

'Dint urt,' he said.

Kids.

I let go of him and bent down to match his height. 'Listen,' I said. 'I've asked you where you got it. Now tell us.'

His bottom lip was going.

'Not mine,' he said. 'Am jus mindin it.'

'Not the knife. This. This bottle.' I held it in front of his face.

'It's me mam's, that.'

'Bollocks. You're lyin.'

'Am not lyin.' He kept his chin up. His cheek was a red sting, hands all twitchy, dying to rub it.

I spoke calmly and prodded his chest after ever word: 'Tell me, mate. It's important.'

'Told yer,' Trenton said. 'It's fuckin Mam's.'

I jumped Vic's gate and tripped on the crazy paving out front. The curtains were shut in the front room. I rang the bell non-stop and knocked on the glass square.

Dog barks from the green.

A decked-out Golf went by too fast – headlights off. The drapes twitched over the road.

It was Jan who took the chain off and half opened Vic's door. The lights weren't on in the hallway.

'Lovey,' she said. 'Thank God.'

I pushed my way in and we stood there in the dark. 'Where is she?' I said.

Jan was shook up, crying her eyes out, chanting gibberish, a cordless phone in one hand.

I said: 'Berta. She give you the tonic?'

'Ah called ambulance . . . Ah dint – ah dint know it'd . . . that Berta said ter put a drop in er . . . oh, fuck.'

I could imagine Berta telling our Jan what needed doing.

Ah say, tek disya an give it dat ooman. She drink dis – den neba look at yah mon again.

'Where's Roisin?' I said.

'Oh, fuck.'

Cold light flashed from outside and lit Jan's face up a treat – turned her hair blue.

The pigs were pulling up with the ambulance – blocking my motor in. I shut the door to and bolted it, watching them through the window square.

Jan scrubbed her eyes, stamping on the carpet. Her hair still looked blue to me. I took her hands away from her face.

Light-sparkle tears, mascara tracks.

I coughed and felt sick. I said: 'You're lookin guilty, love.'

Jan reached out for a hug and when I let her go she pointed to Vic's front room.

45

GHOST OF YESTERDAY

August 1990

I WENT IN Vic's front room. It was roasting – the gas
fire was up too high, hot enough to make me squint.

Billie Holiday – 'Ghost of Yesterday' was playing on
a flash new portable stereo. Cheap elephant horns.
Thumpy bass. Billie sounded drugged up, too tinny –
the cassette was old.

'What yer reckon?' my dad said.

'Bloody mournful,' said Vic, sitting down and taking
his cig back out of the ashtray. He had his trilby on.
'Me uva alf's bin buried four years this munf. Ah went
Southern Cem, Sunday gone. Not what ah bloody need
ter ear, this.'

My dad stopped the tape. 'Fair nuff, Vic. Cav it
anyway – got plenny.'

'Alright,' I said.

Our Gordon nodded and shoved up on the couch to free me a spot.

The telly was on with the sound low – an old Brando film where he was tarted up to look like a Jap. Glenn Ford kept raising his voice.

My dad said hello to me last, finishing a drop of rum. He looked happy. A big win on the horses yesterday – six ton.

'Oo's that barmy sod?' Vic said, pointing at the box. 'Not Brando. Im. The little feller.'

My dad: 'Dunno. Nobody.'

'Nobody?'

'Nobody.'

'Well it's somebody,' Vic said.

Laughter.

'Bloody bugger's bloody buggered.'

Laughter.

'You two goin pub now?' I said.

'This one is,' my dad said.

Vic flicked his trilby rim. 'Aye.'

Old Henry Bane got on his feet and tucked his shirt back in. 'Stay out o mischief, big lad.'

Gordon raised his Carlsberg.

Vic stood up and jabbed the air, sniffing *See that! See that!* He shadow-boxed until Gordon looked up again and said: 'Fuck off.' Vic kicked Gordon's foot and told him to tidy the place up.

Gordon belched. 'Ah do the tidy-up every pissin week.'

'Yer bloody don't.'

'Where you off then?' I said to Dad.

'Home,' he said.

'It's not even nine.'

Gordon yawned, eyes back on Brando: 'Dunt ee know yet?'

'Know what?' I said.

Gordon to Vic: 'Tell im.'

Vic to Henry: 'Tell im.'

Dad looked at me. 'It's yer mam, son. Lola. She's only gone n come back.'

'Where's she now?' I said.

'At the ouse. Unpackin.'

Vic laughed at him – a dog whine that turned into a chesty cough: 'She must av erd bout yer winnins.'

ACKNOWLEDGMENTS

Cheers to: Robin Robertson, Kate Watson and all the staff at Jonathan Cape; Sam Copeland of Rogers, Coleridge and White; my family; my Manchester mates; my UEA mates; and Alexandra, as usual.